Miss Zukas:
I've seen you at work and I trust your train of thought. Time is essential. Un-cover the Raven.

Helma held in her hand Stanley Plummer's letter—postmarked the day his punctured body had been discovered. "Do you know the Raven stories?" she asked.

"There are many in my tribe's traditions," Audrey said.

"If someone said, 'Uncover the Raven,' would that have any significance for you?"

Audrey's face was unreadable. "No," she finally said. "The Raven changes shapes to get what he wants; you wouldn't *uncover* the Raven. He is already what he is: a trickster, sometimes good, sometimes bad."

Was this the Raven Stanley Plummer expected her to un-cover? He'd wanted something from Helma when he was alive, and now he was dead. Had the murderer seen the envelope sitting on his desk with her name on it?

MISS ZUKAS
AND THE
RAVEN'S DANCE

JO DERESKE

AVON BOOKS  NEW YORK

MISS ZUKAS AND THE RAVEN'S DANCE is an original publication of Avon Books. This work has never before appeared in book form. This work is a novel. Any similarity to actual persons or events is purely coincidental.

AVON BOOKS
A division of
The Hearst Corporation
1350 Avenue of the Americas
New York, New York 10019

Copyright © 1996 by Jo Dereske
Inside cover author photo © Teresa Salgado Photography
Published by arrangement with the author
Library of Congress Catalog Card Number: 96-96492
ISBN: 0-380-78243-X

First Avon Books Printing: December 1996

AVON TRADEMARK REG. U.S. PAT. OFF. AND IN OTHER COUNTRIES, MARCA REGISTRADA, HECHO EN U.S.A.

Printed in the U.S.A.

RA   10 9 8 7 6 5 4 3 2

For J.M., P.H. and V.P.

CONTENTS

❧ *chapter one* ❧

MOBILIZATION

By Tuesday, the day Miss Helma Zukas discovered she'd been drafted, the inhabitants of Bellehaven, Washington had seen only eleven minutes of sunshine in the past eight days.

November had blown into town. Winds with gusts of fifty miles per hour cracked Big Leaf maples, crashed giant fir trees, and slanted pedestrians like a pressing hand. Under November's onslaught, the town of forty thousand huddled miserably around its curved bay in the most northwest corner of the most northwest state in the lower forty-eight.

November also brought driving rain so thick and serious it had color. And that color was dull gray, the same as the sky and Washington Bay and the humpy islands disappearing into misty vistas to the west. Behind Bellehaven, the snowy reaches of Mount Baker hadn't been spotted since early October.

Some might have said it was perfect weather for murder. And four days earlier, Bellehaven had been shocked and dismayed by the gruesome death of one Mr. Stanley Plummer. The dead man wasn't personally known to the staff of the Bellehaven Public

Library, but there was no escaping the subject since people insisted on referring to Stanley Plummer as "that murdered librarian."

"No, Stanley Plummer wasn't employed here," Helma Zukas, who was one hour into her three-hour stint on the reference desk, told the young man in front of her, as she'd already explained to a number of inquisitive patrons. "I don't have any details about his death."

The library was permeated with the doglike odor of wet wool. The windows were steamed. Air pressure inside the building rose and fell as the winds swept in and out, popping ears like high altitude and honing the most mild-mannered patron to knife-edged surliness.

In the past hour, Helma Zukas had taken the *Wall Street Journal* away from *both* elderly men who were arguing over who had seen it first, given a generous amount of tissues to a student crying over a book report on *The Red and the Black*, and directed the removal of a shrieking toddler who'd wedged himself into the second shelf of the atlas case.

"My friend Dorothy read that book twice," the gray-haired woman now in front of the reference desk told Helma emphatically, her voice close to desperation. "So it *has* to be good."

Raindrops sparkled on the woman's glasses. A dark mantle of moisture covered the shoulders of her blue jacket.

"I'm sorry," Helma told her, moving the box of tissues closer to the woman. "But without an author or title, it's difficult to pinpoint which book your friend means."

The woman blew out an exasperated sigh. "It's pink and it has a man and woman embracing on the cover. His chest is bare. It takes place in the 1800's."

Helma shook her head. "You might call your friend and ask her for the title."

"She's visiting her grandchildren." She looked at Helma hopefully one more time. "The heroine of the book falls in love with the wrong man."

Miss Helma Zukas never sent a patron from the desk without an answer of some intelligence so she located *Gone with the Wind* in what the staff called the "If you liked *blank*, then you'll like *blank*" book and gave it to the woman to peruse.

"Psst," curly-haired Eve leaned over and hissed in Helma's ear. "The Moonbeam wants to see you in her lair."

"Do you mean Ms. Moon?" Helma asked. The entire staff except Helma had taken to calling the director "the Moonbeam." So far no one had mistakenly addressed her so directly, but Helma believed it was only a matter of time.

"Mm-hmm. I'll stand in for you out here. Have you been getting dead librarian questions?"

Helma straightened the blotter, pencils, and pads of paper on the reference desk as she rose. "Not as many as yesterday."

"Maybe they've peaked then."

Eve, the fiction librarian, dropped into the reference desk chair, tucking one leg beneath her. Eve had taken to heart Ms. Moon's encouragement that the staff wear "personal power clothing" and lived in a succession of oversized sweaters and bright leggings. Helma's own clothing had not changed despite Ms. Moon exclaiming a nice forest green would enhance her aura.

As Helma reached the workroom door, George Melville, the bearded cataloger, pushed it open from the other side, and Helma jumped out of the swinging door's way.

"We need in and out doors," George said, stepping aside and holding the door for Helma, "like in restaurants. Did Eve tell you what's going on?"

"She said Ms. Moon wanted to see me."

There was no privacy in the Bellehaven Public Library, no secrets. Not from marital quarrels, personal cycles, or private memos.

"This is what happens when you skip a staff meeting," George warned. "We all have to be present and accounted for to guard our territory, like jackals around the zebra carcass."

Helma had missed the morning's staff meeting to see Dr. Freier, her dentist. It was her first cavity in eight years and the first staff meeting she'd missed in four years.

Ms. Moon's office, the only work space with a door, was at the far end of the workroom, beyond the crowded librarians' cubicles, next to the tiny staff lounge. Her door, which Ms. Moon fervently swore was "open day or night," was hung with a multi-striped rainbow, a cheery pink "Welcome" sign suspended beneath its arch. The lamp on Ms. Moon's desk was lit against the gray day and the room glowed golden. Through the windows behind Ms. Moon, Helma glimpsed a woman running past in the rain, a baby pressed to her heart and pulling a toddler whose feet barely skimmed the sidewalk.

"Please, leave the door open," Ms. Moon told Helma.

"No thank you," Helma said, closing the door and choosing a chair to the side rather than the chair that faced Ms. Moon across her wide desk.

Ms. Moon had been the enthusiastic director of the Bellehaven Public Library for two years, and during those two years she'd blithely presided over the library's catalog computerization, overnight "camp-outs" in the library, an "adopt-a-librarian" program, a public promise never to let a question go unanswered or a library fine uncollected. Every week she wrote a column called "Biblio Babble" for the *Bellehaven Daily News*.

Ms. Moon had, as George Melville said, "grown

succulent" since her arrival in Bellehaven, her clothing becoming more drapey and robelike to accom-
modate her expanding girth. "I'm exactly where I
need to be at this moment," she liked to say.

Helma crossed her legs at her ankles and opened
the notebook in which she kept notes of meetings,
chronicling their accuracy. Pen poised, she waited
for Ms. Moon to begin.

Ms. Moon clasped her ringed hands together,
leaned forward, and smiled at Helma. Her full
cheeks plumped, rounding her face like a child's
drawing while her blue eyes intently met Helma's.
A blonde lock fell forward against Ms. Moon's
cheek.

"Helma," she said, her voice dulcet but shadowed
by a tense edginess that grew more pronounced the
longer Bellehaven went without sun. "I have the
most wonderful opportunity for you. One which
will enhance both your career and personal development." She shook her head and briefly closed her
eyes. "I'm almost envious of you."

On the first line beneath the date in her notebook,
Helma lightly jotted the word, "almost."

A manila file folder lay open on the desk in front
of Ms. Moon. She lifted a sheet of paper covered
with small print on which Helma recognized the
University of Michigan seal. "I see you received a
B+ in cataloging in library school."

"It brought down my average," Helma said. Normally she wouldn't have volunteered such information but she was still sensitive about the lowest
grade she received in library school. All because of
a corporate cataloging exercise Helma had refused
to change.

"Well," Ms. Moon said, "that's a better grade in
cataloging than anyone else on our staff received."
She held one hand to the side of her mouth and said

in mischievous confidentiality, "including George Melville, our cataloger."

"Although his experience is far more extensive than mine," Miss Zukas said generously.

Ms. Moon clapped her hands together triumphantly and rolled her chair closer to Helma. "That's exactly right!"

Helma laid down her pencil, sharply alert.

"So I know you'll agree that you're the only logical choice," Ms. Moon continued.

"The only logical choice for what?"

Ms. Moon rolled her new, wider chair back to her desk and closed Helma's file folder. "The new cultural center. Surely you've heard about Stanley Plummer's death? Everyone's talking about it." She shuddered and her clothing rippled. "Terrible way to die."

"Of course. The murdered librarian."

Ms. Moon's eyes sparked; her face reddened. She tapped her blotter with her index finger, emphasizing her point. "Stanley Plummer *wasn't* a *professional* librarian. The cultural center board hired him to catalog a collection of specialized books and they didn't care whether he had a master's degree in Library Science or not. He wasn't even certifiable."

Ms. Moon was passionate about librarians receiving their just due and proper respect. She was fearless in her defense of master's degrees, separation of professional and paraprofessional duties, and the equality among, but superiority of, "real" librarians.

"Naturally," Ms. Moon went on, "it's an appalling situation which I brought immediately to the attention of Shelby Eaton, the director of the cultural center." Ms. Moon sighed. "Stanley Plummer had once worked as a clerk in a college library. Can you imagine, Shelby Eaton actually asked me, 'What's the difference?' "

Ms. Moon gazed over Helma's head, then said

fiercely, "The only way he'll appreciate the advantages of a qualified librarian is to actually see a professional at work."

Helma was beginning to understand. "And you feel I'm that qualified professional?"

"You're the logical choice. We need George too much, and considering your grades . . ." She shook her head in admiration. "You'll be released to work in the cultural center on Mondays, Wednesdays, and Fridays and that'll give you two days a week to do your work here. I'll fill in your reference desk hours."

"I'm sorry," Helma said without regret, closing her notebook and rising from her chair. "But I've just begun the new Bellehaven organizations index and I haven't the time."

Ms. Moon raised her hand. A faceted clear stone flashed in lamplight. "You misunderstand, Helma. I'm *giving* you time."

The two women looked at one another without blinking. Finally Ms. Moon smoothed her dress front and said, "Think of it as one more battle in the war for library enlightenment."

"And I'm your first draftee?" Helma asked.

Ms. Moon smiled serenely.

MISS ZUKAS AND THE RAVEN'S DANCE

story with an imagination provoked into the whirl of a wind-crazed pet skeleton.

❧ chapter two ❧

RESEARCH

There would be no changing Ms. Moon's mind; Helma knew that from past experience. Ms. Moon projected a "go-with-the-flow" attitude, but Ms. Moon was the one who set the flow in motion and staff members who didn't paddle along at the ordained speed risked subtle disadvantageous shifts in their duties and responsibilities.

Using the computerized index for the *Bellehaven Daily News*, Helma tapped in the full name of the new cultural center: Colonel Soldier Hooke Northwest Native and American Native Cultural Center. Nine entries zipped across the screen.

Colonel Soldier Hooke had died nine years ago at the grand old age of 101. Born under tragic circumstances on a train coming west from Boston, he'd become a wealthy land developer, a reclusive man interested in astronomy, Native American culture, and turning a little money into a lot of money.

Developing his beloved cultural center had occupied the colonel's waning years, despite the populace's view in the beginning that his center was an oddity akin to a house built of beer bottles or a thirty-room mansion chiseled into the side of a sandstone escarpment.

Along with funds and certain artifacts, Colonel Soldier Hooke had willed his personal library to the center, a reputed treasure trove of Native American books and papers, some irreplaceable.

And that's where the recently deceased Stanley Plummer—and Miss Helma Zukas—entered the picture.

Helma carried last week's newspapers bearing the story of Stanley Plummer's murder through the workroom to her desk, skirting four open umbrellas lining the wall.

Thursday's headline, "Librarian Murdered," had brought an instant protest from Ms. Moon. "Only librarians are librarians," she'd said curtly into her telephone, and the next day's heading had read "No Suspects in Cultural Center Employee's Death."

Stanley Carrol Plummer, forty-six, had been hired six months prior to his death. He was originally from Missouri and most recently employed by the library at the University of California Los Angeles.

Helma held the photograph of Stanley Plummer closer to her desk lamp, studying the thin-faced man with gray temples, aviator-style glasses, and slightly hunched shoulders. He had that faraway academic look that was sometimes mistaken for homelessness.

Helma had never met Stanley Plummer but she'd seen him before, she was sure of it. That pursed mouth, those outdated eyeglass frames. But she couldn't recall when, only that it hadn't been a completely comfortable situation.

Stanley Plummer's body had been discovered in the cultural center and the murder weapon was a five-inch metal spindle for holding papers. The body hadn't been found simply slumped over the metal spindle on Plummer's desk, but in the handicapped access stall of the women's restroom, spindle still inserted to the hilt.

Before Ms. Moon had discovered that Stanley Plummer didn't possess a legitimate library degree, she'd cordially invited him to a joint librarians' meeting on space planning, but he'd neither responded nor appeared. Not only that, Stanley Plummer hadn't bothered to apply for a library card at the Bellehaven Public Library, either.

Helma set down the newspaper. And remembered where she'd seen the murdered man.

Not more than two weeks ago, Stanley Carrol Plummer had spent a Tuesday evening in the library while Helma manned the reference desk. He hadn't spoken to her but he'd settled with a book at a nearby table.

Perfectly innocent. Except that each time Helma glanced his way she'd either caught him watching her or seen his eyes shifting away. She was positive it was the same man. He'd left the library before closing but he'd made Helma so uncomfortable she'd asked Jack the janitor to walk her to her car.

Helma refolded the newspapers and put them in reverse order, the most recent on top. Stanley Plummer's actions had been curious but not that unusual. People were often inquisitive about those in public positions and sometimes even developed disturbing attachments. She wouldn't have expected such behavior from a man involved with books, though.

Short of resigning, Helma had no choice about the cultural center. A collection of 1,500 books, Ms. Moon had said. After six months, Stanley Plummer must have nearly completed the task. She'd bring his work up to professional standards and finish the project in a few weeks. Before Christmas, definitely.

"I wouldn't do it," Harley Woodworth said to Helma across the shelves that separated their cubicles, emphasizing his words with a fist lightly thumped on his desk. "If it's not in the job description, I don't do it. No way."

Harley Woodworth had replaced Patrice, who was no longer a librarian. Helma mentally counted to ten whenever she thought of Patrice or her poodle or Helma's own role in Patrice's departure.

Harley Woodworth, who George Melville referred to as "Hardly Worthit," was Ms. Moon's project. "Imagine how we can change his life," Ms. Moon had rhapsodized when she announced to the shocked staff that she'd hired the glum, taciturn librarian. "We'll share the joys of information disbursement with Harley, watch him blossom into a pillar of this institution. This is a rare opportunity for all of us."

"But he's held four library jobs in three years," Roger Barnhard, the children's librarian, had pointed out.

"Because others have seen his strengths but not developed them," Ms. Moon had cooed.

Beside Helma, George Melville had muttered, "Oh goody, a remedial librarian."

"He doesn't smile," Eve, the fiction librarian, had said.

"He will when he works with us," Ms. Moon had assured her.

"His recommendations are lukewarm," Helma added.

"But he's published," Ms. Moon countered, referring to Harley Woodworth's short but well-documented article on the significance of the crescent on the outhouse door which had been published in *The Stumped Librarian*. A framed copy of the article hung over his desk.

He'd arrived from Arizona, pale and surprisingly young. His first words on meeting the staff of the Bellehaven Public Library had been "I thought you'd all be younger."

Now Harley Woodworth looked at Helma expectantly. His favorite topics were death, illness, and government waste, each discussion accompanied by his habit of opening his jaws while keeping his lips closed, lengthening his already long face into a morose caricature.

"Being a professional librarian requires flexibility," Helma said, choosing not to encourage Harley's confidences.

Harley pointed his finger into his chest and said, "A spindle in the heart. It probably didn't bleed much."

"I wouldn't know, but you could check the forensic medicine book in closed stacks. In the 614's."

Harley's face brightened. "Forensic medicine," he said dreamily, his finger still pressed into his heart.

Helma scanned her notes from her meeting with Ms. Moon. Native Americans. She knew very little about Indians. A few families had lived by the river in her hometown of Scoop River, Michigan. Quiet people who'd disappeared by the time she left for college. Her brother Bruce had found an arrowhead in a field once, then tied it to a Tinker Toy stick and ambushed Helma when she took out the trash. And she remembered the eerie groupings of Indian burial mounds in the woods near the river, which the trees grew around but never on.

"Attention," a voice over the rarely used public address system said. "The owner of a red Mazda pickup. Your lights are on."

A few tribes lived near Bellehaven, the closest being the Nettle Indians, who lived north of Bellehaven on a long curve of Washington Bay. Helma had seen them: sturdy, smooth-skinned adults. Children who seemed older than their years, young people who frequently died too soon. She'd read about their canoe races and politics in a cursory way, as one did events that didn't pertain.

A swirl of cold damp air stirred through the workroom and Roberta, the Washington history/genealogy librarian, entered through the staff door at the back of the library, paused by George Melville's desk, and, with a grim smile, shook her wet umbrella over his untidy mess of papers.

During the past few weeks, there'd been conjecture, in which Helma hadn't participated, about what had changed Roberta and George's soulful glances to scathing exchanges.

Helma's desk phone buzzed. It was Eve at the reference desk.

"Helma, I've blabbed and I'm sorry."

"I beg your pardon?"

"Some guy called and asked what time you finished work today and I told him. It just came out. I know we're not supposed to give out personal information. I'm sorry."

"Did he give you his name?"

"I asked but he said it wasn't important."

"Then maybe it isn't."

"He had a sore throat kind of voice. Be careful when you go home, okay?"

"I will, Eve. Thank you," Helma said and hung up on the always excitable Eve.

Helma left the workroom for the public area. The 970's were at the rear of the nonfiction collection. In the Dewey Decimal classification system, 970.1 was the number allotted to Indians of North America, 970.3 for individual tribes. Perhaps those numbers had been sufficient back in the 1800's, when the Dewey system was devised, about the same time General Phil Sheridan was popularizing the sentiment that the only good Indian was a dead Indian.

But now, with an avalanche of new books covering every aspect of Native American life, from anthropological facts to the imagined, Helma wondered just how adequate those few Dewey numbers were.

"Boning up for the new job?" George Melville asked, passing by the end of the book tier and obviously not having seen his desk yet.

"Just looking. Have you ever seen the cultural center's book collection?"

"I've never been to the cultural center, period," George told her. "All I know is that it's an Indian museum and Colonel Hooke's baby." George frowned. "Well, that's not true. I heard it's been the project from hell from day one. Zoning problems, building code violations, infighting, you name it. And now murdered pseudolibrarians. By the way, I heard a story about Stanley Plummer. A friend . . ."

"Is this gossip?"

"Truth."

"No thanks," Helma told him as she pulled a selection of books from the shelf. "Are the Nettle Indians involved in the center?"

"I don't think so. But I *do* know cataloging can be dangerous work. And let me tell you, I'm keeping my cataloging act as clean as a whistle."

"You're not implying Stanley Plummer was murdered because he wasn't a very good cataloger, are you?"

George grinned. "What other possibility could there be?"

Helma was the last to leave the workroom at five-thirty. The wind gusted against her as she stood on the loading dock pulling on her gloves. The streetlights above the staff parking lot rattled and swayed in the wind, ticking as rain fell on metal. The nearest light had burned out.

From the shadows beside the bookmobile, a man's hand reached toward Helma and she neatly sidestepped it. A watch flashed on his wrist.

"Who is it?" she demanded. "What are you do-ing?"

He kept to the gloomy shadows, his features hid-den by darkness. "I want to . . ." he began in a grav-elly voice.

"Are you the man who telephoned earlier?" Helma asked, recalling Eve's flustered call about the man with a "sore throat" voice. "You asked when I finished working. Well, I'm finished now."

"I'm warning you . . ." he began, taking a step to-ward Helma, who casually raised the pointy end of her umbrella. The man stopped.

"Warning me of what?" she asked in her silver-dime voice.

"Stay away from . . ." he began, when the work-room door banged open and Jack the janitor stepped outside, shaking a dustmop.

"Blowy night," Jack said to Helma.

"Very," Helma said. "Good night," and when she turned around, the loading dock was empty. She glanced toward the parked cars, then the wet street, but there was no sign of the stranger. Another un-stable patron, she decided, like the man a week ago who'd warned her that words were being stolen from volume six of the Encyclopedia Britannica.

Despite the wind and the rain and the fact that it was dark as darkest night, Helma drove in the opposite direction from her apartment, along the northern edge of Bellehaven above the rim of Wash-ington Bay, her windshield wipers on high. The falling rain blew thick and thin in her headlights, like snow.

"Several power outages reported in the county," the radio newsman happily announced. "The Nit-cum River is expected to crest at two in the a.m. so keep your rowboat tied to the doorstep."

To many Northwesterners, any weather to the left or right of moderate was worthy of celebration.

The Colonel Soldier Hooke Northwest Native and American Native Cultural Center was on the edge of town, occupying grounds that sloped down to shallow tidelands that smelled of rank muck at low tide. The building was originally a nursing home that had declared bankruptcy, according to the newspaper, because too many of Bellehaven's elderly skipped the nursing home phase and died healthy.

The car in front of Helma braked, its taillights filling her car with watery red light. She slammed both feet on her brake pedal, stopping inches from the car's bumper, in time to see two dark dogs lope across the road and disappear into the rainy night.

She passed Kelly's Bar and Restaurant, where a green neon four-leaf clover flashed on the roof, and turned left into the center's entrance, tires splashing through puddles. The long low building, a wing sweeping out to either side of the porticoed main entrance, was lit by low light, the type stores left on after hours. Inside that simple building a man had been murdered.

On the lawn to the left of Helma's car, still in the shine of her headlights, stood a towering totem pole. She leaned forward to see the pole's top figure: a looming broad face staring wide-eyed and pupil-less into the night, its expression unreadable. Beneath it was a thick-beaked bird with hooked talons. Helma could point any patron toward 730.89 for books describing Northwest totem poles, but she hadn't read about totem poles herself, and didn't know the significance of the eerie figures.

Movement caught her attention. A figure stood in the doorway of the cultural center. Before Helma could discern whether it was a man or woman, or whether the figure was watching her, the dim interior lights were switched off and the building went completely dark, invisible.

❧ chapter three ❧

MISGUIDED ROMANCE

The wind flipped up a corner of Helma's navy blue coat and she broke stride long enough to smooth it down before she hurried up the outside staircase of the Bayside Arms. From somewhere in the early darkness came the desperate clanging of wind chimes.

During November, Bellehaven grew dark by five and stayed that way until after seven the next morning. And if the clouds didn't break it never truly grew light at all, only less dark.

As Helma reached 3E, Mrs. Whitney's apartment next to her own, the door swung open and a younger woman stepped onto the landing. She pulled back blowing hair and shouted over the wind, "It's me, Cassandra. Can you come in for a minute?"

Mrs. Whitney hadn't mentioned a visit from her daughter, an event usually heralded by weeks of baking, cleaning, and anticipation.

"What happened?" Helma asked, stepping inside Mrs. Whitney's bright apartment.

Cassandra twisted her hair. She was a younger

version of Mrs. Whitney: plump and comfortable, a little scattered.

"Mom collapsed at the senior center this morning. She'll be all right but the doctor's keeping her in the hospital for a couple of days. Meg's here, too. I was going to take a nap before I went back to the hospital." She waved at the quintuplet porcelain baby dolls lining her mother's sofa, identical except for the color of their hair ribbons. "Mom's dolls take up every spare inch. You know Mom and all her dolls." Cassandra's voice caught. "I wanted to tell you what happened. Mom talks about you."

Helma scooped up all five dolls. They filled her arms. She straightened all their little limbs and piled them like cord wood on the floor at the end of the couch. "Please," Helma told Cassandra, handing her an orange afghan from Mrs. Whitney's rocker, "don't hesitate to ask if I can be of any help. Tell your mother hello and let me know when I can visit."

Cassandra nodded and dropped onto the couch, her eyes already closing. "I've been up all day," she said vaguely. "Scared to death."

"I'll let myself out," Helma told her.

A gust of wayward wind blew from the east and Helma put her shoulder against her apartment door to close it. Behind her, the wind ruffled the edge of the paper towel roll and fluttered the pages of the notepad beside her telephone.

She locked and bolted her door, her apartment settling uneasily like an exhaled breath, while outside there continued the bumps and creaks and discomfited moans of the November weather.

Before she did anything else, Helma changed clothes. Every morning since Helma was eight years old, she'd set out her after-school—now her after-work—clothes on her bed so she wouldn't have to waste time considering what to wear when she came home.

A pair of beige slacks, a blue shirt, and a white V-neck sweater, along with appropriate underwear, lay on her bed.

Helma inspected the impressions on her thighs from her latest garter belt. After reading an authoritative article on the unhealthier aspects of pantyhose, Helma had switched to stockings although she had yet to find the perfect garter belt and had so far purchased six of various styles and fabrics, rejecting each one except for the baby blue satin and lace affair she now wore.

That completed, she folded her work clothes, laid them on top of the other folded clothes in her laundry hamper, and headed for the kitchen, turning on the news as she passed her television.

"This weather will continue through Saturday," the weatherman was saying. "Expect a high of forty-five tomorrow and a low of forty-three tonight. Same for Thursday and Friday, and probably Saturday and Sunday, and on into next week."

From her zippered bag, Helma removed the book she'd checked out from the library, titled *North American Indians: An Overview*. The book was thick with glossy pages and bright drawings and several solemn sepia photos.

Filtering through the discordance of the wind came the single meow of a cat. In Helma's living room, the shade on the sliding glass doors to the balcony was raised a few inches as it usually was so Boy Cat Zukas could peer in.

Boy Cat Zukas hunkered on Helma's balcony, his wet and scraggly body pressed against her glass door, his head drawn in and eyes half-closed. She tapped on the glass; he didn't move.

"Oh, Faulkner," she said, looking down at the miserable cat. She pulled the wooden dowel from the door track and slid the door open far enough for Boy Cat Zukas to squeeze through. The wind moaned past the door with the sound her brothers used to make blowing over empty pop bottles.

Boy Cat Zukas belonged to no one, although there *had* been times when Helma was forced to take responsibility for the battered black cat's well-being.

During a severe cold spell the winter before, Helma had placed a wooden cube inside her balcony door, the opening turned away from her living space and one of last year's towels inside. Only when the weather was severe did she offer Boy Cat Zukas use of the cube.

With his ears and tail low, the wet cat slunk inside and into the cube without acknowledging Helma. Ignoring Helma wasn't unusual but rarely did he slink with such humility.

Helma's doorbell rang and there stood Walter David, the manager of Bayside Arms, his face grim, water beading on the brim of his Seattle Mariners cap.

Walter David was in his late thirties, close to Helma's age. He was overweight and favored leather jackets and t-shirts and rumbled around Bellehaven on a glossy black motorcycle, no matter the weather.

But so serious was the normally shy Walter David's face that Helma's first thought was that the rumored decision was true: the Bayside Arms was being turned into condominiums. Walter David stepped inside onto the mat and Helma closed the door on the wind.

"That cat." Walter David tugged off his cap. "That cat that hangs around your balcony."

"What about him?" There *had* been a no-pets policy in the Bayside Arms which had relaxed when Walter David, who owned a white Persian cat himself, took over.

"Where is he?" Walter David demanded.

"On a night like this, I *know* he's found somewhere warm and dry," Helma told him.

Walter David glanced around Helma's apartment. The wooden cube might have been a modern end table, not exactly Helma's style, but not completely incongruous with her furnishings, either.

"I'm calling animal control the next time I see him."

"What did he do?" Helma asked.

Walter David shifted uncomfortably from one black leather booted foot to the other. "The wind blew the screen off a window I accidentally left open and he got inside. I caught him with Moggy and they were . . . well, I was too late."

"Isn't this the wrong time of year for cat mating?" Helma asked.

"Moggy is a purebred," Walter David said, as if that explained everything.

Helma had never seen this mild man so agitated. Walter David wrung his cap like a wet sock.

"Is Moggy upset?" Helma asked delicately. "Was she . . . forced?"

"No. She's in her bed, asleep. But that tomcat, I'd like to . . ."

"If it *were* my fault," Helma said sympathetically, "I'd certainly apologize for his behavior."

"Apologies won't fix it."

"Truly, I *would* be sorry," Helma said.

Walter David softened; his jaw unclenched and he slapped his cap against his pant leg. "Yeah, I guess I'm a little upset. Sorry. Moggy was scheduled to breed with a Persian in Seattle. No offense but your cat is a pretty scuzzy specimen."

"He's not actually my cat," Helma said, suddenly and unaccountably irritated herself.

"Then you wouldn't care if I had the animal shelter pick him up?" Walter asked.

"It wouldn't be any of my business."

"I'll call them in the morning."

"Would you call them if he were neutered?" Helma asked.

"Probably not, if he behaved."

"I'll look into it," Helma told him. "He doesn't seem to be an annoying cat otherwise."

"Thanks." Walter David said. "I appreciate it." He clapped his cap back on his head. "Rotten weather, eh? I haven't seen a scrap of sunshine in a week."

"Actually, we had a little sun four days ago," Helma reminded him. "In the late afternoon, around three."

"I must have blinked."

After Walter left, Helma checked the open side of the wooden cube. Boy Cat Zukas had burrowed beneath the old blue towel inside the box and was now merely a lump of blue terrycloth.

"I suspect you're guilt . . ." she began and then stopped, realizing she was conversing with the back of an animal buried beneath a towel.

Instead, Helma went to her phone and tapped out her friend Ruth's telephone number. Her phone had an automatic dialer but Helma didn't use automatic dialers, convinced they robbed the mind of one more useful skill: the ability to memorize. Helma Zukas believed in memorization. She still recited her multiplication tables—onesies straight through to twelvesies—and occasionally an alphabetical list of all fifty states *and* their capitals when she couldn't sleep.

"Call me back later," Ruth answered the phone, skipping the "Hello" segment.

"No," Helma said firmly. "I need advice."

"What?" Ruth yelped in her ear. "*You're* asking *me* for advice? It must be about love."

"It's about neutering cats."

"Oh. They use a knife—or maybe a tiny pair of shiny sharp scissors. Can't you look it up?"

"Boy Cat Zukas is in trouble and if I don't have him neutered immediately, the manager's calling the animal shelter."

"Where is he?" Ruth asked.

Helma glanced over at the cube. She hadn't seen or heard any movement since Walter David left. "He's in his box."

"I can't wait to hear the details on this one. I'll be right over with Max's cat carrier."

"You can pick him up tomorrow," Helma said. "He'll be here."

Ruth laughed her deep hiccupy laugh. "Believe me when I say he *already* knows you've got something nasty in mind. Whatever you do, don't let him out. I'll be right there—if my car starts." And Ruth hung up.

Helma jumped as Boy Cat Zukas yowled a single strident meow. She hesitated and he yowled again. Louder. What did Ruth mean, he already knew? Boy Cat Zukas was a *cat*, an animal devoid of language skills. She was halfway across the room to the sliding glass door; Boy Cat Zukas had stuck his head out of the box in preparation—when she pictured Ruth stomping through Helma's door with her cat carrier. If Boy Cat Zukas were gone, Ruth would be more annoying to listen to than Boy Cat Zukas's screeching.

Instead, she put the soundtrack from *Camelot* on her stereo, turned up the volume, and sat at her dining table to wait for Ruth, ignoring Boy Cat Zukas's petulant cries.

Helma thumbed through the Indian book, pausing at a nineteenth-century depiction of feathered savages gleefully dismantling a railroad track on a lonely prairie. In the distance, a train steamed innocently toward them, the windows filled with the sweet trusting faces of little white children and their helpless, pale, soft mothers. Not a man in sight except the kindly old bearded engineer who obviously wouldn't hurt a fly, let alone a papoose. She closed the book, wishing she'd investigated the book's interpretation more thoroughly.

On Helma's bookshelves next to her baby book, sat a row of library school textbooks. *Fundamentals of Cataloging* was shelved between *A Philosophy of Librarianship* and *Serving Man: Recipes for Patron Satisfaction.* Tomorrow she'd begin refamiliarizing herself with the immutable rules of book cataloging. She didn't doubt her skills but it *had* been a long time since she'd cataloged a book.

The doorbell rang. Ruth couldn't just press the button once; somehow she managed to make the electric chime *jangle.*

"You let him out, didn't you?" Ruth asked, stalking inside with the white cat carrier open like a trap.

Ruth's jeans were blotchy with various shades of red and blue paint. A frayed black sweatshirt hung below the hem of her corduroy jacket. Ruth's normally bushy hair was blown into an exaggerated effect she sometimes spent hours trying to attain.

"You said not to let him out," Helma told her.

"So when did that make any difference?" Ruth shrugged off her jacket, dropping it on the floor. "I'll keep him in my kitchen tonight and drop him off at the Meow Medic's tomorrow."

Ruth swore by the Meow Medic and had even painted an icy blue painting which she claimed to be the soul of a cat to hang in the Meow Medic's waiting room.

Ruth knelt and peered into the cube. "What did you do, you bad kitty kitty?" she asked.

"Walter David said he mated with Moggy, his Persian."

Ruth smiled widely into the cube. "Hot stuff, Boy Cat!" she said in approval. Then she sobered. "So that's why he has to be . . ." She made scissors motions with her fingers. "Love with a cat from the wrong side of the cat box. He might as well end his career on a fling with a purebred; we should all be so lucky."

Ruth rose from her knees and dropped into Helma's rocker. "Let's grant him a few more minutes of precious freedom. What's new in library land?"

Helma explained her new assignment at the cultural center. Ruth's eyes grew round; the corners of her mouth raised. She leaned forward, avidly listening.

"Is it true about the dead librarian?" she asked.

"It is. He wasn't actually a professional librarian at all."

Ruth wrinkled her nose. "Librarian shmibrarian. Who cares? No, I mean was his body really found in the women's john cradling a buxom Barbie doll?"

"I believe he was found in the women's restroom but I don't know anything about a doll."

"Can't you ask your favorite cop?"

"I don't inquire into his official business."

Ruth stuck out her lower lip and blew upward. She was always interested in the most salacious aspects of crime. A man was *dead* and Ruth was curious over a silly story about a *doll*.

"Let me know. I bet everybody at the center's talking about it. But you don't exactly sound thrilled about this golden opportunity."

"I'm not," Helma admitted to Ruth. "I'll have to postpone a project I just began at the library. And I haven't cataloged in years."

"But you've had the same job for sixteen years, Helma. This'll be like traveling to another country."

"I don't know anyone at the center. Do you?"

Ruth put a fingernail between her front teeth. "I know old Colonel Soldier Hooke's grandsons, Aaron and Darren. Can you imagine naming a baby *Soldier*? She might as well have named him Captain.

Aaron's single—again. But they're not really *at* the center, just connected by birth. Carrying on the old man's wishes so they can keep their piles of money. When their mommy dearest got divorced she changed her name *and* her sons' back to her maiden name. I've seen the director: a chubby Nordic type. White guys. They're all white guys. You'd think an Indian cultural center would be run by Indians."

"Maybe it will be once it's completely organized."

"Then I hope somebody got it in writing. So you're going to put little numbers on the books?"

"Catalog and classify."

"What's the difference?"

"In cataloging, you record all the bibliographic information: author, title, publisher, subject headings. In classifying, you give the book a unique number so it stands on the shelf with other books on the same subject. The work's mostly standardized now, done from computerized databases, but the center's collection is so specialized . . ."

Ruth clicked the cat carrier open and closed, open and closed. Helma suspected Ruth wasn't listening. She glanced at Ruth meaningfully and she stopped playing with the carrier, mumbling, "Sorry, Helm."

"Helma," Helma corrected.

"Yeah, yeah," Ruth muttered and stared off toward what would be the view of Washington Bay, if the drapes hadn't been drawn, if it hadn't been dark outside.

"Do you think I made a mistake?" Ruth asked, her face turned so Helma couldn't see her eyes. Not explaining but Helma knew what she was referring to—again.

"Not if it's what you really felt," Helma told her.

"He's not going to wait for me to change my mind, you know."

"Probably not," Helma said, believing that honesty was what was called for rather than empty encouragement.

Ruth went back to distractedly clicking the cat carrier lid and this time Helma ignored it.

"I couldn't live in Minnesota," Ruth said in the absent way of people repeating an argument so many times it had become meaningless. "Start all over again? I'm just getting to be a Northwest art goddess. What would I do back there: enter my stuff in the county fair?"

"What about Paul?" Helma asked. "What does he think?"

Ruth threw up her hands. "I haven't talked to him in two weeks. It wasn't like he gave me an ultimatum: move here with me or get out of my life. But that's what it feels like, you know?"

Boy Cat Zukas poked his head around the corner of the cube, twitching one torn ear. When he spotted Helma watching him, he pulled back inside.

"*Live* with him?" Ruth went on. "He'd make me quit drinking out of milk cartons. I'd have to use clothes hangers and eat at the table and go to sleep just because it was night." Ruth shivered and sat up straighter. "No. I *know* I made the right decision."

It had been a continuing conversation for six weeks and Helma knew it by heart. For two years, Ruth had been unaccountably drawn to a man from Minnesota, a man with whom Ruth claimed she had absolutely nothing in common but with whom she'd maintained a bewildering long-distance relationship anyway. Helma didn't doubt Ruth's confused ambivalence but Ruth *had* already made the decision. Why didn't she just put it behind her?

Helma had known Ruth most of her life, each of them having made their separate ways from Michigan to Bellehaven. Always, Ruth had allowed herself to be consumed by her passions, often to the exclusion of everyday life.

"Well," Ruth said now, sitting up straight and clapping her hands together once. "Let me drag myself out of my maudlin life for a minute here and quiz you on your chief of police."

"He's not *mine*."

Ruth nodded sagely. "One of the walking wounded, afraid to commit."

"I'm not wounded," Helma protested.

"Not you, *him*. Nasty divorce and all that. There *you* are, waiting patiently for a sign and he probably still goes to the drugstore and can't decide which brand of toothpaste to buy. You need to shake him up a little."

"Ruth," Helma said. "I don't intend to 'shake up' anyone. And I also don't believe *you're* in a position to count yourself an expert on commitment."

Ruth dramatically clutched her chest and rocked backward. "I'm injured. *Everybody* plays games; that's how we get through our allotted time in this wasteland, doncha' know? You lose most, win a few, and then you die. Whoopee."

"That's very pessimistic and cynical," Helma told Ruth.

"I'm shocked you think so," Ruth said, the gleam returning to her eyes. She stood, leaving the rocker swaying behind her.

"Enough philosophy. Let's capture your kitty for his mutilation rites."

Ruth set the carrier on the floor beside the cube and reached inside. "Give me a hand, would you?" she asked Helma.

"I don't touch cats."

"Ow!" Ruth said, jerking her hand out of the cube. "Damn . . . Can you grab my gloves out of my jacket?"

Helma retrieved Ruth's blue leather gloves from the pocket of her jacket, causing a cascade of gum wrappers and scraps of paper to fall out with them.

She scooped up the paper and threw it in her trash basket.

Gloved, Ruth cautiously reached into the cube and, with a resolute face, pulled out Boy Cat Zukas, her hands beneath his shoulders. Boy Cat Zukas had managed to shape himself like a horseshoe, all four legs stiff and braced against Ruth's arms. His eyes weren't wild or terrified, just gloomily burning straight into Helma's.

Ruth squeezed him a little to fit him into the carrier and quickly latched it closed. From inside came a single hiss and then silence.

Ruth stood triumphantly. "When next you see this bad-tempered mangy wretch he'll be as docile as a lamb. Huggable even."

"Only if you're ordering a lobotomy."

Ruth laughed. "The vet only operates on one end at a time."

At the door, Ruth said, "Let me know how it goes at the cultural center. And don't forget to find out what the fake librarian was doing playing with dolls." She lowered her voice. "And how he ended up in the women's john, too."

"My only responsibility will be to catalog Colonel Hooke's library collection," Helma told her. "That's all."

"Hooke's books. See ya!" And Ruth was gone into the wind, the cat carrier swinging casually from her hand.

Helma gave the Indian book one more chance. She randomly opened to a photograph of a miner standing beside a log cabin, an Indian woman by his side and two children with Indian features in front of them, the miner's hands resting on the shoulders of a young boy with straight black hair. "Early miners were tolerant of Indians," the caption read, "as portrayed in this photo of a miner having his photograph taken with a visiting Indian family." Helma studied the identically shaped mouths on the man and boy and closed the book.

In the morning she'd begin her work at the Colonel Soldier Hooke Northwest Native and Native American Cultural Center and she was apparently on her own.

❧ chapter four ❧

TAKING STOCK

Before leaving her apartment, Helma opened her drapes. Morning light was turgidly rising, seeping into the darkness. Along the curve of Washington Bay, mists and rains washed the shine of street lamps and automobile and house lights, forming overlapping nimbuses of light.

Outside, the air smelled of the sea; it was heavy, saturated. Surely if she moved too slowly she'd find herself drenched by its sodden weight. When Helma turned on her Buick's engine, the windows steamed and she impatiently waited inside the fogged automobile rather than wipe the windows and risk streaked glass.

As soon as Helma pulled into the line of traffic heading toward town she was forced to swerve around a hunched bicyclist whose rear tire had thrown up a stripe of water from his seat to his neck. A lone, hooded jogger splashed through puddles along the upper shore and beneath him the gray water of Washington Bay was riffled by whitecaps, empty of boats and commerce.

At the last minute she turned out of the traffic onto the library's street. She might as well drop off the Native American book before she went to the center.

"Keep your coat on," George Melville advised Helma when she entered the workroom. "Something's wrong with the heat and our fearless janitor is clinging to the roof trying to fix it."

"The roof?" Helma asked, puzzled.

"The cap on the chimney pipe blew off and Jack thinks a dumb and now dead animal tried to descend it."

"We're lucky nobody got carbon monoxided," Harley Woodworth commented, his long face glum. "We all could have died. You can't smell carbon monoxide, you know. You don't have a clue what's happening—until you're dead."

"Aren't you supposed to begin your new assignment today?" George asked Helma, ignoring Harley.

"I'm returning a book first," Helma told him.

"Cataloging books at a murder scene. That's a new one. At least *you'll* have a little variety in your life for a few months. Pity the rest of us."

Roberta entered, unzipping her jacket. "Wind's coming up again," she said and then when she realized Helma was talking to George, she sniffed and turned away, her head high. George grimaced and wordlessly slunk to his desk in the cramped cataloging area of the workroom.

Helma carried the Indian book to the still-closed public area and found Eve sitting at the circulation desk, wearing a pink and black ski jacket with old lift tickets pinned to the zipper, frowning at the computer screen.

"Computer problems?" Helma asked.

Eve held up her pink-gloved hand. "No. It's just hard to type in gloves. Oh. You start at the cultural center today. I think it's mean that the Moonbeam's making you finish a dead man's job. Be careful; the murderer might still be there."

"If he is, the police will arrest him soon."

"Did your policeman friend tell you that?"

"The police rarely share privileged information with the public."

"I'm glad it's you and not me. I couldn't catalog *Curious George* without going back to library school."

Helma glanced at her watch. The cultural center was open. If she waited much longer it would be obvious, even to herself, that she was avoiding the first day of her new assignment.

Ms. Moon stood beside Helma's cubicle. Ms. Moon had a way of holding herself that was, George said, as if she were receiving distant signals in a forgotten language from an extinct people. In the beginning, the staff had mistakenly thought it meant Ms. Moon wasn't paying attention.

"Oh, Helma," she crooned, crossing her hands over her heart. "Your first day. Indians are one with the earth, children of the Great Fathers. We can learn much from them, how to live and love, and," she paused dramatically, "how to die."

"I certainly hope Stanley Plummer had that opportunity," Helma said. "Excuse me."

Ms. Moon stepped aside so Helma could retrieve a fresh spiral notebook.

"You'll have so much to share with us after this experience, Helma," Ms. Moon went on. "Stay open."

As Helma passed George Melville's desk he solemnly waved and softly whistled the theme from *The Bridge On the River Kwai.*

Helma drove north above the rim of the white-capped bay. The wind and rain had increased and the opposite side of the bay had disappeared behind cobweb-gray skies. She turned up her heater and the speed of her windshield wipers.

Cedar branches waved like flapping arms. A garbage pail lay on its side at the end of a driveway, its contents a spill of fluttering color drifting down the sidewalk, startling in its brightness.

By day the cultural center more closely resembled a nursing home: long and low to the ground, institutional, definitely less mysterious than the night before. Even the totem pole towering in front of the main entry now appeared benign, hulkingly cheerful. Helma parked closer to a gray Mercedes than a brown station wagon with billowing and tearing plastic taped over the rear window.

She dashed under the portico and inside, pulling the plate glass door closed behind her.

From an upholstered chair behind the reception desk, a small yellow dog watched her approach, its tail wagging cheerily.

Four closed doors were arrayed behind the desk, and halls proceeded off to the north and south of the central area. Another, smaller totem pole stood in the south hallway. Muted voices came from behind one of the closed doors. Women's laughter.

Helma cleared her throat. No one appeared. The dog's desk was covered with papers. The top desk drawer was ajar, holding an opened bag of potato chips.

There was no bell or buzzer.

"Are you the animal in charge?" Helma asked softly and the yellow dog sat up and gave a single happy bark.

Immediately, one of the office doors opened and a black-haired young woman leaned out. She glanced at Helma without surprise, then walked slowly to the desk and took a chair beside the dog, whose entire rear wiggled in pleasure.

"I'm Miss Wilhelmina Zukas and I'm here to see Mr. Shelby Eaton," Helma told her.

"Are you starting today?" the young woman

asked. She had a pleasant round face and dark eyes that briefly met Helma's before glancing away.

Helma never provided information to unauthorized personnel, so she merely asked, "Is Mr. Eaton in?"

The woman's expression didn't change from polite disinterest. She turned in her chair and pushed a button on the desk phone. An intricately beaded barrette held back her black hair.

"Shelby, the new librarian's here," she said into the phone.

Instantly, one of the other doors opened and Shelby Eaton, director of the cultural center, emerged.

He wore a dark suit and beaded mocassins. A turquoise ring decorated the pinky finger of the hand he held out to Helma, more turquoise stones the size of bubble gum wads graced either side of his wristwatch.

"Miss Zukas," he said, shaking her hand heartily. "You've arrived. Your boss said you were a real whiz-bang librarian."

Shelby Eaton was in his late fifties, not a big man but a man with a large cushiony frame, his remaining hair yellow-blond and his eyebrows and eyelashes hardly darker than his skin. He had boyishly pink cheeks and puffily rounded features.

Helma had never heard herself referred to as "whiz-bang."

"I'm a well-seasoned professional librarian," she told Shelby Eaton.

"Exactly what your Ms. Moon said we needed." He turned toward the woman sitting at the desk beside her dog. "This is Audrey Dubois, from the Nettle tribe. She'll help you when she has free time."

"And her little dog, too?" Helma asked.

One corner of the solemn young woman's mouth

raised. She patted the dog's head. "And Tillie too," Audrey replied.

"Let me give you the grand tour," Shelby Eaton told Helma, sweeping his arm in front of him. "Disgusting weather, isn't it? My wife and I booked Thanksgiving in Mazatlan. We may forget to come back." And he laughed, holding the rim of his bifocals as if they might fly off.

They walked first down the north wing to the right of the desk. Walls and doors had been knocked out and realigned to form two large exhibit rooms.

"This is our non-Northwest wing," Shelby Eaton said. "Naturally, most of the materials in the center deal with Northwest Native culture, although Colonel Hooke had an interest in all Native American tribes."

He ushered Helma into a light-filled exhibit area lined with cases of bead and leather work, necklaces and arrowheads. Mannequins wore the leather dress of the Plains Indians. Tightly woven baskets were tumbled together in an artistic display.

Edging one wall was a row of glass-enclosed dioramas. Helma walked from one to another, admiring the intricate scenes. Figures the size of dollhouse characters portrayed everyday Indian life: teepees and wigwams and cookfires, ponies and travois, from earliest times to a train chugging along a cliff, a puff of cotton steam rising from the engine while three Indians at the edge of a lake warily contemplated the train's passage.

"Are these from Colonel Hooke's personal collection?" Helma asked, stopping to admire the diorama of a buffalo hunt, the illusion of dust created by gossamer threads of wire.

"He had a special fondness for dioramas," Shelby Eaton told her, pointing to the canny miniature scenes. "He constructed these himself. A fascinating man, I understand. Private. Dabbled in astronomy, too. His daughter told me he was so excited by the moonwalk in '69 he had a heart attack. He was already eighty-three then but he lived to be 101. Think of what he saw, the changes."

"You arrived in Bellehaven after Colonel Hooke's death?"

"Two years ago," Shelby Eaton told Helma. "I was the curator of the Pioneer Museum in St. Louis."

At the end of the hall, enshrined by a golden art light, hung a portrait of Colonel Soldier Hooke in middle age, his hair already snowy white above a broad forehead and large nose. His eyes pierced down the hallway. Helma had a sudden urge to dodge to see if his eyes would follow her the way the saints' eyes in St. Alphonse's used to, "watching your every move," the nuns had warned.

"Makes you feel like you should salute the old boy, doesn't it?" Shelby Eaton asked when he saw Helma studying the likeness.

"He does appear to be a man of military bearing," Helma observed, glancing to see if she recognized the artist's name. She didn't.

"He was sickly as a child but sharp as a tack and as straight-backed as a new recruit until the day he died, I understand," Shelby Eaton said with proprietary pride. "He lost his leg in World War I; they say that's what turned him into a recluse."

As they passed Audrey and her dog Tillie on the way to the south wing, Audrey tossed a potato chip into the air and Tillie caught it between snapping teeth.

Beside Audrey's desk stood a handsome man with thick black braids. On a leather thong around his neck hung a tiny doeskin bag that rested against his chest, plainly visible because the top buttons of his flannel shirt were undone. He stood cross-armed, gazing past Helma and Shelby Eaton with solemn indifference.

Shelby Eaton glanced at the braided man once and Helma saw Eaton's shoulders stiffen, his lips purse. Audrey paid no attention to either of the men. It was curious.

"This is the south wing, the Northwest Native exhibits," Shelby Eaton explained.

"It seems more logical to have placed the Northwest Native exhibits in the north wing, rather than the south," Helma commented. "Mnemonically, I mean, to align north with Northwest."

"Yeah, well, logic doesn't always get to ride in the front seat around here," Eaton said tersely.

This exhibit room was painted flat black with track lighting, holding Northwest Native artifacts: decorated boxes, ceremonial containers, Salish weavings and argellite carvings, carved masks, portions of totem poles and door posts. And more of Colonel Hooke's dioramas.

"The Plains Indians used every scrap of the buffalo," Shelby Eaton said, speaking like a tour guide. "The Northwest Indians used red cedar from birth to death, for every aspect of life: clothing, medicine, homes, transportation, you name it."

The mannequins here, dressed in traditional woven cedar clothing, stood with faces invisible: heads bowed, women in woven cedar bark capes and skirts, their eyes shaded by basket hats or raised hands or partial masks. The effect was unsettling, secretive.

"The colonel collected these costumes," Shelby Eaton was saying. "All authentic, by the way. And of course, his dioramas."

The dioramas in this wing were as cunningly detailed as those in the north wing. Tiny Northwest Indians fished from rocky river banks, raised totem poles, danced in tiny cedar lodges, raced long cedar canoes in blue artificial water, camped on the shores of Washington Bay.

"I had no idea the collection was so extensive," Helma said.

"Not many local people do," Shelby Eaton told her. "You know that saying about not being appreciated in your own hometown. We have more visitors from afar than from this county." He flicked a piece of dust from his sleeve. "Of course, local attendance has definitely risen since . . ."

"The murder," Helma supplied.

The man winced. ". . . our unfortunate incident. But now I suppose you'd like to peek at your domain."

"I'm only temporary," Helma reminded him, pausing in the hallway to note the winged totem pole that stood no taller than she did.

"I'm aware of that. And don't think the center's board of directors isn't grateful."

At the end of the south wing, he opened a door marked "Reading Room" and ceremoniously held it for Helma. "The police had it cordoned off until this morning. Nobody could go in. I haven't had a chance to look it over since . . . but Audrey tells me everything's in order."

Helma stood inside the doorway, taking it in. Floor-to-ceiling windows faced the south but the overhang outside the Reading Room kept the sun from directly shining in. Although at the moment, "sunny day" sounded like an alien term.

Four tiers of oak shelves with scrolled tops filled two-thirds of the room, crowded with books of every size. A shrub-sized jade plant stood in a corner. In the other third of the room an oak desk and a small library table monopolized the space.

All tidy and impersonal except for a snakeskin cup of pencils sharpened to perfect points and a goggly-eyed ceramic turtle teabag holder sitting on the desk.

"Plummer's," Shelby Eaton said when he saw

Helma glancing at the desk items. "He had . . . odd tastes. I'll have somebody get those out of here. The police took everything else, his personal papers and . . . you know, his body." He waved in the general direction of the restrooms they'd passed.

"If you'll show me his notes," Helma told Shelby Eaton, "so I can determine how he was cataloging the collection."

"Who knew *what* Stanley Plummer was doing back here," Shelby Eaton said stiffly, his face reddening. "Plummer acted like the crown prince, fussing and fidgeting over 'the collection.' He wasn't much of an advertisement for librarians." He held up his hand before Helma could protest. "I know. Your director made it clear Plummer wasn't a 'real' librarian, so according to her, I should have been thrilled he could read and write."

"Didn't you hire him in the first place?" Helma asked.

Shelby Eaton shook his head. "Blame the board of directors. Plummer had a connection to Miriam, Colonel Hooke's daughter, a distant relative or something, so the board went along with it, whatever Miriam needed. And look where it got them: a dead body in the women's restroom. Not the kind of publicity they wanted after all the other setbacks."

Shelby Eaton was coming dangerously close to sharing gossip with Helma. The center's "setbacks" weren't any of her business, at least not yet.

"I don't see his computer," Helma said, removing her notebook from her bag and glancing at the beige electric typewriter on a typing stand beside the desk.

A sympathetic expression crossed Shelby Eaton's shiny face. "Didn't Ms. Moon tell you? The colonel expressly requested there be a *physical* card catalog, with cards, pull-out drawers, the whole shebang. No computers. We're lucky he didn't demand that the cards be hand-printed with a quill pen." He pointed to a small oak card catalog Helma hadn't noticed.

"Then I'll expect a support staff," Helma told him.
She'd hoped she'd seen the last of paper card cata-
logs when the Bellehaven Public Library recycled
theirs in the wake of their conversion to computer.
"For me to type and file catalog cards is a waste of
my professional time."

"Sure. As I said, Audrey will be available to you."
His eyes shifted and Helma suspected he was making this up as he went along. "And there's also Julianna. Julianna can type," he added in a tone Helma
interpreted as hopeful.

Helma wrote "Staff" on the first page in her notebook and beneath it: "Audrey" and "Julianna,"
turning her paper to be sure Shelby Eaton saw his
words in writing.

"Well," he said. "That's it. I'll leave you here to
. . . do whatever librarians do. Let Audrey know if
you need anything."

Shelby Eaton saluted her, one finger to his brow,
and hastily departed, leaving the door open behind
him.

Helma slid her hand over the honey-colored wood
of the oak desk. Had Stanley Plummer been sitting
here when the murderer accosted him? Had he raced
through the center in panic, desperately and vainly
trying to hide himself in the women's restroom?

She tucked thoughts of murder in the back of her
mind and began the more pressing business of library work.

After five minutes of perusing Stanley Plummer's
arrangement of supplies and materials, Helma realized with surprise that there was no way she could
improve on Stanley Plummer's organizational skills.

Commonly used items stood at the front of cabinet
shelves; less used, behind. Paper clips were stored
in holders according to their size, pens by ink color.

Taped to a cabinet door was a list of contents, with hatch marks indicating each item removed.

Plummer's desk drawers were just as orderly, stripped of all personal effects except for a book of crossword puzzles and anagrams, all completed in ink. She skimmed the book for anything personal and then dropped it in the trash basket.

The telephone on Helma's desk rang. She gasped in surprise but picked up the receiver and said in her official library voice, "Reading Room. May I help you?"

"I tracked you down. How about that?"

"Hello, Ruth. That was very clever of you."

"Well, *I* thought it was. Don't you want to hear about Boy Cat Zukas's eventful morning?"

"It all went well?"

"He's been successfully deballed and is in recovery even as we speak."

"Thank you for taking him to the veterinarian, Ruth, really."

"Unless there are complications, I'll return him to your tender loving arms tonight. Did you find out about the dead guy's Barbie doll?"

"No and I don't intend to ask, either. It's none of our business."

A soft sound came from behind Helma. She turned to see Tillie, Audrey's yellow dog, sitting in the doorway watching her, pink tongue hanging out the side of her toothy mouth. Helma resolved to bring her can of flea spray on Friday.

"It'll come out anyway," Ruth was saying. "Things like that always do."

After Helma hung up she turned toward the door again to see Audrey holding Tillie in her arms.

"I didn't hear you," Helma said.

"You're not supposed to. I'm an Indian."

"That's part of the mythology, isn't it?" Helma asked. " 'Silent as an Indian'?"

Audrey shrugged and her dark hair gleamed in the flourescent light. "There must be some truth to it."

"Do you always bring your dog to work?" Helma asked.

"Not always. Sometimes Tillie gets bored and waits in my car."

"Mr. Eaton said you'll be available to help with clerical duties."

Audrey's facial muscles didn't move. Helma was looking directly at her. So why did Helma have the impression Audrey was rolling her eyes?

"You and . . ." Helma flipped back to the first page of her notebook. "Julianna."

Audrey's eyebrows did raise a fraction of an inch this time. "Julianna?" she repeated.

"Yes. Is she here today?"

"I doubt it."

"Isn't she an employee of the center?"

Audrey shrugged. "I'll tell her to come see you."

"Who was the man standing by your desk a while ago?" Helma asked. "The man with the braids?"

"Nobody," Audrey said, and when Helma continued to wait expectantly, she added, "He's not from here. Shelby doesn't like him." Audrey pointed to the snakeskin pencil cup and turtle teabag holder. "I'm supposed to get rid of those. They were Stanley's."

"You can leave them," Helma said, looking at the odd but scrupulously clean items. "I can use them."

"You *want* to?" Audrey asked.

"It'll save me bringing my own."

"Oh," Audrey said but Helma caught her expression of distaste.

"Were you here when his body was discovered?" Helma asked Audrey.

"Yes," she said.

A fleeting shadow of sadness crossed Audrey's

face and Helma asked, guessing, "Did you find him?"

Audrey nodded.

"That must have been horrible for you."

"It was a surprise," Audrey said.

❧ chapter five ❦

INTERRUPTIONS

Helma perused the center's collection of books, working without breaks, surprised to discover that Stanley Plummer had written the bibliographic information—author, title, publisher—for many books on 3 × 5 cards and left the cards in the creases of the title pages. And even more surprising he'd penciled in the information in the exact same format on the 3 × 5 card as it would appear on a library catalog card.

She scrutinized Plummer's cards for errors but found none, not even a comma out of place. He had produced perfectly, impeccably rendered cards in typewriter-neat handwriting. It was a surprising feat for an untrained man. No doubt *he* would have received an A in cataloging if he'd bothered to attend library school.

Plummer's cards held bibliographic information, but not the call numbers. Nowhere could Helma find Stanley Plummer's notes that would explain what type of call numbers he'd intended to assign to each book. Considering Plummer's detailed handiwork, she couldn't believe he hadn't made copious notes.

"Ask the police," Audrey told her. "They took anything they wanted."

Once when Helma used the women's restroom, she inspected the handicapped stall, wondering if it had been used since the murder. It was clean; both rolls of tissue were full, the tile floor was spotless. No stains. In fact, the entire restroom was exceptionally clean. Antiseptic even.

A young boy appeared beside Helma's desk, gravely regarding her. He was about twelve, not very tall but with shoulders already filled out. Raindrops sparkled on his black hair.

"May I help you?" Helma asked.

The boy shoved his hands deep in his jeans pockets, his eyes warily on hers. "I was just looking. The cops wouldn't let anybody come in here."

"This isn't actually the crime scene," Helma told him.

"Yeah, but I can't go in *there*."

"Look around all you like," she invited him.

He studied her desktop. "Are all the spindles gone?"

"I believe the police removed them." When he still waited expectantly, Helma asked, "Did you see the spindle?"

The boy nodded. "I bet it was the biggest one," he said and moved to the oak card catalog, bending low to examine the ornately carved drawer pulls and Helma settled back to her tasks. When she looked up again he was gone.

The books in the Reading Room ranged from yellowed disintegrating cheap broadsides to gilt-edged leatherbound beauties to newer editions of glossy photographs. Examining them, Helma felt a physical stirring, like anticipation before a holiday dinner. With the tip of her finger, she traced the embossing on the cover of a beautifully bound book titled *Life Among the Indians*.

"I see you're enjoying my father's collection," a voice said from the doorway.

The woman was in her late sixties with that sleek look of self-preservation and good posture that, at first glance, defied time. Smooth blonde hair, brows defined like commas, skin artfully lotioned, powdered, and stretched taut around her nose. Her navy pants and pale blue sweater were understated—and very expensive.

"I'm Miriam Hooke," the woman said, smiling and offering her hand to Helma. Helma shook hands gently so as not to hurt Miriam or herself on the multistoned rings that studded Miriam Hooke's fingers. "You may know me better as Miriam Hooke Anderson," the woman volunteered. "But I dropped Anderson a few years ago. So many women retain their maiden names these days. Is Zukas your maiden name?"

"Yes it is," Helma told her.

"Good for you." She glanced around the room, smiling fondly. "What do you think of Daddy's collection?"

"It appears very . . ." Helma began.

"It is," Miriam cut her off, nodding. "Some of these books are priceless, irreplaceable." She pointed gracefully to the book Helma had been admiring. "That Barrett volume, for instance. Daddy paid ten dollars for it twenty years ago and now it's worth hundreds."

"Did you help him acquire his library?" Helma asked politely, shifting her eyes away from the thin scar beside Miriam Hooke's ear.

Miriam laughed. "Oh no. No one *helped* Daddy. You've seen his dioramas?"

"They're beautiful."

"And authentic," Miriam Hooke told her. "His research was scholarly, no matter that he didn't have a degree. A fact that causes some to take his work less seriously than it deserves," Miriam added sharply. She paused and her eyes misted. "This was my father's dream. This was why he lived such a long life."

"And you're on the board because you share his interests?" Helma asked, squeezing in her question while Miriam took a deep breath.

Miriam hesitated. "I agree with his mission of preserving a bygone culture. Those of us with the means owe it to the less fortunate, don't you think?"

"I've heard that sentiment expressed," Helma said.

"My father's family can be traced to the founding of this country," Miriam went on in a pleasantly lilting voice. "Are you aware he was born on a train coming west from Boston?"

"And his own father died on . . ." Helma began but again Miriam cut her off as if Helma were usurping her tale.

"That's right. In Nebraska. Death and birth in the same little town. Such tragedy in those days. My grandmother is legendary in both the East and West Coast branches of the Hooke family. There she was, a beautiful grieving young widow carrying on her husband's dream of going west, new babe clutched to her breast. Oh," Miriam breathed, gazing through the unshaded windows toward the west, hands clasped to her bosom as if she clutched a sleeping infant. "Westward, ever westerward."

"Legendary," she repeated softly. She smiled at Helma. "But I'm here to welcome you to the center. We're grateful Daddy's work will continue. Mr. Plummer's accident was a terrible shock."

"I understood his death wasn't an accident," Helma said. "I understood it was a murder."

Miriam fluttered her hands, her face distressed.

"We're trying not to dwell on the incident. Stanley Plum . . ."

Shelby Eaton rushed into the Reading Room, his face abeam, arms out as if he were preparing either to hug Miriam Hooke or prostrate himself at her feet.

"Miriam," he said. "The receptionist told me you were here. So you've met Miss Zukas?"

"I believe our little Reading Room is in good hands, don't you?" Miriam asked.

"Yes, definitely," Shelby Eaton agreed, turning his beam on Helma.

Since Helma agreed completely, she said nothing, but acknowledged their faith with a slight inclination of her head.

After Miriam and Shelby Eaton left, Helma caught sight of a figure standing on the center's sloping lawn. It was a man, gazing toward the west, over the waters of Washington Bay. She recognized the braids and upright posture of the man she'd seen standing beside Audrey's desk. He stood in the rain with his arms crossed, unmoving. He might have been a statue.

Helma followed his gaze and saw only the gray curtain of mists and rain obscuring any view of the islands, as if the world ended right here, right now.

Suddenly, the man gracefully turned and without a moment's hesitation, looked directly at Helma. Her immediate instinct was to step back, away from the window. Instead, she remained where she was, motionless, her eyes meeting his while shivers prickled at the back of her neck.

Helma wasn't surprised to be interrupted again. People frequently read open doors as open invitations.

"Hi!"

The casually dressed man entering the Reading Room was only a few inches taller than Helma. His tan face was prematurely and attractively wrinkled around the eyes. His tan was real, not "fake and bake" as Ruth called the bronze skin bought at tanning salons, and Helma had a quick image of Hawaii where the sun was probably shining at that very moment.

"I'm Aaron Hooke, grandson of the colonel, son of Miriam," he said as if invoking names of the legendary. He took Helma's hand before she offered it and shook it in a firm grip while studying her face with such an open expression of curiosity Helma found herself helplessly returning his smile.

"I'm Miss Helma Zukas," she said.

"That's what I heard. Mother says you're going to whip this place into shape." He waved an arm around the Reading Room. "Old Stanley dropped the ball, to Mother's chagrin. Not only did he drag his heels on Gramps's books but he embarrassed her by getting himself killed in the women's restroom. Unforgivable, especially after she championed him for the job."

"It's a pleasure to meet you, Aaron," Helma said, releasing her hand from Aaron's.

"What are you doing for lunch?" he asked, fingering a gold chain around his neck. "Can I take you to the Yacht Club? They've got a great salad bar."

"I brought my lunch, thank you. I'd like to use every minute I'm here to complete this job."

"You obviously aren't being paid by the hour then."

Aaron Hooke vibrated with enthusiasm, curiosity, and disruption. Helma set down her pencil and closed *American Aboriginals*, certain she wouldn't get any work done while Aaron remained in the room.

"Do you know your grandfather's collection very well?" Helma asked. "Was it inventoried before it was moved from his house?"

"Beats me. I don't read much. Maybe a thriller now and then. When I was a kid he used to read me Indian stuff. That was great. He was always stuck in his books or those little whatchamacallits . . ."

"Dioramas," Helma supplied.

"Right. I'm surprised he took the time to die." Aaron smiled his disarming smile and sat on the edge of the oak table. "Was that crude? He kept up a crazy pace to the last minute. That's what guilt does for you: extends your life, if you even care to live to be a hundred, which he was dying to do. Ha ha; that was a joke. Made it to a hundred and one. Like the Dalmations."

"Guilt?" Helma asked, thinking that the Colonel Hooke depicted in the portrait in the north wing didn't appear the type to harbor a vestige of guilt.

"Yeah. Gramps got rich off Indian land. He bought up acres of waterfront property cheap between the two world wars and then made his fortune selling it for about a million times more than he paid for it."

"I didn't know that."

Aaron put a finger to his lips. "It's common knowledge but Mother prefers it tucked under the rug. Land scamming used to be considered smart investing; now it's criminal and worse than that in Mother's eyes, it's politically incorrect."

"But your grandfather wanted to make amends?"

Aaron nodded. "Yeah, once he was richer than God and it looked like he might not live forever like he'd planned. It was too late to give back the land so he thought he'd give back their culture. Nifty, huh?"

"You sound as if you don't approve of the center," Helma said.

"Maybe if Gramps was in charge." Aaron squinted at the ceiling. "Nobody'd dare muck up the place with a murder if Gramps was still around."

Aaron plucked a paperclip from the plastic holder, straightened it to a long piece of wire, and held it up. "Paperclips amaze me: a little piece of wire like this twisted up to be useful."

Aaron tossed the ruined paperclip in the trash and Helma moved the remaining paperclips out of his reach. "I'm curious about Stanley Plummer," she said. "He seems to have been exceedingly well organized."

"That's an understatement. He thought the rest of the center could be better organized, too. And didn't mind telling Mother or Shelby Eaton, either. When Plummer pulled his nose out of his books, that is. Weird little guy." Aaron stood and put his hands in the pouch of his sweatshirt, grimacing. "Creepy, isn't it, to think a murder happened here? Does it bother you? I mean, there you are, sitting in *his* chair."

"No, it doesn't bother me," Helma told Aaron. "Bother" wasn't the right word. She wasn't bothered by the proximity of Stanley Plummer's death, but she admitted to herself she *was* curious.

"No lunch then?" he asked.

"No, but thank you."

"Well, I'll ask you again next time I see you." He smiled, showing perfect teeth. "Be prepared."

"You wanted to see me?"

An exotic creature stood in front of Helma. A big woman dressed in bright blue leggings and a voluptuous tunic of gold, red, and black that hung to her thighs. Pudgy red-nailed hands that she waved gracefully in front of her like a musical conductor in slow motion. Her black hair was dressed in corn rows, each tiny braid ending in a leather and bead tie. Her features were indefinable: brown eyes slightly tilted, flat cheeks, wide nostrils, and a wide mouth above a prim and girlish chin. Her skin was dusky, not quite Native American, yet not black either. She was more arresting than beautiful. She looked Helma up and down in mild curiosity.

"I'm Julianna and before you bust your brain figuring out how to politely inquire about my background I'll tell you my mother was black and Samoan and my father was more or less northern Paiute. I was raised in Cleveland until one day my daddy took me to Albuquerque where I also spent one miserable year at the University of New Mexico on a scholarship. I'm racially confused and I'm currently exploring my Native American roots. I'm employed here because it's to my advantage. I rarely do anything that's not to my advantage."

Julianna stopped and closed her mouth, hands still gently moving, eyes blatantly challenging Helma to lay the groundwork for their future relationship. This moment was crucial.

"That's very interesting," Helma said carefully. "But can you type?"

Julianna's face flushed. Her mouth tightened. For a long moment the two women silently faced one another. Julianna easily outweighed Helma by a hundred pounds.

Julianna lowered her hands. A spark flickered deep in her dark eyes. She readjusted her tunic. "I can type," she said. "Probably faster than you can."

Helma relaxed. It was going to be all right. "That's mainly what you and Audrey will be doing. Typing and filing. I wish it could be more interesting."

"I'll make it more interesting," Julianna said, smiling.

TEARS AND RECOVERY

Lights glowed from behind Mrs. Whitney's curtains. On impulse, Helma stopped and rang the doorbell. It wasn't Mrs. Whitney's daughter Cassandra who answered but a thinner, more closely coiffed version.

"Hello, Meg," Helma said. "How's your mother feeling?"

"She's stable," Meg said. Meg was an air traffic controller and she spoke with the clarity and brevity of a woman accustomed to averting disaster.

"Will she be coming home soon?"

"Not here," Meg said curtly. "Home to California—with me."

"But your mother's lived in Bellehaven all her life."

"I'm aware of that but now it's time to consider her safety."

Meg's course was set and there certainly wasn't anything *Helma* could say to impress Meg, so she asked, "Is she well enough for me to visit her?"

Meg's face softened slightly. "She'd like that. Don't bring her anything with cholesterol."

"I'll stop by the hospital tomorrow night, about six o'clock?"

"I'll tell her."

Despite herself, when Helma stepped inside her own apartment, she glanced first toward the sliding glass doors, expecting to see Boy Cat Zukas pressed against the glass. But of course, Ruth hadn't brought him back from the Meow Medic's yet.

Helma was exhausted. Not overwhelmed by her day at the cultural center, just exhausted—and slightly gritty feeling. She left her mail on the table in a neat stack to read later, when her mind was clearer.

Normally, Helma bathed evenings after nine o'clock but tonight she immediately slipped out of her work clothes and drew a hot bath even before she prepared dinner.

Arms pink and buoyant in the hot water, head against her blow-up seashell pillow, she considered the daunting task of producing cards for a card catalog again, closing her eyes and visualizing the components of the printed catalog card: Author, title, sub-title, edition, place, publisher, date, notes, tracings. Creamy white, single-holed, 10-point rag card stock. Card after card. One after another. Ninety cards to the inch. Z after Y after X after W after . . .

Helma awakened to the jangling of her doorbell. She splashed, dislodging her pillow and sliding down the floor of her bathtub. Her fingertips were wrinkled and the bath water had definitely progressed to cool. She resignedly climbed out of the tub, knowing Ruth wouldn't give up if she suspected Helma was inside.

To the pealing of the doorbell, Helma toweled dry and pulled on a flowered robe Aunt Em had sent for her birthday.

Ruth was scowling. She held the cat carrier against her body with her jacket unzipped and protecting the barred ends. Her hair was held back in a pony-tail by a garbage bag tie. She pushed past Helma, speaking rapid-fire, her voice low and hot.

"So isn't it criminal enough you have your cat's jewels whacked off, you make us both stand out here until we get pneumonia?"

"You could have phoned first," Helma said, closing the door.

"I had my hands full with your beast from hell. If I'd known he was such an ingrate I'd have stopped by the animal research night deposit."

A long low growl followed by a hiss emitted from the cat carrier.

"Easy, sweetheart," Ruth said nastily. "You're back in the bosom of your dysfunctional family."

"Does he need to be inside tonight?"

"Yes, he needs to be inside tonight," Ruth mimicked, fixing Helma with a drop-dead stare. "He's probably in just a little bit of pain. Have a heart, would you?"

Each step resounding with unnecessary weight and force, Ruth carried the plastic box over to the cube and set it on the floor with a thump that brought another hiss from Boy Cat Zukas.

"How much did it cost?" Helma asked.

"More than you can ever repay."

"Ruth, what's wrong?"

"Nothing's *wrong*. I'm just sick of your damn cat."

"You're the one who talked me into taking care of him in the first place."

"So you were deranged to listen to me. How sweet. You put in a new cushion," Ruth said as she opened the carrier and Boy Cat Zukas stiffly climbed inside to the very back of the cube, ignoring both Ruth and Helma. Ruth glanced at Helma's flowered robe. "You should have used that god-awful rag you're wearing. What is it: a nursing home reject?"

Helma crossed her arms and squared her shoulders. "Ruth," she said sternly. "Stop this right now. What's wrong with you?"

"What makes you so . . ." Ruth began with a sneer and then her angry face suddenly slid to naked sorrow. Her lips quivered. Tears filled Ruth's eyes and slid down her cheeks, smearing her considerable eye makeup. She dropped cross-legged to the floor, elbows to her knees, head on hands, sobbing in unfettered gulps, her shoulders heaving.

Helma always kept clean tissues in her left pocket and used in her right. Luckily, the left pocket of her robe was stocked. She pulled out one unused tissue and shoved it into Ruth's clenched hand. Then she hurried to her bathroom for the pop-up box of tissues on her sink counter and set it on the floor in front of Ruth. Ruth cried on in what Helma could only classify as abject grief.

She filled the kettle for tea as Ruth's sobbing approached the level of keening. But then Helma stopped, leaving the kettle in the sink.

This was a situation requiring more serious comfort than tea. Behind Helma's alphabetically arranged spice wheel and the vegetable and olive oil, stood a bottle of brandy which Chief Gallant had brought over one evening to celebrate the completion of a difficult case Helma had accidentally become involved in.

She placed a cushion from her couch on the floor across from Ruth and sat down on it, tissues, brandy, and glasses between them.

"What happened, Ruth?" she asked gently.

Ruth drew in a ragged breath, then wiped her nose on her sleeve. Helma nudged the box of tissues closer to Ruth's knee before she poured them each a jewel-colored measure of brandy.

"I called him," Ruth wailed and burst into tears again.

"Drink this, Ruth," Helma said.

Ruth downed the brandy in two swallows and turned the glass in her hands, covering the top with her palm and tipping the glass back and forth like a cocktail shaker. Her face was red and blotchy and smeared beyond ruin. Tears tracked her cheeks.

"I *know* I'm being unreasonable," she said. "Just because I turned him down, I can't expect him to check into a monastery."

Helma sipped her brandy, silently agreeing. Boy Cat Zukas was invisible in his cube. No hissing commentary; no movement.

"There was a woman there," Ruth continued. "A woman. In his house. I heard her voice. 'We were just having dinner,' he told me. 'So what's for dessert?' I asked. And he didn't even get pissed. He treated me oh so politely. *Polite*, like I was his great aunt Matilda calling at an inconvenient time."

"Ruth, you could probably still change your mind," Helma said as she had several times already in the past six weeks.

"That's just it, Helm. I don't *want* to."

"Why?" Helma asked as she had several times before.

"Because I don't. I just don't. I couldn't. I'd end up in the kind of world where my goal in life would be matching recliners with an electric massage feature."

"I'd hold out for the manual massage feature if I were you," Helma said.

Ruth blinked her teary eyes at Helma. She frowned. "What did you say?" she demanded.

"Nothing important," Helma told her.

"Oh," Ruth said, back to her jeremiad. "It wouldn't work. We've been together enough to see how different we are; we'd end up hating each other. And I couldn't stand *that*." She looked up at Helma's ceiling. "All I want is to have it both ways—what's so complicated about that?"

"I believe that's what we'd all prefer."

"Yeah." Ruth finally removed a tissue from the box and smeared at her face. "I guess we choose the least potent of our poisons."

"More brandy?" Helma asked.

"Definitely." She heaved a breath that caught in her throat and held out her glass. "Sorry I took this out on you."

"It's all right."

"You're entitled to a reciprocal cry on my shoulder."

"I doubt . . ." Helma began.

"Ah, ah, ah," Ruth warned, shaking her finger. "Be careful what you doubt. It's like wishing; sometimes it comes true with a vengeance."

"Thank you for the offer," Helma said judiciously.

"You're welcome. How was your first day on the reservation?"

"The cultural center isn't on the reservation."

"Just joking." Ruth wiped her face with another tissue and studied Helma for a moment. "It's going to be a big job, huh?"

"Bigger than I expected. Colonel Hooke stipulated there be a real card catalog. White cards on brass rods filed in oak drawers."

"Ah, a man who believes in access to knowledge even when the electricity goes down." Ruth's lower lip quivered dangerously and she bit it hard before she spoke again. "What do you think of glad-handing Shelby Eaton?"

"He *is* a hearty man," Helma conceded.

Ruth nodded. "One of those please-all-the-people-all-the-time men. Did he tell you why he left his last job?"

"It wasn't my place to ask, Ruth, and I'm really not interested in gossip."

"This isn't gossip; I heard it was the truth. Mr. Nice Guy caught some punk goofing off in a covered wagon display and knocked him silly. Beneath that hearty heart . . ."

"We all have our breaking point."

"Don't I know *that*?" Ruth agreed, her breath catching on a hiccup. "As for your dead librarian impersonator, I also heard he and Shelby Eaton didn't get along."

"Animosity between library employees and their directors isn't uncommon. I did meet Colonel Hooke's daughter."

"Grand dame Miriam? Did she have her 'boys' in tow?"

"No. Her son, Aaron came in a little later."

"Aaron and Darren. They're twins, not the identical kind but both good-looking. Miriam bought Darren that little insurance business by the marina and he's soooo grateful. Aaron's no Einstein but he's sweet, loves a good time."

"Have you been researching their backgrounds, Ruth?" Helma asked.

"Uh uh. Miriam bought one of my paintings for Darren's wedding a couple of years ago. She's very proud of her family's pedigree. Mayflower or Pilgrim's Progress or whatever."

"She's justifiably proud of her father's . . ." Helma began.

"Hobby," Ruth supplied. "When you've got big bucks like that you get to turn your hobby into an institution."

Ruth sipped her brandy and went distant.

Helma saw the moisture welling again in her eyes. "What are you painting?" she hastily asked.

Ruth sighed and replied, "Nothing. Not a thing. Nada. Yes, we have no bananas. If the juices don't start running pretty soon, I may have to take up painting cute snow scenes on store windows for Christmas."

"You'll be all right as soon as you come to terms with . . ."

"With being jilted?"

"He didn't jilt you, Ruth," Helma reminded her. "*You* decided against moving to Minnesota with him."

"I don't want to hear it. I prefer my own version." Ruth rose to her knees. "Guess I'd better go home and clean paintbrushes or something." She thumped the top of Boy Cat Zukas's cube with the heel of her hand. "Hang in there, little buddy," she said. "I know a few guys who'd make better eunuchs than men."

"Ruth."

"Sorry. Momentary lapse of good taste." She stood and ran her hands through her damp hair. "Thanks for your solace to the lovelorn." She fished a piece of paper from her jacket pocket. "Here are the details of his surgery, when to call the ambulance, that sort of thing."

"Thanks, I . . ."

"Don't mention it. But really, Helma, isn't it time you made Boy Cat Zukas an honest cat? Adopt the little beggar. You could buy him a nice collar with his name on it. Give him flea baths."

"He likes being a stray cat," Helma said with certainty.

"None of us likes being stray. Think about it. See ya."

Helma stood holding her door ajar, feeling the moist night touch her face and watching as Ruth descended the stairs and walked across the parking lot to her car parked in the middle of the driveway, neither hurrying nor trying to shield herself from the rain and wind, her usually straight shoulders slumped, her head bowed.

*   *   *

When her phone rang at two minutes to seven, Helma expected the caller to be her mother, but it wasn't.

It was Chief of Police Wayne Gallant. Helma touched her hair and stretched the phone cord to her table so she could sit down.

"Seeing how you've landed yourself in the middle of a crime scene again, Helma," he said, "and knowing your curious nature, how about if we get together to discuss the crime."

"You're *offering* to share police details with me?" Helma asked incredulously, so surprised she neglected to make the point that she definitely hadn't "landed herself" in the middle of anything, and especially not "again."

"The details I *can* discuss." Helma pictured Wayne Gallant, able to tell from his voice that he was smiling. "Also," he went on, "the details I'm sure you'll ferret out. Can we discuss it over a walk Friday night?"

"A walk?" Helma questioned. "In this weather?"

"If you don't mind walking in circles around the college gym. We'll get something to eat afterward. Can I pick you up about six o'clock?"

"Six-fifteen would be better."

"Fine. I'll see you then."

Helma hung up and straightened the telephone on her counter. She pushed in her dining room chair so its back just touched the table edge like the other three. She absently restacked her ceramic coasters, then pulled aside her drapes and stared unseeing out into the black wet night. Her beige cotton pants would be better than the navy wool.

Although her mail wasn't wet, the envelopes were limp with moisture. Helma sorted out the ads and threw them away unopened, leaving her phone bill and a single legal-sized envelope.

The envelope was addressed in three different inks in three different hands. Her name was written precisely in black ink: *Miss Wilhelmina Zukas*. But the address was scrawled. One line written at a rough angle was crossed out; it was her mother's address. Beneath it, in still another hand, it read, "Try 3F Bayside Arms."

The upper left corner was blank. No return address. With a shiver of distaste, Helma slit the envelope with her letter opener and removed the single sheet of paper, thinking if she were looking at an anonymous letter, *this* time it was going directly into her trash.

Miss Zukas:

I've seen you at work and I trust your train of thought. Time is essential. Un-cover the Raven.

She picked up the envelope and studied the postmark. It was smudged but the letter had been mailed in Bellehaven a week ago.

A week ago. Even if there'd been no signature, Helma would have recognized that clear, precise handwriting.

It was signed *S.C. Plummer* and postmarked the day Stanley Carrol Plummer's punctured body had been discovered in the women's restroom of the Cultural Center.

A few minutes later, when Helma's mother *did* call, Helma still stood beside her table, distracted, holding Stanley Plummer's letter.

"Wilhelmina dear," her mother said. "That nice thin librarian, Roberta? After her genealogy workshop at the senior center this afternoon, she told me you were working at that Indian place where that librarian was murdered, is that right?"

"I'll be doing temporary work at the Colonel Hooke Cultural Center, Mother," Helma said, smoothing out the brief note: *I've seen you at work . . .*

"Right there where he died?"

"No," Helma assured her mother. "In another part of the center."

Helma's mother's name was Lillian and she'd moved from Michigan to Bellehaven shortly after Helma's father died, rekindling a degree of interest in Helma's life unexperienced since high school.

"Well, that's a relief. I don't know anything about Indians except for that one your father and I adopted. Well, actually I did."

Helma stared at the phone. "You adopted an Indian?" she asked. "When?"

"When you were a little girl. Through Father Phil's mission in Wyoming; an eight-year-old boy. We sent money every month and got to name him, too."

"Didn't he already have a name?"

"I guess not. Why else would Father Phil say *we* could name him? I called him Elliot Alexander. I think his last name was White Bear. Doesn't that sound nice: Elliot Alexander White Bear?"

"What happened to him?"

"I don't really know. It was a one-year commitment."

"I'll only be cataloging books at the center three days a week," Helma told Lillian. "I don't expect I'll be adopting anyone, or even meeting very many Indians."

"I met the murdered man."

"You did?" Helma asked, pulling her hand away from Plummer's letter. *Time is essential.*

"He gave a talk at the senior center last month. We've had so many better presentations since I became head of the program committee. You know Sara James, the retired French teacher who lives down the hall? She thought Mr. Plummer was 'darling,' but you know how *she* is. Anything in pants. I wasn't so charmed by him myself. Your father would have called him *Išdidus*."

Išdidus meant arrogant in Lithuanian. Helma closed her eyes, hearing her father's voice.

"What was the topic of his speech?" Helma asked.

"Old dolls."

"Old *dolls*?"

"Mm hmm. What was valuable, what wasn't. You'd be shocked at what some of those dolls are worth. Even plastic ones, especially if they're in their original boxes and nobody's played with them." Lillian gave a heartfelt sigh. "This rain is like torture, isn't it? My skin's going all puffy."

Helma vaguely listened to her mother, trying to reconcile the information that Stanley Plummer might be an authority on doll collecting, with the image she'd seen in the newspaper and the orderly remnants of his work in the cultural center.

And now this letter from the very dead Mr. Plummer who claimed to trust her train of thought.

❧ chapter seven ❧

DISTANT MESSAGES

On Thursday morning, Helma picked up the twigs and dead leaves that had blown onto her balcony and ground them up in her garbage disposal.

Then she drove to the post office through a misty rain that hovered and gently fell, softening the landscape. No angles or straight lines in sight.

"Can you explain where this letter came from and why it's in this condition?" Helma asked the young blonde woman at the postal counter.

The young woman took the envelope, inspected it front and back, and said, "It looks like it's been through dead letters."

"That's appropriate," Helma said.

"Pardon?"

"Nothing. So the addresses on this envelope were written by postal employees?"

"Not the name, but they probably added the addresses. The sender dropped it in a mailbox without addressing it. People do that. Are you Wilhelmina Zukas?"

"Yes."

The woman beamed with pleasure. "That's great!

You'd be surprised at some of the stuff that comes through. No way it ever finds its home."

George Melville sat on a book truck beside Helma's cubicle, his eyes eager. "How's life at the cultural center?" he asked. "Did you find yourself slogging through biblio-chaos?"

"Quite the contrary," Helma told him. "Stanley Plummer was very organized." She paused, then added generously, "And also very knowledgeable."

"Horrors. So we can rule out Mr. Plummer being murdered by the Association for Excruciatingly Correct Cataloging?"

"Definitely. You said earlier that a friend told you a story about Stanley Plummer?" Helma removed her navy heels from her zippered case and set them beside her desk, waiting until George left before she changed.

George leaned forward. "You want to hear it?"

"Only as information."

"You bet." George made himself more comfortable on the book truck, flexing his shoulders, scratching his beard and settling his bottom. All he lacked was a pipe and an attentive little circle of children.

"You know how my doctor coerces me into exercising at the Y? A month ago, Tom Chany, who works out with me, cut Plummer off in traffic and it seems Plummer followed Tom home, right on his tail the whole way. So they get to Tom's house and Plummer parks behind him, gets out, introduces himself, and informs Tom he's an 'inept and dangerous' driver."

"What did your friend do?"

George shrugged. "Knowing Tom it probably wasn't a cordial exchange. But two days later Tom got a phone call reminding him he'd enrolled in a senior drivers' refresher course, and then a call thanking him for the generous donation he'd pledged to a safe drivers' club and then he received books and magazines in the mail about good driving habits."

"And Stanley Plummer was responsible?" Helma asked.

"What do you think? Tom couldn't prove it but it's a pretty powerful coincidence, isn't it? A guy who'd work that hard for a little piece of revenge had his share of enemies, you can bet."

George rubbed his chin through his beard. His eyes went serious. "He was cataloging the same material you'll be cataloging in the same place, Helma."

"And?" Helma asked.

George leaned forward and said, "Watch your back."

"I always take certain precautions no matter where I am."

"Glad to hear it. What cataloging system was he using?"

When Helma explained how Colonel Hooke had specified a physical card catalog, *not* a computer catalog, George's fingers absently moved as if they were flipping through a drawer of catalog cards. "I'd be glad to generate some of the cards for you off the databases here," he offered. "What kind of card catalog cabinet do you have?"

"Oak. It's actually quite beautiful. The drawer pulls are carved in . . ." She stopped when she saw how George's sharp features had softened. "Why George! I didn't know you missed our old card catalog."

"I don't. Not really. Well, maybe once in a while. It's like loving your Corvette but lusting after a Model T in perfect condition."

Lusting after cars made just about as much sense to Helma as lusting after plastic dolls still in their original boxes.

Harley Woodworth emerged from the staff

lounge, his jaw extended even longer than normal.

"What's the problem?" George Melville teased. "Did you run out of fatal diseases to research?"

Harley waved toward the window. "It doesn't do this in Arizona," he grumbled.

"That's why we call this state Washington," George said.

After George left, Roberta stopped beside Helma's cubicle. Slender Roberta appeared thinner—if that were possible; one-dimensional, like a stick figure. "How do you like working all by yourself at the cultural center? Nobody staring over your shoulder? Just you and you alone? It's worth a murder or two."

"I've only been there one day," Helma told her. She thought of Miriam Hooke. Roberta was the genealogy librarian. "But I did meet Miriam Hooke. She seems very interested in genealogy."

"That's an understatement. Her charts are so complete that if there was a heavyweight division in genealogical research she'd be Muhammad Ali."

"I didn't realize genealogy was so competitive," Helma said.

"Isn't everything?" Roberta glanced at George who was rocking back in his desk chair, then out the window. "Do you remember what a sunny day feels like?" she asked wistfully. "When you have to squint? And you can't find your sunglasses? And you only need one layer of clothing?" Roberta wandered off toward the public area, her face melancholy.

Eve looked up from her cubicle next to Helma's. "It's the weather," she said. "It's making everybody cranky." She flashed her bright smile. "Except for us natives, of course. We're in our element, just waiting for the rest of you to cry uncle and go home."

Helma pulled Stanley Plummer's letter from her purse and discreetly reread it. *I've seen you at work and I trust your train of thought. Time is essential. Uncover the Raven.* A game. Stanley Plummer had chosen Helma Zukas as his partner in a game she wasn't exactly eager to play.

She retrieved the issue of the *Bellehaven Daily News* that held Stanley Plummer's tale of death. The only family listed was a sister in Miami: Frances Jay.

She remembered how Stanley Plummer had spent an evening in the library watching her. He *had* seen her at work. Was the Raven he expected her to uncover the Raven of Northwest native tales, the trickster and bringer of light?

And the word "un-cover"? She wouldn't have expected such a fastidious man to hyphenate "uncover."

Time is essential. Time was immaterial to Stanley Plummer now but when he'd written the note, he'd been concerned about its passage. Urgency was implied, more than that, it was "essential." But why? He'd *wanted* something from Helma when he was alive, and now he was dead. Something to do with her work as a librarian? And there was the matter of the letter being mailed after Stanley Plummer's death.

Helma had long ago discovered that her mind frequently worked out complicated problems if she stayed out of its way, so she turned her attention to designing a form to be rush printed, for use between herself and George Melville in creating catalog cards. Helma had an uncanny flair for creating forms and had single-handedly designed an Interlibrary Loan form fourteen years ago that was still in use and in fact had been copied by six other regional libraries and won her accolades in the state's library community.

"Are you working late?" Eve asked as she emerged from the women's restroom in jogging clothes and baseball cap.

"Only a few more minutes," Helma told her. "Good night."

"See you tomorrow. We're doing six miles tonight."

Helma glanced into the rain and near-dark and watched Eve bolt off, reflectors shining on her heels and hat, and forming a happy face on the back of her sweatshirt.

In the empty and silent workroom, Helma ate two plain M&Ms—sucking them, not chewing—and then dialed directory assistance in Miami.

The phone was listed under Frances Jay's name. A widow, Helma guessed. Mrs. Jay answered on the first ring.

"This is Miss Wilhelmina Zukas," Helma told her. "I'm employed at the cultural center where your brother Stanley Plummer worked. We still have a few of his effects. Should we mail them to you?"

"Is there anything personal?" Frances Jay asked, her own voice decidedly impersonal.

"No," Helma said, thinking of the snakeskin pencil cup and turtle teabag holder. "He was very tidy."

Mrs. Jay laughed, barked really. "Stanley turned 'tidy' into the eighth deadly sin, didn't he? Give those things away. I've got what's left of him down here; *that's* plenty for me."

"Are there other family members I should ask?" In the background, Helma heard the twittering of parakeets, lots of parakeets.

"No one. Mother died twelve years ago; that's the last time I saw Stanley. Here one day, gone the next. He never could sit still very long."

"No friends?" Helma asked.

That laugh again. "Not Stanley. Always played by himself; always cleaned up after himself. All his games. Mother called him a 'self-contained boy.'"

"What did you call him?" Helma inquired politely.

"A stinker," Frances Jay replied without hesitation.

Meg and Cassandra, Mrs. Whitney's daughters, sat on either side of the hospital bed, eyes solicitous on their mother, who lay plumply beneath white sheets, on her face an expression of embarrassed pleasure.

"How are you feeling, Mrs. Whitney?" Helma asked.

"Well enough to go home, if only Dr. Coin would release me."

Meg and Cassandra exchanged quick glances which Mrs. Whitney surely saw.

"My dears," Mrs. Whitney told her daughters, "go get a bite to eat." She smiled sweetly, her cheeks dimpling. "You've been so loyal, here every minute. Go on now. Shoo."

Meg looked questioningly at Helma.

"I'll be here half an hour," Helma told her.

When the daughters were gone, Helma removed a box of Frango mint chocolates from her bag and set it on the bed next to Mrs. Whitney. Mrs. Whitney glanced toward the door of her room and hurriedly opened the green six-sided box.

"My favorites." She unwrapped one of the little oblongs of chocolate, bit into it, and leaned back against her pillow in contentment. "Meg wants me to go home to California with her," she told Helma.

"What do *you* want to do?" Helma asked as she tucked a corner of loose sheet beneath Mrs. Whitney's mattress.

"Stay here in Bellehaven," Mrs. Whitney said with certainty, even a little defiance. "I've lived here for seventy-four years."

"Then that's what you should do."

"Meg thinks it's dangerous to live alone at my age." A man holding a bouquet of roses peeked in hopefully, apologetically waved, and disappeared.

Helma unwrapped a Frango and took a small chocolatey bite. "My Aunt Em is eighty-five years old and she lives by herself. People check on her. She has help. There's always a way."

"Do you really think so?"

"Yes," Helma said. "I do."

"Thank you, dear," Mrs. Whitney said as if the matter were completely settled. "And how's your work in the library?"

"I'm beginning a project at the Colonel Hooke Cultural Center," Helma told her.

"I remember his books," Mrs. Whitney said, taking another Frango. "Books everywhere. And those little scenes he made."

"You've been to Colonel Hooke's house?" Helma asked in surprise.

Mrs. Whitney smiled. "I know. That family's a little out of my league. Years ago, the colonel's son James and I were . . . well, we weren't engaged but I had hopes. He's the reason I married late. I waited four years for him."

"What happened?" Helma asked softly. Beneath Mrs. Whitney's nostalgic smile, Helma glimpsed a young girl's longing, before hope was lost.

"He never came home from the war." Mrs. Whitney gazed out the window at the streetlight shining on wet pavement. "There have been so many wars, they don't say 'the war' anymore, do they? World War II. The Battle of the Bulge. The colonel was more tolerant of me after Jimmy died, as if I was a connection. I visited him every month or so, right up until he died. He loved those oatmeal cookies I make, the crunchy ones with the raisins."

"What was the colonel like?" Helma asked.

"Lonely, I think. His wife died when the children were young. Always busy, making things or trying to understand the world. He liked puzzles."

"I understand he was reclusive," Helma said.

"Not really. He didn't want pity over his missing leg. Men can be so sensitive, can't they?"

"Did you know Miriam too?" Helma asked, trying to imagine Miriam Hooke and Mrs. Whitney sharing a girlish giggle.

"Only to exchange hello's. I wasn't the kind of young woman she'd have for a friend."

"I'll take you to visit the cultural center when you're stronger," Helma offered. "All his dioramas are on display."

"It's so sad that librarian got himself murdered there." Mrs. Whitney raised her hand to her mouth. "Oh, I nearly forgot. The day before this silliness began, that handsome policeman friend of yours came by and asked me about Barbie dolls."

"That's curious," Helma said carefully. "Maybe he's buying one for his daughter."

"No, he asked about *old* Barbie dolls. They're valuable, you know. I loaned him a price book. He's *such* a nice young man."

When Helma's half-hour was up, Mrs. Whitney asked her to slip the box of Frangos in the bottom drawer of her bedside table. "It's cooler there, but can you leave three pieces behind that vase where I can reach them? A little more to the right, dear, so they're not quite so visible."

Helma said her good-byes and, eschewing the elevator as she always did, walked toward the stairwell at the end of the mauve-carpeted corridor. Halfway to the stairway door, she heard the low buzz of voices. Many voices.

The hallway turned beyond the stairwell door and a crowd of people stood outside a hospital room. Dark hair, dark skin, leaning forward as if the hospital room were packed to capacity. The doors of the other rooms along the hall were closed and except for this crowded room, the short corridor felt vacant, deserted by hospital staff, turned over to the Indians.

Three children sat on the floor, bent over a *National Geographic*.

One of the adults at the edge of the crowd—a woman—turned and looked at the children and then at Helma. Helma recognized Audrey, the receptionist from the cultural center. Her eyes were sorrowful.

Audrey looked at Helma without acknowledgment or recognition, then turned back toward the hospital room.

❧ chapter eight ❧

LINES OF COMMUNICATION

"**W**here's Tillie this morning?" Helma asked Audrey when she spotted the empty chair beside the receptionist.

"It's my ex-husband's day to have her," Audrey explained.

"Is Julianna here?"

"Not yet," Audrey said, for some reason glancing over her shoulder.

"Is someone in your family ill?" Helma asked Audrey. "I saw you at the hospital last night."

"My great aunt," Audrey told her. "We keep vigil. It's taken a few years but the hospital's finally used to it. When someone from the tribe gets sick, the nurses put them in the biggest room they have."

Helma nodded, thinking of her aunts and uncles and cousins who'd once grasped at any excuse to gather, now scattered across the country, coming together most often after the fact, for funerals.

Voices sounded from the north wing and Shelby Eaton emerged from the Plains Indians exhibit, lead-

ing a group of six visitors. A white-haired man leaning on a cane was saying, "I wish I could remember
the details but who pays attention when they're
kids, right? It was Cherokee, definitely Cherokee, I
remember that. Great-great grandmother, somebody
back there. Lot of that going on a hundred years
ago."

As she passed the slightly eerie Northwest Exhibit
in the south wing, Helma was surprised to find the
door of the Reading Room standing open. She returned to the reception area and told Audrey, "The
janitor left the Reading Room unlocked."

"I don't think there *is* a key," Audrey told her.
"Ask Shelby."

"Then the Reading Room is always unlocked?"

"Except when the police locked it."

"Do you monitor who goes in or out or what materials are removed?"

Audrey looked steadily over Helma's shoulder.
"Is something missing?" she asked.

"I wouldn't know unless an inventory was made
at the time the collection was given to the center.
Was there?"

Audrey shrugged and nodded toward Shelby Eaton who was helping the center's visitors with their
coats. "I'll tell Shelby you want to talk to him."

Helma sat at her desk and opened Stanley Plummer's letter.

Miss Zukas:

*I've seen you at work and I trust your train of
thought. Time is essential. Un-cover the Raven.*

S. C. Plummer

Then she removed his hand-written bibliographic
note from *At Home on the Plains* and laid it next to
the letter.

The handwriting was unmistakable: the same slant, the identical lower loops of the f, the printed capital I. Both specimens were definitely executed in Stanley Plummer's hand.

Un-cover the Raven, he'd advised. The Raven was one of the most prevalent and favorite figures in Northwest native folklore. The bringer of light, the trickster, the shape-changer. Hundreds of variations of the tales existed.

She scanned Colonel Hooke's shelves of books, removing volumes dealing with folklore or the Raven, fanning the pages, examining them for underlining or notes or inserts, finding nothing unusual.

Then she set the tales aside to read later and inspected the Northwest exhibits, stopping before a raven bowl and a raven ceremonial rattle, then a wooden raven mask trimmed with cedar bark rope, a small mask intended to be worn on the forehead, with shiny black eyes reflecting pranksterish curiosity.

Uncover. The underside of the mask was clearly visible; only smoothly carved wood.

Momentarily thwarted, Helma returned to the Reading Room and once again considered Stanley Plummer's unfinished cataloging project.

The publishing information that would make up the body of the catalog cards was the least of Helma's concerns; most could be easily found on computerized databases. The complications arose with the call numbers to be printed on the spines of the books.

She picked up the Stewart book titled *Cedar*, on the uses of cedar by Northwest coast Indians. If the Dewey classification number on the *Cedar* book was taken to its fullest sense, which would be necessary in such a specific collection, the book's call number would be 674.089970795. Helma tapped one of Stanley Plummer's pencils on her paper. The number wouldn't even fit on the spine. And trying to shelve a book with a number that complex . . .

The rustle of paper at the back of the Reading Room caught Helma's attention. She rose and warily approached the far corner, holding her hardbound copy of *Anglo-American Cataloging Rules 2* in both hands.

A boy sat curled on a shiny blue jacket beneath the window, a book of totem pole photographs balanced on his knees, the same boy who'd been in the Reading Room on Wednesday. He looked up without surprise at Helma, his straight black hair falling damply across his forehead, his dark eyes preoccupied. He placed a less-than-spotless finger to the illustration of a carved salmon atop the outstretched arms of a carved woman. "Did you see this?" he asked.

"Do you like it?" Helma asked.

"Sure. I'm going to carve like that."

"How did you get in here?"

"I walked." He flipped a page and pressed his face closer to a totem pole painted in red, black, and yellow.

"Is today a school holiday?" Helma asked.

"No, but I got kicked out for two weeks."

"Why?"

"Carving," he said and bent back over the page.

Helma had been dismissed. She moved the subject of the Reading Room key to the highest priority on her mental list.

"What's your name?" Helma tried.

"Young Frank," he answered without looking up.

"Do you belong to someone who works in the center, Young Frank?"

He shook his head and turned another page.

Helma, exasperated, said, "These are valuable books. Please check with me before you take any from the shelves."

Halfway back to her desk she heard Young Frank say, "I just like to come here. It's nice." When she looked back, his head was still down, deep in the book of totem poles.

Helma took down the first few books that Stanley Plummer had arranged in alphabetical order and with one of Plummer's keenly sharpened pencils, began to fill out her freshly printed forms for George Melville.

Shelby Eaton harumphed and pulled at his sleeve cuffs as he entered the Reading Room, announcing himself. "I just passed Young Frank Portman leaving the center. Was he in here again?"

"He was reading."

Shelby puffed his pink cheeks and blew outward. "Keep an eye on him. He's a little hellion."

"He told me he'd been expelled from school for carving."

"Hah. That's half true. He carved a totem pole on the leg of a 'time-out' table. It was bad enough he smuggled a lethal weapon inside the school but then he set the shavings on fire, too." Shelby Eaton shook his head. "Fire trucks, kids standing in the rain. Complete disruption."

"He was perfectly well-behaved here, except for removing a book from the shelf," Helma stopped and acknowledged, "which he *did* return to its proper place. But the point is I'd like the key to the Reading Room."

Shelby Eaton shook his head. "The colonel expressly willed his collection would only go to the center if it were in a fully accessible unlocked room."

"I can't maintain control over this material, some of which is irreplaceable, if the room is open to anyone who comes along."

"I know, I know. Stanley Plummer didn't like it, either. But we have to follow the provisions of the colonel's will."

"When I arrived this morning," Helma explained, "this stack of water rights treaties had been disturbed."

Eaton glanced at the booklets and government documents Helma referred to. "People hang out here sometimes. Ask Audrey who's interesed in water rights." Eaton looked out at the dripping shrubbery and glossy rocks. "Although we have more water than anybody on this earth has a right to."

Shelby Eaton smiled and for a moment Helma thought he was going to heartily clap her on the back and acquiesce. She moved a step away.

"You'll figure out a way to keep this place in control," he said cheerfully. "That's what being professional is all about, isn't it?"

"Stanley was going to sell some of the books," Julianna announced calmly as she walked through the tiers of shelving, lightly running her hands along the book spines.

"From Colonel Hooke's private collection? Helma asked in surprise. "Did he tell you that?"

"Almost."

"And *did* he sell any of them?"

"I don't know." The big woman pointed to the cardboard box on the floor that Helma had yet to inventory. "Look in that box. I saw him put some really old books in there."

A series of small explosions came from outside the building. Helma rose from her chair.

"It's just Young Frank," Julianna said, pointing out the window.

"Fireworks are illegal," Helma said.

"Not on the reservation," Julianna reminded her.

Young Frank stood on the sloping lawn, smiling at spots of smoke trailing upward across the lawn and melting into the mist that hung in the trees.

"I don't know how he gets those things to work when it's so wet," Julianna mused.

Helma turned from the window and asked, "Did you know Mr. Plummer very well?"

Julianna inspected her bright nails. "Not very. He was fussy with a capital F. He had these *things* he did. Sharpen *all* his pencils before he sat down, wear different shoes to and from work, eat only white bread sandwiches. His socks always matched his tie and he put everything in straight lines, weird stuff like that."

Helma didn't see what was "weird" about Stanley Plummer's behavior; perhaps it was a cultural difference.

"Do you know about any dolls?" Helma asked.

"Yeah, he talked some about dolls," Julianna said. "That was weird, too. He even gave me one; it was still in a box, just like brand new but it was old. I sent it to my niece for her birthday." Julianna shook her head. "But he was, I don't know, stuck up. Nobody *really* liked him. Even Tillie growled when he walked by. It was no big surprise he was getting fired so you could take over."

Helma couldn't stop herself. "What are you talking about? Stanley Plummer wasn't fired; he was *murdered*."

Julianna relaxed into the role of the woman who has the information. "Stan was murdered *before* he could be fired. He already knew it was going to happen and you'd take his place."

"How could he? That wasn't decided until after his death."

"Oh yeah?" Julianna asked, her smile growing.

The conversation had escaped into gossip and was catapulting into unknown territory. Ms. Moon. Helma needed to talk to Ms. Moon as soon as possible. Julianna had misunderstood Stanley Plummer.

Ms. Moon was the proper person to give Helma the correct version of *this* story.

Helma cleared her throat and gave her copy of *Catalog Card Filing* to Julianna, who took it reluctantly, holding it away from her body. "Study this and you'll learn the proper format for filing catalog cards. Conformity is vital."

"Maybe in some things," Julianna commented, opening the booklet and closing it without glancing at the pages. "I'm dying for a cup of coffee. Want some?"

"No thank you."

Julianna paused at the door and looked back at Helma. "Do you drink tea like Stan did?"

"I do prefer tea," Helma told her.

Julianna snorted with satisfaction and left the Reading Room.

Helma sat at her desk and breathed deep regular breaths. In for four, hold for four, exhale for eight. This was why Helma Zukas disliked gossip. It distorted the patterns of information and threw everything into unfounded confusion. Gossip, that's all Julianna was relaying, gossip. How could Stanley Plummer have possibly known she'd replace him?

Helma turned the ignition key again, pumping the gas pedal, but her Buick wouldn't start; it sat as useful as a stone in the center's parking lot, not emitting a single encouraging sound.

She pulled the key from the ignition and sat back as rain pounded on the roof and sheeted down her already steamed windshield. Helma and Audrey had been the last to leave the building and Audrey's taillights had just disappeared over the hill.

A pay phone, that was what she needed now. Across the road the green and red neon of Kelly's Bar and Restaurant winked at her in the darkness. She had no choice.

She removed a dry plastic rain hat from her glove compartment and secured it over her hair, then positioned her bag over her shoulder, preparing to dash through the rain to Kelly's.

The lock button was down and Helma reached to pull it up, at the same time wiping a clear space in her steamy window.

And that's when she saw a figure approaching the car from the direction of the center. She couldn't see who it was, only that the person moved slowly, cautiously, from an angle she wouldn't have seen unless she'd turned in her seat, and suddenly Helma remembered the man on the library loading dock, the way his hand had reached out toward her.

She slammed the lock button down with the side of her hand and frantically searched in her bag for the can of pepper spray Ruth had given her for her birthday. The wan light of the street lamp barely penetrated through her steamy windows.

As her fingers touched the cool pepper spray container, knuckles rapped sharply against her window. Helma gasped and raised the spray, rolling down her window one cautious inch.

"Stand back," she called out in her silver-dime voice. "I have a weapon."

"Don't shoot," a voice answered. "It's me, Aaron Hooke."

"Step away from the car," Helma told him.

He did and Helma rolled down her window two more inches, still holding the pepper spray.

Aaron Hooke stood five feet from the car, wearing a hooded sweatshirt spotted with rain. "Car trouble?" he asked. "Or is this a stick-up?"

"Why were you coming from the center?" she asked. "It's closed."

Aaron looked behind him toward the murkily lit building. "I wasn't at the center. I was just leaving Kelly's," he said, pointing in the opposite direction, "and I saw your car sitting here so I walked over to investigate."

"It won't start," Helma told him.

"Come on. I'm no mechanic but I *can* give you a ride."

Helma hesitated and Aaron bounced on the balls of his feet like a prize-fighter, splashing rain water. "You can tell my mother if I misbehave," he offered.

"Could we go inside the center to use the phone?" Helma asked.

"Sorry. I don't have a key. I'll take you home."

"I don't think..." Helma began and Aaron stopped bouncing. "Actually," he said. "If you *really* want a phone, I've got one in my car."

Before she unlocked her door and stepped from her car, Helma jotted on the notepad she kept in her car: *Helma Zukas accepted a ride from Aaron Hooke*, along with the time and date and left it on the car seat.

With Aaron's hand on her elbow, they hurried through the rain beside the line of vehicles parked along the road, stepping to the shoulder each time traffic swished past.

He opened the passenger side for her, tucking in her coat before he closed the door.

"You thought you saw somebody?" Aaron asked as he fastened his seatbelt. "Who was it?"

"I couldn't tell," Helma told him.

"Might have been shadows from the traffic," Aaron said. "Go ahead and use my car phone if you want."

Instead of calling road service, Helma phoned Ruth.

"Your voice sounds funny," Ruth said. "Where in heck are you?"

"In a car."

"Whose?" Ruth demanded.

"Could you please pick me up at the library in ten minutes?"

"Are you sitting beside our chief of police?"

"No."

Ruth whooped in her ear and in the quiet car Aaron took his eyes off the wet road long enough to raise his eyebrows at Helma.

"I'm on my way," Ruth said and hung up.

"Lucky I stopped at Kelly's, eh?" Aaron asked Helma. "You'd be soaking wet by now."

Helma sniffed delicately but couldn't detect the odor of cigarettes and beer she associated with bars.

"I'm surprised you saw me and realized I was having car trouble."

"It's a habit of mine: whenever I'm near the center, I give it the once-over, just to check on Gramps's investment."

"Weren't you at work?"

"Do you mean, am I employed? I'm between jobs and I mean that seriously, although Gramps left me a nice pile. I don't have to *really* work if I don't want to."

"How fortunate for you."

"It really is," he said, completely without irony.

Aaron reached the edge of town and sped through a yellow light, headlight beams from legally stopped cars flashing into the car's interior.

"I usually stop for yellow lights," Helma said, glancing over her shoulder as the traffic light turned red.

"You do?" Aaron asked as if that were a novel and charming idea. "Find anything interesting in the Reading Room yet?"

"Such as?"

Aaron shrugged. "Beats me. Maybe whatever old Stanley was doing back there instead of his job?"

Had he heard Julianna's gossip? No, Helma decided, of course not.

"I do believe Mr. Plummer was making headway; it just wasn't apparent to nonlibrarians." Helma winced, remembering that Stanley Plummer wasn't a librarian either.

"I bet you're better than he was."

"It's a safe wager, I suspect. You missed the library's corner," she pointed out. Aaron had a disturbing habit of turning his eyes from the road to Helma as he spoke.

"I hoped you wouldn't notice. Are you sure I can't take you home? Or how about Tweed's for a drink?"

"No thank you."

Aaron made a tire-squealing U-turn in the middle of the street and pulled into the handicapped slot in front of the library. Helma noted with relief that Ruth's car wasn't anywhere in sight.

"Then how about a raincheck?" Aaron asked.

"I'd agree to a raincheck," Helma said as she raised her umbrella.

The library workroom was empty except for George Melville, who was just turning off his desk lamp.

"Sorry, Helma," he said. "Our beloved Ms. Moon snuck out of here an hour ago. Off to a weekend retreat to put the world back in balance. If we're lucky, she'll come back in better balance herself." George's grin faded. "You okay? Any problems at the center? News about the murder?"

Tonight was Helma's walk with Wayne Gallant and it was already 5:28. "Just an issue I need to verify with Ms. Moon," Helma told George.

"Uh oh, sounds serious. She's not up to another one of her schemes, is she?"

A car horn blared three times in front of the library and Helma headed for the workroom door, withdrawing her umbrella from its scabbard. "I'll talk to her on Monday. Have a good weekend."

"You, too. I'm holing up in the desert with

Lawrence of Arabia," George said, "and I'm not looking out the window once."

"So who was it?" Ruth asked.

After Aaron's Lexus, Ruth's car felt like America's first automobile. Invisible things crunched and crackled beneath Helma's feet; the interior lights, including the dash lights, were burned out and she couldn't verify how fast Ruth was driving.

"One of the center's patrons," Helma said. "He gave me a ride."

"I don't believe that for a second, Helma Zukas," Ruth said, raising her chin. "You won't tell me because you think I'll give you a rough time."

"Wouldn't you?"

"Well, yeah."

One more time, after she'd changed her clothes and before she finished her hair, Helma checked her balcony, standing in the wind and shining the flashlight from her storm kit on the other balconies, but there was still no sign of Boy Cat Zukas. She briefly considered calling him but she'd never called the cat and wasn't sure what to say and doubted he'd answer anyway.

When her doorbell rang, Helma met Chief Gallant, her jacket buttoned, her purse over her shoulder.

"You're ready," he said unnecessarily, smiling in surprise.

Helma glanced at her watch. "It *is* 6:16," she said.

His eyes twinkled in that irritating way. "I knew I shouldn't have stopped for that yellow light," he said and moved aside so Helma could step in front of him.

"Windy the past few days, huh?" he asked as they drove toward the college.

It seemed a rhetorical question but Helma answered anyway. "Yes," she said.

As if in emphasis, they passed a house where early Christmas lights had blown loose from the eaves and now swayed in the dark night like a brilliant jump rope being warmed up for a good twirl.

Marching music blared from ceiling speakers in the brightly lit college gym. And around the room, a crowd of people moved counterclockwise as in a roller skating rink, some walking, others jogging, a few with babies on their backs.

Side by side, Helma and Wayne Gallant merged into the throng between a vigorous gray-haired couple and two college-age girls in Spandex. Conversation steadily swirled around the room, creating a hum that insured more privacy than if there'd only been a few people in the gym.

"Has anyone at the cultural center mentioned the murder to you?" Wayne Gallant asked as they matched strides.

"It's come up but I have the impression people prefer to avoid it."

"It's not the kind of attention the board's been working toward."

"Do you know *why* Stanley Plummer was killed in the women's restroom?" Helma asked.

"The murderer either chased or followed him inside."

"The killer was a man," Helma said.

"Why do you say that?"

"If it had been a woman, Plummer wouldn't have run into the women's restroom to hide."

The chief smiled at Helma and made an "okay" sign with his thumb and forefinger.

"And the weapon was a paper spindle?" she asked.

"Plummer had a collection of antique spindles. There were five of them sitting on his desk. The murderer chose the best one for the job."

"Wayne!" a woman jogging past called. She

turned, running backward for a few steps, ponytail bobbing, until the chief waved back. Helma noted the expression in the chief's eyes, which was merely friendly, and she waved at the woman, too.

"I did understand he was a collector of sorts," Helma said, and told Wayne Gallant her mother's story of Stanley Plummer's doll-collecting lecture. She hesitated for a moment and then, hoping it wasn't gossip, she told him what Julianna had said about Plummer selling rare books.

Chief Gallant wasn't surprised. "Plummer *was* a professional collector. He moved around, boning up on a subject in one city and then passing himself off as an expert in another, buying and selling pieces to contacts he'd made along the way. So far we've verified he collected dolls, paper spindles, model trains, mechanical banks, Limoges enamels, and nineteenth-century spurs."

"So while he was employed at UCLA, he was boning up on library cataloging to prepare himself for the cultural center."

"Probably. We haven't uncovered any illegal activity but the words 'unsavory' and 'unethical' do come to mind."

"I'm curious what he was studying during his tour in Bellehaven," Helma said.

"My guess is Native American artifacts but he was only here six months. He had a storage locker for his collections. Everything organized, labeled and valued."

Helma and the chief split up to pass a woman with a cane.

"He didn't leave anything personal in the Reading Room," Helma said, "unless the police took it."

"His effects were all impersonal," the chief agreed.

"Or concealing," Helma suggested. "Did you speak to his sister?"

Wayne Gallant paused mid-stride, nearly causing a jam-up behind them. "Why do I have the feeling you spoke to her yourself?"

When Helma only smiled, he asked, "What do you say to ten more circuits and then we get something to eat? Do you like Italian food?"

"As long as it doesn't entail long strings of pasta," Helma told him.

It wasn't until they were seated in Tony's Italian Cafe—the chief eating spaghetti and Helma a salad—that Helma asked, "How is the Barbie doll connected to Plummer's murder?"

Wayne Gallant shook his head. "Rumors get out no matter what, don't they? What's that saying about secrets?"

"Benjamin Franklin said three people could keep a secret if two of them were dead," Helma provided. Beside Helma's chair sat her purse and in her purse the letter from Stanley Plummer, a message from the dead: *I've seen you.*

"Right."

"Then it's true? Stanley Plummer was cradling a Barbie doll?"

"Maybe not 'cradling' it, but it was close to his body. A valuable one, according to a local doll collector. 'Barbie #1,' she called it, a 1959 model. At first we suspected the obvious: that the murder had involved doll collecting, but . . ." Wayne Gallant took a breath. "This is confidential."

"Of course," Helma said, surprised he felt it necessary to say so.

"We believe whoever left the doll knew that Plummer was a collector and wanted to be sure we uncovered that fact."

"So the murderer wanted to make it appear a collector was involved?" From the kitchen came the clatter of a dropped tray. Three college-age boys at a nearby table applauded.

"Possibly."

"And do *you* believe a collector was involved?"

"From what we've found so far, Plummer had created more than his share of ill will in that crowd."

"Mmm," Helma acknowledged. She set her fork on the rim of her plate and reached for her purse. "I received a note in the mail I'd like to show you."

Wayne Gallant wiped his mouth and hands on his napkin and eagerly took the letter.

" 'I've seen you at work and I trust your train of thought. Time is essential. Un-cover the Raven,' " he read aloud. He looked at Helma. "Do you know what this means?"

"I don't. Not in the least. But you can see the signature: S. C. Plummer. It's from Stanley Carrol Plummer himself, and it's postmarked the day Plummer's body was discovered."

"When did you receive it?"

"The day before yesterday. Since my address wasn't completed, he hadn't decided whether to send it to my home or the library. The clerk at the post office said it went through their dead letter office."

"That's why it took a week to reach you. You didn't know Plummer?"

"I never met him, although I saw him in the library one evening. I'm certain he was watching me."

" 'I've seen you at work,' " the chief read again. "Could the Raven refer to the Raven tales? Maybe a book in the center?"

"That was my first assumption. I've searched the collection, and the exhibits, too."

"Nothing?"

Helma shook her head. "Not yet. And 'time is essential,' " she added. "When he wrote this, he felt under pressure. Whatever the Raven is, he hoped I'd uncover it soon; he was urging me to hurry."

"And then he died," the chief said, sounding as if

he were talking to himself. "Why would he have been watching you?"

"There is a rumor . . ." Helma began. No, Julianna's claim still had to be verified.

"What?"

Helma shook her head. "At this point that's all it is. I'll inform you if it's true."

"Does verifying this rumor involve any danger to you, Helma?" he asked.

"None at all," Helma assured him.

"Maybe Stanley Plummer isn't actually the author of this."

"I compared it to his handwriting at the center and it matches perfectly."

The chief frowned. "At first glance it may appear similar but to the trained eye . . ."

"I'm certain it's his," Helma said, picking up her fork.

"I'm not saying it *isn't*," Wayne Gallant said hastily, "but I'd like to have someone at the lab look at it. Can I take this?"

"You may."

His eyebrows raised. "You're giving it to me that easily?"

"I already made a very good photocopy of both the letter and the envelope."

Chief Gallant tipped his head, looking at Helma intently. "If you found anything . . . unusual, you'd let me know, wouldn't you?"

"Anything?" Helma asked.

The chief smiled. "Anything pertaining to nefarious activities, murder and mayhem, that sort of thing."

"Certainly," Helma said. "And if you were to find already in police possession any material that had to do with Stanley Plummer's cataloging intents, you'd inform me, wouldn't you?"

"Of course."

"Shelby Eaton implied Plummer was hired through an association with Miriam Hooke," Helma said.

"He convinced her they were related, going back several generations, so you *could* say he was hired because of family connections."

"And there weren't actually any connections?" Helma guessed.

"None that can be proven," the chief said.

"He had to have done a credible amount of research to convince a genealogy expert like Miriam," Helma said.

"He did. I'm not sure which Miriam feels most: embarrassment or relief."

After their walk and a glass of wine Helma was so relaxed she ordered a piece of cheesecake with wild blackberry sauce and laughed lightly when Chief Gallant told her she could afford to eat cheesecake better than he could.

They didn't discuss Stanley Plummer's death or the letter again. Chief Gallant walked her to her apartment door, tenting his jacket above her head to protect her from the rain.

As he lowered his jacket in front of her door, his arm fell across Helma's shoulder. She stood very still, waiting. Expectant.

"Do you want me to read it?" he asked.

"I beg your pardon?"

"The note taped to your door."

Helma ran her tongue between her lips and pulled off the yellow piece of paper taped above her dead-bolt.

"I have your cat," it read, and was signed "Walter."

Walter David answered the door so quickly he must have been watching for her through his window. He nodded to the chief, looking preoccupied.

A woman wearing black boots and jeans stood at his shoulder. She looked closely at Helma, her eyes narrowing, then she disappeared deeper into Walter's apartment.

"He's in here," Walter said, waving inside. "He was sitting on my patio in the rain. You weren't home and I saw you had the job done so I let him in. He was sopping wet," he added in an accusatory tone Helma ignored.

Boy Cat Zukas lay curled pathetically on a towel beside the patio door, his fur still damp and matted. He paid no attention to the humans invading the living room.

Moggy, Walter David's white Persian, sat regally on a velvety cushion on the back of Walter David's couch, her round eyes blazing at Boy Cat Zukas, her flat face disturbingly humanoid.

"I'll carry him upstairs for you," Wayne Gallant said. "I don't have a cat myself but he's a beauty," and the chief went to Moggy, gently lifting the perfectly groomed Persian in his arms.

"Not her," Walter David said. He pointed to Boy Cat Zukas. "Him."

Chief Gallant blinked. He looked from Helma to Boy Cat Zukas, his brows drawn.

"I'm surprised," he said.

"Ruth, can you come over? I'd like you to see something."

It was Saturday afternoon and Helma's opaque shades were closed, not to block light but to block her view of the day which was identical to the day before and the day before that and so on for the past two weeks.

"What?" Ruth asked.

"A letter."

"From a man?"

"Yes."

"Who?" Ruth asked.

"Ruth, can you just come over?"

"Okay. I'm tired of staring at blank canvases anyway."

When Ruth arrived she handed Helma a foil packet of kitty treats. "These are from Max, cat-to-cat sympathy present. Where is he?"

"I haven't seen him since this morning but he appears fully recovered."

"Don't overlook his bruised psyche. So what's this mystery letter?" Ruth asked, already leafing through Helma's unanswered mail in her letter holder.

"Here," Helma said, handing her the page from a file folder marked "Plummer—Correspondence." "This is a photocopy."

"What happened to the original?"

"I gave it to Wayne Gallant last night."

Ruth nudged Helma with her elbow. "I'll ask you about *that* later." She dropped onto Helma's couch and studied the letter, reading it silently but moving her lips. "S. C. Plummer? This is from the dead guy?" she asked, shaking the paper. "He's seen you at work? This is really weird, Helma. Creepy. 'Uncovering the Raven' sounds ver-y kinky to me. He wrote 'uncover' wrong, too."

"It was mailed the day his body was discovered."

"I thought you didn't know him."

"I never met him." She told Ruth about Plummer watching her in the library.

Ruth chewed her thumbnail. "He *wants* something from you, Helma. What we have here is a dead man asking you to do him a little favor. And he wants it done fast. 'Time is essential.' "

"He *wanted* something from me *before* he died."

"But you're curious."

"Of course I am."

"He should have mailed this letter to you a little sooner. By the way, what about the doll?"

"The chief said it's confidential."

"Just tell me if it's true or not."

"It's confidential," Helma repeated.

"So it's true." Ruth turned her attention back to the letter. "Are you sure Plummer wrote this?"

"I compared it with notes he left at the cultural center."

"It looks fussy," Ruth said.

"Precise," Helma amended. "Everything Stanley Plummer did was carefully planned and precisely performed."

"Too bad he's dead. He sounds like your soul mate."

"There's the remotest possibility he knew I was replacing him. He could just be wishing me luck. He 'trusts my train of thought.'"

"No. I think he's asking you to figure out who killed him."

"I doubt if he expected to be murdered when he wrote it," Helma said.

"Yeah, victims usually don't plan that part. Why doesn't he just come out and *give* you the facts? Why be cryptic?"

"Maybe he feared someone else might read the note."

"So?"

"So 'the facts' might be dangerous."

"Or worth a zillion bucks." Ruth set down the letter. "I only know one thing: this guy's deader than a doornail. Let's talk about more interesting stuff, like your date last night."

"Your car's ready any time you want to pick it up," the mechanic told Helma.

"Did it need a new battery?" Helma asked, reaching across the telephone to adjust the pleat in her kitchen curtain.

"Nope. The battery cable was disconnected; that's all. Cheap fix."

Helma's hand froze on the knife-sharp pleat. "Disconnected? Is that a usual occurrence in a parked car?"

"Not very," he told her.

❧ chapter nine ❧

INTRUSION

Helma arrived at the Bellehaven Public Library before Ms. Moon on Monday morning. While she waited for the director, she discreetly carried a book titled *Cat Ownership* from the public area to her desk, tucking it beneath a flyer advertising a CD-ROM-a-Month club.

"Is the weather like this every November?" Harley Woodworth asked her as he took off his jacket, gloves, and two wool scarves, draping them around his cubicle to dry.

"Sometimes."

He rubbed his hands together and put them under his arms. "I slept through Sunday and I couldn't tell you a single thing I did on Saturday, not for a million dollars. This weekend never happened." He sat down, mumbling, "I might be getting the flu."

With a flourish, George Melville leaned into Helma's cubicle and presented her with a two-inch stack of catalog cards. "Here you go. I printed these for the center using the forms you filled out. Save you a little typing. No call numbers on the cards just like you asked. Look good, don't they?"

"Yes, they do," Helma agreed, thumbing through

the creamy, computer-printed card stock.

"Have you decided what kind of call numbers to stick on these babies?"

"Not yet. The Dewey Decimal system is . . ."

"Overkill," George supplied. "Numbers so complicated you'd have to hire mathematicians to shelve the books."

Helma slipped the rubber-banded catalog cards into her bag. "Thank you again, George."

Ms. Moon finally hurried in, banging the workroom door and dropping her bag, unusually frazzled and late. Her normally curly hair was flat, her eyes red. If Helma hadn't had such pressing questions she might have allowed Ms. Moon more time to repair herself.

Instead, she followed on Ms. Moon's heels to her office. "I'd like to speak with you regarding my assignment at the cultural center," Helma said.

Ms. Moon, still wearing her coat, dropped into her chair, splaying her arms across the chair's arms. "I thought we already had."

"Was my 'loan' to the cultural center arranged with Shelby Eaton and the center's board of directors *before* Mr. Plummer's death?"

Helma fully expected Ms. Moon to laugh gaily and assign Julianna's claims to permanent rest. But Ms. Moon's eyes shifted to the open door as if this were one time she'd appreciate it being closed. She picked up one of the crystals on her desk and turned it between her palms, breathing on it and then wiping her breath away. "The center has a rare collection of books and manuscripts," she said.

"I'm aware of that."

"The only way *our* reading public could have access to the collection is if they went to the center itself and used their card catalog."

It was as if a sudden burst of sunlight had struck Helma. "You're saying you made a *deal* with the center?" she asked, her voice helplessly rising. "You traded *my* cataloging skills for access to the center's collection?"

"That's an unharmonious way to put it."

"That's the only way to put it."

"Once you complete the project we'll add your cataloging to our computer system." Ms. Moon smiled. "Think of our grateful patrons. Rare information at their fingertips."

In dismay, Helma sat in the chair opposite Ms. Moon. "Stanley Plummer was actually being fired so I could take his place?"

Ms. Moon gazed sadly into the gray morning. "He didn't have an accredited degree. He'd misrepresented himself to Miriam Hooke. And his energy was contrary to Shelby Eaton's. With or without our agreement, Stanley Plummer was going to be terminated."

"*That's* true enough," Helma said.

Ms. Moon raised her hands to her heart. "If only we'd moved a few days sooner his essence might still be with us."

"I resent not being told the truth about the situation," Helma said.

"It was destined to happen," Ms. Moon said. "Only the time frame was altered."

Helma stood. "It was hardly fair dealing."

"Not a lot in life is," Ms. Moon said, heaving a deep sigh and standing her crystal on end.

When Stanley Plummer had "seen her at work," he'd already known of Ms. Moon and Shelby Eaton's scheme. He'd been watching Helma, judging her as his successor.

Roberta looked up as Helma passed her desk. "It's raining," she said.

Tillie lay sleeping on her chair beside Audrey, issuing little dog snores. Julianna sat on the edge of Audrey's desk, a steamy cup that smelled herbal in her hand, dressed in yellow leggings and high heels and a t-shirt that reached her knees.

"Did you have an opportunity to study the booklet on card catalog filing over the weekend?" Helma asked Julianna.

Julianna sniffed. "I don't get paid on weekends. I might look at it today."

Helma turned to Audrey, but Audrey was busily picking a tangle from the soft fur behind Tillie's ear.

Helma raised her pencil from her form, recognizing the hiccupy laugh rising above other laughter in a distant part of the center. She glanced at her watch. Ruth was usually home painting this time of day.

When ten minutes had passed and Ruth still hadn't appeared in the Reading Room, Helma went looking for her.

And found her coming out of the men's restroom, her hair bushed out, wearing a red paisley outfit that brushed the heels of her slingbacks.

"Helma Zukas!" Ruth said when she saw Helma. Ruth broadly smiled but there was a tense swagger to her walk, a glitter in her heavily made-up eyes that made Helma wary.

"What were you doing in the men's room, Ruth?"

"You don't use the women's, do you?" Ruth asked.

"Of course I do," Helma told her.

Ruth held a hand to the side of her mouth. "*Nobody* does. That's where they found the *body*."

"It isn't there now."

"That doesn't make any difference."

"Yes it does," Helma told her. "If you avoided every spot where a body had lain, you'd hardly be able to walk anywhere on earth."

"Only fresh bodies, Helma. It wears off after a while."

"What are you talking about?"

Ruth shrugged. "I don't know. I'm just trying to get into the spirit of . . . I don't know." Ruth wound down. Her shoulders sagged.

"Are you okay?"

Ruth straightened. She was "on" again. "Sure. This is a bodacious institution, don't you think?"

"Were you looking for me?"

"Not particularly. I wanted to see what the fuss was about. Murders and stuff."

"I thought you'd be home painting."

Ruth shook her head. "My abundant talent has gone into hiding." She laughed hollowly. "Maybe I lost it for good this time."

A door banged and Ruth jumped, her eyes wide and startled. The whites of Ruth's eyes were touched by red; dark shadows sagged beneath her makeup.

"Ruth," Helma asked her quietly. "Are you drinking too much?"

"Just enough to get by," Ruth said.

"Ruth," a tall man in braids and flannel called in a deep voice from the door of the room Helma knew to be an informal lounge used by staff and visitors alike. "Coffee?"

Helma recognized him as the man who'd stood behind Audrey's desk, the man she'd seen on the center's lawn, who Audrey had called "Nobody." His eyes passed over Helma as if she weren't standing beside Ruth at all.

"Be right there," Ruth said. "Want to join us?"

"No thank you," Helma told her, wondering how Ruth had already managed to meet the braided man. "I have work to do."

"Pity."

A few feet before the women's restroom, where Helma intended to fill a glass of water for the overly dry jade plant in the Reading Room, she was stopped by the sight of a rectangular brass plate mounted in the wall at shoulder height, an open slot in its burnished center. "U.S. Mail," the raised brass letters read. How had she missed it?

She fingered the cool metal, wiggled her fingers in the slot, then approached Audrey at her desk. "Is the mail slot in the wall near the restrooms in use?"

Audrey nodded. "It was there when the building was bought, when it was an old peoples' home."

"What's on the other side? Which room is it in?"

Audrey led the way to a door in the hallway behind her. Tillie followed close behind, head high, eagerly sniffing.

Behind the door was a windowless room, half storage, half office. An ancient duplicating machine sat in the corner next to an obsolete electric typewriter and boxes of computer paper. A canvas mail bag was opened on a stand beneath the mail slot. Envelopes pushed through the slot simply fell into the bag.

"Do you sort through the mail before it goes to the post office?" Helma asked Audrey.

"No. I just close the bag and give it to the mailman every afternoon, then replace the bag. It would be easier to have in and out boxes on my desk but Shelby thinks that's too public."

"Did the mail go out the day Stanley Plummer's body was found?" Helma asked.

"Probably. After I found . . . I didn't stay."

"I see. Thank you." Helma left the mailroom and walked back toward the restroom, continuing her mission of water for the jade plant, following Stanley Plummer's path past the letter slot and into the women's restroom, picturing it.

"I trust your train of thought," he'd written. Now she knew *how* the letter had been mailed but she wasn't sure the *why* could be so easily answered.

*   *   *

Once again, Audrey and Helma were the last remaining employees in the center. Audrey was tidying her desk when Helma casually approached her.

"On Friday night when we left the center together, did you see anyone else in the parking lot?"

Helma had grown accustomed to the way Audrey briefly met her eyes and looked away, as if maintaining eye contact overlong was an intrusion. "No," Audrey answered. "Did you?"

"I thought I did. My car wouldn't start and when the mechanic inspected it, he discovered the battery cables were disconnected."

Audrey's face didn't change. She listened politely, without comment, and after a few moments of silence, said, "Somebody tampered with your car."

"Unless the cables were jostled loose, which seems unlikely."

"That may be," Audrey said. "Tonight I'll wait in the parking lot to be sure your car starts."

"Thank you, but I think I'll stay a while longer."

"Everybody's gone."

"It'll only be for a few minutes," Helma said, accompanying Audrey and Tillie to the north wing where Audrey switched off the lights. "The front door locks itself, doesn't it?"

"You'll be alone," Audrey warned, turning on low-wattage recessed lights that barely illuminated the exhibits.

"I don't mind. May I ask you a question?"

Audrey nodded.

"On the night Stanley Plummer died, did you turn off the lights in the center?"

"Except for the night lights," Audrey told her. "Like now."

When Helma heard the front door close behind Audrey and Tillie, she sat down at Stanley Plummer's desk. She put both feet flat on the floor and folded her hands on her desktop.

It was dark outside and raindrops patted the roof. The heating ducts pinged as the center cooled down and from somewhere else there came the gentle thumping of wood against wood. Helma glanced out the door into the low-lit hallway.

Sounds traveled so easily in the building surely Stanley Plummer had heard his murderer approaching. He'd worked late, staying on after the rest of the staff went home. And then he'd been surprised: stalked and murdered.

Helma removed a clean envelope from her desk drawer and set it on the desk, pretending it was the note Plummer had chosen to write to her. She pictured the envelope lying on his desk with her name on it. Had the murderer seen the envelope? Read her name? There was a quarrel, a confrontation. Shouting maybe.

Helma stood and picked up the envelope. Purposefully. Plummer wouldn't have just snatched it up. Even during grave danger, she guessed, his actions would have been deliberate.

The letter wasn't addressed. Why? Perhaps he'd never intended to mail it—rather to *leave* it in the Reading Room for her to find. He'd known she would be his replacement.

Helma left the Reading Room, moving consciously, without panic, seeing what the dead man had seen.

The same lighting. To her left, the shadowy Northwest exhibit, figures glimpsed from peripheral vision, their faces invisible. Shapes of totem poles and eyeless masks, the silent north wing stretching dimly beyond the reception area.

She turned toward the restrooms, not looking over her shoulder, her pace strong and purposeful, reaching out her right arm and shoving the unaddressed envelope through the mail slot, not breaking stride.

Helma was one step from the women's restroom

when she heard the sound. A door opening some-where in the building. She froze, listening so hard her ears rang. Someone was in the building. Had Audrey returned? With her breath held, Helma waited for a voice to call out.

But all she heard was the slightest whisper of movement, so soft a stirring she couldn't tell from which direction it came. Whoever was in the build-ing was moving stealthily through the halls.

Carefully, her breath still held, Helma took the re-maining step to the women's restroom, soundlessly pushing open the door and slipping inside.

It was pitch black. No windows, not a glimmer of light, the sounds of her movements suddenly hollow against the tiled walls. Helma reached toward the light switch, then pulled back her hand.

No. The light might show beneath the door, real-izing even as she thought it, that this was also Stan-ley Plummer's experience. He wouldn't have risked turning on the light, either.

Holding her arms out in front of her in the dark-ness, Helma bumped into a sink and careened to the left against a stall post and helplessly into a stall, struggling to maintain silence, fighting to keep her balance.

She spread her arms, disoriented. Only one hand touched a wall and she knew she was in the hand-icapped stall where Stanley Plummer had died with a metal spindle through his heart.

She stood stock-still, afraid to move, listening for the sounds of the intruder approaching the rest-room. Surely, he or she had heard Helma's clumsy entrance into the handicapped stall.

She had no idea how long she stood in the pitch-black stall, listening and waiting, hearing her own breath. She couldn't hear any movement outside the restroom. Had the intruder left?

Finally, Helma took a few cautious steps, thinking

she was approaching the door of the stall, but instead she bumped into a corner of cool tiles. She turned, pressing her back into the corner, and wrapped her arms around her body, her breath rising and falling in harsh gasps, her eyes straining into the blackness as Plummer's must have. Waiting. What next?

Silence, not even the sounds of the falling rain reached into the restroom. Helma was so cold. She slid down the wall—and her elbow hit the toilet handle.

The gurgle and swirl of water through porcelain resounded through the restroom like an explosion, crashing and then subsiding and dying away. Helma took a deep breath, stood upright, and with her suddenly restored sense of direction, unerringly found her way out of the handicapped stall, hearing as she reached the restroom door the clatter of footsteps and the banging of a door.

She pushed into the reassuring light of the hallway, already running toward the front entrance, knowing whoever had been inside was escaping.

The front door was closed but the air still smelled of the rainy night that had briefly blown into the building. Helma peered outside but saw nothing but darkness and passing traffic.

She returned to Audrey's desk, flipping on lights and reaching for the telephone. She glanced at her watch. Only eleven minutes had passed since Audrey and Tillie had left the building.

Four policemen emerged from two patrol cars—none of them Chief Wayne Gallant—followed closely by a very flustered Shelby Eaton, his bulky body curiously attired in a jogging suit.

"What does it mean?" he asked Helma and then without waiting for her response, swept off after the policemen who were poking and prodding around the building.

"I'm ready to assist you in inspecting the Reading Room," Helma told officer Sidney Lehman, whom she knew from previous encounters involving Bellehaven mayhem.

"Great, Miss Zukas," the young policeman said, brushing back his blond hair. "I'd appreciate it."

Helma halted in the doorway and surveyed the Reading Room while two policemen and Shelby Eaton stood behind her. Her middle desk drawer gaped open. The cardboard box of books Helma had planned to sort through was dumped onto the carpet, the volumes splayed. Loose pages scattered the floor, corners of the brittle paper broken into pieces.

"*Now* can this door be locked?" Helma asked Shelby Eaton.

"It wouldn't have mattered if the door was locked, Miss Zukas," Shelby Eaton said soothingly. "Whoever did this *broke* in through the service entrance. If they'd been determined to enter the Reading Room, they would have *broken* in here, too."

"A locked door is seen by some as a challenge," a man beside Shelby Eaton said.

Helma hadn't noticed this man's arrival. He was an Indian in his late forties, his graying hair pulled back in a ponytail, wearing jeans and a Reebok sweatshirt that was too small. Massive shoulders and a broad chest accented by relatively short legs. He was nondescript, but Helma observed the way Shelby Eaton physically deferred to the man, similar to the way he treated Miriam Hooke.

"I'm Raymond Corbin," he said to Helma, nodding briefly.

"How do you do. I'm Helma Zukas," she said, duplicating his brief nod.

"He's with me," Shelby Eaton provided. "He's a fisherman."

That was probably true but Helma guessed Raymond Corbin was definitely more than a fisherman.

"Does this have anything to do with Stanley Plummer's murder?" she asked Officer Lehman directly, ignoring Shelby Eaton's shocked intake of breath.

"It looks like simple vandalism, and not much of that."

Raymond Corbin regarded Helma without expression, then glanced away, reminding Helma of Audrey.

"What was vandalized in the rest of the center?" Helma asked.

Officer Lehman flipped the pages of his notebook. "Nothing, except the service door entrance."

"That's all?" Helma asked.

"All we've discovered," Shelby Eaton said, wringing his plump hands.

"The Reading Room was the intruder's target, then," Helma announced. "He was searching for an item in here."

"Or else you interrupted him before he could get any further," Officer Lehman suggested. "Tell us what's damaged or missing in here, if you would."

Helma turned her considerable skills of observation to the Reading Room, her head erect, nose flaring. She walked from one side of the room to the other, alert, examining for order and disruption.

"Obviously these books have been disturbed," she said, pointing to the overturned box. "The pencil cup should be to the left of the phone." Helma rested one hand on the first shelf of books. "These books are out of order." She moved to the next shelf and the next. "These also. I had a few dollars in change in my desk drawer; that's disappeared. I'd say this room was definitely the intruder's target."

They were interrupted by excited voices from the hallway and in glided Miriam Hooke, her calm features pinkly animated, and behind her, two men of the same age, one of them Aaron Hooke. He winked at Helma.

"Who's responsible?" Miriam Hooke demanded. "Can we keep this out of the newspaper?"

Shelby Eaton's hands patted the air around Miriam as if trying to soothe her without touching her. "Just minor vandalism," he said. "The police have it completely under control. Everything's fine, just fine."

Miriam turned to Helma. "The books. My father's books. Are any missing?"

"I don't believe so, but . . ." Helma pointed to the books tipped from the cardboard box.

Miriam gasped and raised a hand to her mouth. The man beside her patted her shoulder. "It's all right, Mother."

Aaron Hooke stood just behind Helma. He leaned so close to Helma, his breath feathered her hair. "That's Darren," he whispered. "My twin. Mummy loves him best."

She turned and looked into Aaron's twinkling eyes. He shrugged. "But it's okay," he whispered. "I got the looks."

Helma had to admit Aaron was right. He *was* better-looking than Darren. They were the same height and had similar facial characteristics, but where Aaron had defined, almost sculpted features, Darren's were filled in and softer, his chin rounded, his mouth smaller. Aaron's athletic body contrasted with Darren's indulged businessman's body. Darren's demeanor was gentler, more solicitous to their mother.

Miriam patted Darren's hand and faced Officer Lehman. "I trust the police department will give this case a high priority."

"We're giving it every attention it deserves," Officer Lehman said.

"That 'other matter' still isn't solved," Miriam reminded him.

"You might want to talk to Chief—" he told her.

"I will," Miriam interrupted, and turned to Shelby Eaton. Perspiration shone on his forehead. "You'll inform me as soon as you have a complete list of missing items?"

"Certainly, certainly," Shelby Eaton assured her.

Miriam glanced from face to attentive face and shifted her pose, heel against arch, model-like. "It's obvious I'll only hinder your investigation if I remain here. Good evening, everyone."

She glided from the room, Shelby Eaton hurrying behind her.

"Hello, Raymond," Aaron said to Raymond Corbin.

"Aaron," he acknowledged. Nothing more was said but Helma felt the undercurrents of conversation between the two men.

Aaron motioned from Helma to his brother. "Miss Zukas, may I present my other half, Darren."

"Hello," Darren said, turning a quick appraising smile on Helma, the kind of smile that heightened his resemblance to Aaron but which Helma recognized as not particularly interested, the same acknowledgment he'd give her if they were introduced in a few weeks or months, having forgotten this encounter.

"She's the *librarian*," Aaron said.

Darren looked questioningly at Aaron.

"Check her out," Aaron whispered mischievously.

"I assure you, that's an old joke," Helma told him.

"Not to me," Aaron said. "This is the first time I've ever had the chance to say it."

"If you gentlemen are finished here," Helma said, "I'd like to take a few minutes to straighten my desk and then go home."

Officer Lehman returned his notebook to his

pocket. "If you discover more missing items," he told Helma, "you have the chief's number."

Helma gazed at him steadily and Sidney Lehman blushed. "Sorry, ma'am. I didn't mean anything by that."

Helma tidied her desk and then gingerly approached the books spilled onto the carpet, lifting the brittle loose pages on the flat of her palm and placing them to one side until she could return them to their proper paginated order.

As she sorted through the books from the carton, she realized they weren't all old; but they *were* all damaged. Broken bindings, torn pages noted for repair.

Stanley Plummer hadn't set these books aside to *sell*, he'd intended to *repair* them.

A methodical force had visited the Reading Room. The invaders hadn't been idly vandalizing; they'd been searching the Reading Room. Had they found what they were looking for? She turned in a circle, studying the confines of the simple room. Whoever had been here had leafed through the books and then returned them to the shelves, only not as neatly as Helma would have if she'd hoped to go undetected.

❧ chapter ten ❧

LOONS

Helma informed Ms. Moon she needed to resolve urgent business at the cultural center that day instead of attending to her library responsibilities, and drove to the center during a pause in the rains. The landscape shone with weighted dampness.

An air of excitement permeated the center. A knot of employees stood near Audrey's desk, speaking in urgent voices. The man with the braids stood a few feet behind the group, listening, his eyes half closed.

Julianna broke away and walked with Helma to the Reading Room. "That juicy police chief was here," she said, eyeing Helma speculatively. "Is he a friend of yours?"

"We're both city employees."

"He asked for you," she said, raising her eyebrows. " 'Miss Zukas,' he called you."

"That's my name."

Julianna grinned and gave Helma a thumbs-up sign. "Don't worry; he'll be back."

"I'm sure he will be," Helma said. "He's very tenacious where his cases are concerned."

"Right," Julianna said. She stepped inside the

Reading Room and gazed at the disturbed books on the floor. "The guy who broke in last night was looking for something in here, wasn't he?"

"It looks that way to me," Helma conceded. "This is the only room that was disturbed."

Julianna ran her hand through her cornrows. "Do you think Stanley Plummer hid something in here?"

"Do you?" Helma asked.

"Maybe. Stanley was a sneaky little guy. He liked secrets, do you know what I mean? I always felt like I'd better watch what I said around him."

"Did other people seem uncomfortable around Plummer?"

Julianna shrugged and smoothed her tunic top. "Probably. *He* complained about everybody here at one time or another, except Audrey. He liked Audrey."

"And the man with the braids?" Helma asked.

Julianna gave a short laugh. "Tall Darkheart? Isn't he a specimen? He looks like he should live in a teepee with a spotted pony parked out front, doesn't he?"

"Is he an employee?"

"More of a permanent visitor. He drifted in from the Plains a month ago." Julianna pulled a long face and crossed her arms over her ample breast. "Heap big brave. He takes himself *very* seriously."

"But did he and Stanley get along?" Helma persisted.

"I don't remember ever seeing them speak to each other." Julianna's face grew more serious. "I like your friend, Ruth," she said. "But I don't know if Tall Darkheart's the man to heal her broken heart."

Helma closed her desk drawer on her purse and said, "Ruth's never been one to welcome advice, especially if it's in her best interest."

"Warn her if you can, would you?"

"Why? Is Tall Darkheart dangerous?"

Julianna shrugged. "That depends on how you define dangerous. He's already left a few women crying in their morning coffee."

Anyone glancing into the Reading Room and seeing Miss Helma Zukas at her desk might have suspected she was taking a break, but actually she was deep in serious thought. In her left hand she held a perfume ad from a magazine of no relevance to the center. With her right hand she worked a pair of scissors around the image of a lush fern, expertly excising each tiny leaflet of each tiny frond, holding to the lines with fastidious precision.

Her scissors snipped faster the deeper her contemplation. By the time she'd cut to the base of the fern's rhizome, leaving an equally precise negative space in the perfume ad, she'd made up her mind.

She rolled back her chair and prepared to drop the excised fern in the trash basket beneath her desk.

"If you're going to throw that away, can I have it?"

It was Young Frank. He held a brown grocery sack so well used its top had gone as soft as fabric. His hair was tangled and his eyes were dark, as if he hadn't slept.

"What will you do with this?" Helma asked, holding out the paper fern.

"Look at it for a while." Young Frank took the fern and held it on his palm. His fingers were scarred with tiny cuts. "This is like carving," he said. "Cutting like this." He glanced up at Helma and she caught the slightest hint of approval.

"Do you know the center was broken into last night?" she asked.

It was a mistake; that was obvious at once but too late to retract. Young Frank closed his hand over the paper fern, crumpling it like a candy wrapper and shoving it in his jeans pocket.

"Is Aaron here?" he asked.

"I haven't seen him. Ask Audrey."

Young Frank held the grocery bag closer to his body and turned, leaving the Reading Room without another word.

Helma sighed and opened her notebook to a clean page. Notebook in hand, she marched toward the offices at the center of the building, passing Young Frank, who sat with Tillie the yellow dog on his lap, his cheek resting on top of her head, the worn paper bag at his feet.

Shelby Eaton's office door said "Director" on it. No name. Helma rapped smartly three times.

"Come in," he said.

His office was a mix of Native American artifacts: Chilkat blankets, Woodlands Indian baskets, masks, arrow quivers from the Plains, a miniature birch bark canoe, Acoma pottery. Black and white Curtis photographs the size of posters hung the walls. The universal Indian room.

"Miss Zukas," Shelby Eaton said, rising briefly from his chair and settling again. A gust of wind rattled the window behind him, the lights flickered, and they both stilled until the electricity held steady.

"Did you discover something else missing?" He turned a sheet of paper toward her. "Write it down here, if you would."

Helma positioned herself squarely in front of his desk. "I'm aware of the negotiations that led to my appointment here, the trading of my services for public library access to the center's collection."

"Ah," Shelby Eaton said, smiling. "Advantageous for both institutions."

"But you planned to fire Stanley Plummer and draft me, without consulting either of us."

"There was hardly time before his death."

"Then how did Stanley Plummer know of the mediations?" Helma asked in a manner intended to deter him from questioning how *she* knew.

The director's eyes shifted away from Helma. "I *may* have dropped a hint or two, but only in hopes he'd be more . . . cooperative."

"I can no longer be of any assistance to the cultural center," Helma said and paused to allow the director's eyes to widen; "unless certain steps are taken."

Shelby Eaton leaned back in his chair. "You sound like you're giving me an ultimatum."

"I am. I want the Reading Room locked every night and, until I have the entire collection cataloged and processed, I want it locked whenever I'm not here."

"But the colonel's will . . ."

"I *know* the colonel would agree with me. When I'm finished you can operate the Reading Room however you like. Until then, if you expect me to administer this collection, the Reading Room must be locked."

Shelby Eaton's face reddened. His smile fluttered and went flat. "I'll have to discuss it with the board."

"Fine. If they agree, I'll also add Tuesday and Thursday afternoons to my schedule."

Shelby Eaton rubbed his head with the tip of his finger. "Could we compromise on . . ."

"No. No compromises. Either I'm allowed to lock the Reading Room or there's nothing more I can do to help the center."

With a sharp click, Helma retracted her mechanical pencil. "Now I'll leave so you can speak to whomever needs placation. I'll expect a key before I leave this evening. If the board prefers another alternative, please inform me by four o'clock so I can leave notes for my replacement."

Helma had clearly stated her position; the rest was up to him. She left his office, notebook held close to her side.

And nearly bumped into Ruth and Julianna who crouched outside Shelby Eaton's office door like two characters listening at the keyhole in a silent movie, gleeful expressions on both their faces.

"Doesn't she inspire you to bare your breast and storm the Bastille?" Ruth said to Julianna.

Julianna applauded softly, bowing toward Helma.

"I don't appreciate your eavesdropping," Helma said.

"Didn't expect you to," Ruth told her. "Did you leave the man with any self-respect at all?"

"I don't know what you mean."

"Never mind. But look here, Helm. This is Tall Darkheart."

Standing this close to him, Helma realized he *was* tall, taller than Ruth, which most men weren't. He had the still, silent demeanor that Helma had grown up associating with Indians. His hair was black, his eyes brown, his body lean and graceful as if he might casually leap onto a bareback pony and gallop across the prairie toward the setting sun.

But there was something . . . Helma couldn't think what it was so she let it go. Her mind was still occupied by her conversation with Shelby Eaton.

Tall Darkheart inclined his head toward Helma. Helma wouldn't have been surprised if he'd raised his hand palm outward and said, "How."

"Hello, Helm," he said solemnly.

"My name is Helma or Wilhelmina, not Helm," Helma told Tall Darkheart. "And you can call me Miss Zukas."

"Watch out," Ruth told Tall Darkheart. "She's still on the . . . Never mind."

It was then that Helma realized Audrey sat at the receptionist's desk, her back to the four of them, her hands folded in front of a magazine. Tillie had moved from her chair to the floor at Audrey's feet where she lay just as still as Audrey sat. It was curious and obvious.

"May I speak with you in the Reading Room, Ruth?" Helma asked and without waiting, still confident from what she sensed to be a victory with the center's director, she returned to the Reading Room where she sat at her desk, her eyes becomingly bright.

Ruth entered the Reading Room, her chin raised, her shoulders back, her eyes focused to the left of Helma's ear.

"Ruth, what are you doing here?" Helma asked.

"This place is open to the public, isn't it?"

"Yes."

"Well, I'm the public and here I am." Deep in Ruth's eyes a light flickered dangerously, revealing how close she was to losing control. "Am I bothering you? Interfering with putting all your cutesy numbers on the books? Messing up your shelves?"

"You know you're not, Ruth," Helma said evenly.

"Oh. So then this is a preemptive strike? Get me out of here in case I *embarrass* you?"

Helma said nothing, knowing only silence would defuse Ruth. She opened *Everyday Life Among the Anasazi* and turned to the verso page, keeping an eye on Ruth.

Ruth stared out the window at the glistening wet thicket of blackberry bushes at the edge of the property line. "I don't want to be home alone right now," she said. "And I can't stand being out there in the world where all the Christmas decorations are already dangling in your face every step you take. Ho ho ho. It isn't even Thanksgiving; it's sickening."

"For many people, Christmas is the most joyful time of the year," Helma said. "That's why they stretch out the celebration."

"You sound like your mother. Isn't that what she always says?"

Despite herself, Helma winced. Lately, she'd caught herself voicing the exact phrases her mother used. Out of nowhere. It was completely unintentional and dismaying.

Ruth's eyebrows raised. "It's okay to sound like your mother. It only bugs you when she's alive. After she's dead, I assure you hearing your mother's voice fall out of your mouth gets to be a comfort."

Ruth's own mother had died while Ruth was in college and she rarely spoke of her. Ruth went on to ask, "What do you think of Tall Darkheart?"

"He's tall," Helma commented.

"Yeah, a priceless commodity. I think anyone that tall deserves to be investigated a little more closely, don't you?"

"You don't know anything about him, Ruth. What if . . ."

"Oooh," Ruth said. "Do I hear prejudice coming from Helma Zukas?"

"No," Helma said emphatically.

"Besides, I'm tired of sleeping with the enemy," Ruth said, twirling a pencil between her fingers like a baton.

Ruth always said that when there was no love interest in her life.

Ruth sat on the library table and crossed her feet on a chair seat. "I heard you were here while vandals roamed the halls last night," she said. "Were you scared?"

"No." Helma thought a moment and amended, "Yes, I was."

"Let that be a lesson to you: don't hang out alone in dark buildings." She paused and added more seriously, "Really. Do not. Any more letters from dead men?"

"No, but I've discovered how the letter was

mailed," Helma said and described the mail slot so close to the women's restroom.

"That's weird, isn't it, that Plummer's last living act while he's being hunted down by a killer is to risk his life sending a love note to a librarian he doesn't even know?"

"But he's seen me 'at work.' "

"And admired your skills to death."

Helma's phone rang and Ruth took the opportunity to depart the Reading Room, waving her arm in a quick arc.

It was Shelby Eaton. "Miss Zukas, I've convinced the board that the Reading Room should be locked. I believe this is a wise move for the protection of the collection. You can come get the key anytime."

"I agree with you," Helma said. "Please have Audrey bring the key when she begins her four hours in the Reading Room."

After a moment's silence, he said heartily, "Certainly, certainly."

Helma hung up, smiling.

Ruth returned an hour later. "Peace offering," she said, setting a paper plate on Helma's desk.

"What is it?"

"A fry bread taco. Audrey and Julianna made them. Indian frybread with taco filling. A very happy cross-cultural marriage. Try it."

When Ruth left, Helma picked off the thickest of the cheese and cautiously lifted the hot food, holding the frybread folded to contain the filling. She took a bite. Helma had never eaten a taco or frybread but the combination of dense friedbread and spiced meat was delicious. She surprised herself by eating it all.

Audrey set the key on Helma's desk. It was brass and a round tag attached to it read "RR." "You're locking up the books," Audrey accused her.

"Only while I'm putting them in order. We can't have security worries at the same time we're trying to inventory and catalog the collection."

Audrey slowly scanned the Reading Room. "What do you want me to do?"

Helma gave Audrey the rubber-banded sets of cards George Melville had printed. "Could you file these sets in the first drawer, alphabetically by the first line of the first card in each set?"

Audrey nodded and took the cards. She sat in front of the oak card catalog, her long black hair spreading across her back. Helma thought Audrey might be twenty-five or twenty-six, but her composure was far beyond her years, giving her an air of self-containment, almost concealment.

"The person who broke in last night must have watched you leave." Helma said.

"They didn't realize you were still in the building," Audrey agreed.

"Do you think they were looking for something Stanley Plummer hid before he died?"

Audrey turned and briefly regarded Helma. "Stanley Plummer was more likely to take than to hide," she said.

"What do you mean?"

Audrey shrugged. "That's the kind of man he was."

"Do you know the Raven stories?" Helma asked.

"There are many," Audrey said. "There's a time for telling them."

Helma heard the unspoken, "and this isn't it."

"But can you tell me more about the Raven itself?" she asked.

"The Raven is a trickster, sometimes good, sometimes bad," Audrey said quietly and Helma heard the faint lilt of the storyteller in her voice. "He never uses force, only trickery so well planned it's like a dance, but sometimes he's so smart he outsmarts himself. He loves beautiful shiny things. There's a tale of the Raven turning himself into a baby so he could trick an old lady into giving him the moon she kept locked in a box." Audrey stopped and moistened her lips, bringing herself back from thoughts of a tale she obviously loved.

"Thank you," Helma told her. "If someone said, *'uncover* the Raven,' would that have any significance for you?"

Audrey's face stilled in thought, her expression unreadable. "No," she finally said. "The Raven changes shapes to play tricks and get what he wants; you wouldn't *uncover* the Raven. He is already what he is."

"I've read some of the Raven tales. Have they all been transcribed?"

"There are people who've tried to write all the variations, but some should only be told," Audrey said. "Not written."

Both women worked silently until Helma grew aware of a figure standing at Audrey's shoulder. It was Young Frank.

"My chain broke," he told Audrey.

"I didn't drive today," Audrey responded. "Christa brought me."

Young Frank looked at the clock on the Reading Room wall. It was 1:50.

"What time did he tell you?" Audrey asked.

"Two," Young Frank said. He scuffed one sneakered foot. "I don't care anyway."

"Ask Julianna," Audrey suggested.

Young Frank shook his head.

Helma immediately read the situation. "I'm taking a break now," she said. "Can I give you a ride?" she asked Young Frank.

Young Frank nodded without surprise and left the Reading Room. Audrey looked after him. "His father . . ." she said and shrugged, bending back to her filing.

"You're suggesting I make my best effort to get him home by two," Helma said, already reaching for her coat.

Young Frank didn't speak until Helma had pulled out of the center's parking lot and was heading north toward the Nettle reservation. The wind was stilled but the afternoon brooded in light without direction, a light so gray it was nearing blue.

"My cousin has a car like this but he took off the doors." He pinched up a fold of the clear plastic seat cover. "What's this for?"

"To protect the upholstery."

"It's like new," he agreed, letting go of the plastic and rubbing his hands back and forth on the seat, "but you can't touch it."

They drove the curving two-lane road through a dripping stand of bare-branched alder and maple, past small pastel houses and fallow fields, over the dangerously high and swiftly flowing dark river that bounded the reservation. A fading hand-painted sign in front of a partly hidden house read "Gillnet hanging. 1.50/fathom."

Around a bend, in a meadow of tall brown grasses still plumed like wheat, Helma spotted three figures, one following after the other. She slowed her Buick, blatantly staring. The first figure wore an oversized mask: big-beaked, painted red and black, strands of cedar fringe hanging from its neck. Behind the first figure, two black-haired children walked single file, one carrying a staff, the other an object held in front of her. From the sizes of the three figures Helma surmised they were children between ten and twelve.

The three children moved in a slow easy pace, slipping through the grasses as if they followed a path. Behind them the dark sky touched the mist-fingered trees.

She glanced at Young Frank who looked out his own window in the opposite direction.

"What are those children in the field doing?" Helma asked him.

"Just playing," he said, adding in a tone that disallowed any more questions. "It's private."

"Where do you live?" Helma asked him, dropping her question about the children in the field.

"You passed it. I changed my mind."

Helma pulled her Buick off the road at a clearing beside a collapsed fireworks stand.

"I don't think I'll drive aimlessly up and down the roads. Where would you like to go?"

Young Frank pointed a thumb over his shoulder. "Back there."

"Will you tell me when to stop before we get there?"

"Okay."

Helma turned a neat, two-stage policeman's turn, the way her father had taught her: back up, go forward. Young Frank nodded in approval.

The field where she'd seen the figures was empty. Not even the grasses rippled. Young Frank stared straight ahead.

They approached a mobile home and Young Frank slid lower in his seat. Still able to see, he eyed two cars in the driveway parked beside a pickup with a black dog sprawled beneath it. Three men leaned against the hoods of vehicles, standing out in the drizzle and drinking cans of beer.

"Here?" Helma guessed.

"No!" Young Frank said fiercely. "Keep going." And Helma knew she was right.

They drove across the river and off the reservation. A few hundred yards past the river, Young Frank said, "Here."

Helma stopped. There was no house, no driveway, not even a turnoff. Blackberry bushes crowded the ditches and threatened the cracked road. Pale moss draped from pine boughs. Rotting vines twisted through the man-high bushes.

"There's nothing here," Helma protested. "I'll take you back to the center."

Young Frank pointed into the dark forest. "My grandfather's house is in there. The path's back a little ways."

Helma backed up her car until she discerned a faint depression through the brambles. She peered down the path, through the bushes and giant fir trees, looking for a house, but all she saw was more dark vegetation.

Young Frank opened the car door and jumped out. Before he slammed the door louder than was necessary, he said, "It's a secret."

Helma reached over and locked the passenger door before she drove back to the center, thinking Young Frank's life was surrounded by secrecy.

Aaron Hooke lounged at Helma's desk in the Reading Room, his legs stretched out toward Audrey, who still sat in front of the card catalog.

"I like your hair like that," he told Helma.

She touched her hair, which was styled in the same becoming fashion she'd worn since she was sixteen.

"Did you get the little felon home on time?" Aaron asked.

"Are you speaking of Young Frank?" Helma asked.

"Who else?"

"He changed his mind. I dropped him off at his grandfather's."

"Back in the woods. This side of the river?"

"Yes."

"That's where his grandfather used to live. He's dead. Young Frank hides out there. Scares the other kids off by telling them it's haunted."

"How do you know?" Helma asked.

"My son goes to school with him, that is, when Young Frank's living in town with his mother and they allow him *in* school."

Aaron tapped the wrinkled brown grocery bag on Helma's desk, the same bag Helma had seen Young Frank carrying. "Did he show you this?"

"No."

Aaron gently, reverently, opened the bag and with both hands pulled out a wooden carving. He set it on Helma's desktop.

It was a loon, carved from alder, unpainted except for a touch of golden stain on its eyes but possessing the illusion of black and white. The checkering and barred necklace all accomplished by intricate knife cuts that changed the reflection of light on the wood's grain. It was exquisite. Head gracefully raised, smooth neck stretched and beak pointed upward, its back glossy and sleek as if it had just risen from a dive beneath the surface of a still lake.

"I asked the kid to carve a duck decoy, not a piece of art," Aaron grumbled, smiling. "No way I'd let this beauty touch water."

"I trust you paid him its true value," Helma said.

Aaron grinned sheepishly. "I will though."

Audrey stood and pointed toward the card catalog. "I finished," she said. "I'll be out front for the rest of the day."

"Bye, Aud," Aaron said, leisurely waving one hand after Audrey.

"Young Frank isn't even in his teens yet and he can carve like this," Aaron said to Helma, gazing at the loon. "It's all he wants to do. Can you imagine having a goal like that before you're a teenager? Puts you in the fast lane for life, that's for sure," he said wistfully.

"Who's teaching him?" Helma asked.

"He's teaching himself now, I guess, but his grandfather was a master. He carved the totem pole out front."

"Do you understand the figures?" Helma asked.

Aaron shook his head. "I recognize a couple of the common ones, like the frog and killer whale, but they mean different things in different tribes. Mostly they're figures from mythology or family tales. Gramps used to tell me about them, but I forgot. Each totem pole tells a private story. It belongs to a family, usually." Aaron laughed. "One thing I *do* know: you know that saying, 'high man on the totem pole'? Like 'top dog'? That's totally wrong. The most important figure is usually on the *bottom* of the totem pole, holding up every other figure. Pretty good joke on us, huh?"

"I didn't know that," Helma said.

"It's the truth."

"Excuse me but you're sitting at my desk," Helma told Aaron.

"I know it," he said, stroking the back of the loon. "I've come to visit."

"I've already taken a longer break than I intended."

"That wasn't a break," Aaron said. "That was a good deed. It deserves a reward."

"Such as?"

"Lunch tomorrow?" Seeing her hesitation, Aaron hastily continued, "A brief lunch. Right here. I'll bring it. You don't have to do a thing. Just be here."

"How do you know what I like to eat?"

"Trust me."

Aaron turned to put the wooden loon back in the bag and caught his knee on the edge of Helma's desk. The loon slipped from his hand and both he and Helma dove for the precious carving, each grabbing it at the same moment, Helma stumbling in the process, and Aaron catching her by the shoulders. Her cheek brushed against his cashmere sweater.

"You okay?" he asked, still holding her by the shoulders.

There was a sound of throat clearing at the door of the Reading Room.

Helma turned in Aaron's arms and encountered the surprised and very puzzled face of Chief Wayne Gallant.

❧ *chapter eleven* ❧

CONFUSION

"**H**ey, Chief," Aaron said, releasing Helma. "How goes the world of criminal catching?"

Chief Gallant, normally articulate and in command of any situation, was strangely at a loss for words. "Yes," he said, still frowning. "Am I . . . interrupting?"

"We were just playing at art criticism." Aaron held up the carved loon. "Look at this beauty, would you. Kid carved it for me. Young Frank."

"Portman?" Chief Gallant asked.

"You know his work?" Aaron asked, handing Wayne Gallant the loon.

"Not his carving." The chief gently stroked the bird's head. "This is beautiful."

"If I had a mantel, that's where I'd put it." He took the loon from the chief and tenderly replaced it in the paper bag. "I'd better get going. See you at noon tomorrow, Helma." He turned back to the chief. "You still play racquetball?"

"Some."

"Catch you on a slow-crime day sometime."

When Aaron was gone, Wayne Gallant glanced

around the Reading Room. "It looks like you've put everything back in order."

"Nothing was taken except change from my desk," Helma told him. "A few books were on the floor but the damage was minimal. Someone *searched* the room more than vandalized it."

Wayne Gallant sat in the chair by the card catalog. Helma waited for him to pull out his notebook but instead he idly opened the first card catalog drawer and looked inside. "You're making headway," he said, glancing at the cards Audrey had filed.

"I hope it'll go faster now that I've developed a system," Helma said. "You *don't* know who's responsible for this mischief, am I correct?"

The chief closed the catalog drawer, then opened the next one and the next. "Empty," he said.

Helma waited. Wayne Gallant pushed in the last catalog drawer, rose from the chair, and stood in front of the windows. The concrete patio beneath the overhang was wet from the rain slanting in. Green moss edged the corners and grew along one jagged crack, water splattered down the drain spout and fanned out on a concrete spillway into the lawn. It might have been morning; it might have been afternoon. The light came from nowhere.

"Why were you alone in the building last night?" he asked, turning, his forehead creased.

Helma told him about reenacting Stanley Plummer's last minutes. "I've discovered how he mailed his note to me." She explained the proximity of the mail slot to the women's restroom, finishing with "that's why the envelope was postmarked the next day: because the outgoing mail is picked up every afternoon by a postal employee."

"Neither snow, nor rain . . ."

"Nor murder," Helma added.

"We'll take a look at it. Good deducting, Helma."

"Thank you. *Do* you have any new information on the break-in?"

He shook his head. "Either this room was the target or their starting point. If it was the starting point, then the cultural center's the target, not anything in here."

"On Friday evening," Helma told him, "my car wouldn't start."

"You didn't mention that on our walk," the chief said.

"It didn't seem noteworthy at the time; my car *is* over twenty years old. But the mechanic said the battery cables were disconnected."

Wayne Gallant pursed his lips and looked out the window. "Any suspicions?" he asked.

"I thought I saw a figure near the center, but it was raining. I'm not absolutely certain."

"How did you get home?"

"Aaron Hooke gave me a ride."

"I see. From now on," he said, his eyes cool, "call the office if you feel uncomfortable and I'll send a car to pick you up."

He removed a sheaf of papers from inside his suit pocket and set them on Helma's desk. "These appear to be Plummer's cataloging notes you asked about. We took them from his desk. Could you look them over? Tell me if he's written anything here that *doesn't* pertain to books?"

There were five unlined pages filled with concise, razor-straight rows of writing in black ballpoint pen.

At first Helma skimmed the pages and then she returned to the first page and began reading in earnest.

Helma Zukas was not a person who was blind to another's sterling qualities just because he or she might be of unsavory character.

Stanley Plummer had pinpointed the very weaknesses in the library classification systems that

Helma had observed. And he hadn't been a professional librarian; he was a layman, although of superior analytical nature. This confirmed her suspicions of why he hadn't actually begun to catalog the collection: Stanley Plummer was a man who studied a situation from all angles before he acted. She could appreciate that.

The last two pages held a brief outline of the call number system Stanley Plummer had created for Colonel Hooke's collection, a modified Dewey Decimal system: divisions by subject and then by tribes. No decimal points to the tenth place; easy for anyone to shelve the books properly. One call number for folktales and beneath that number the name of the tribe and then the author. Three short simple lines. And the same for Art and Law and every other subject.

Maybe unorthodox but it was simple. Simple and yes, she acknowledged: ingenious, more than adequate for the collection even if it grew in years to come.

"You seem excited."

Helma jumped. "May I photocopy these?" she asked Wayne Gallant. "They contain only cataloging information and they'd save me a great deal of time."

"Go ahead. No hidden clues?"

"None that I can see."

"I was afraid of that."

Julianna stepped into the Reading Room and gave Wayne Gallant the kind of look Helma thought might be called "smoldering." She held her wrists out to Helma as if expecting handcuffs. "I'm yours for the next four hours. Put these magic fingers to work."

"You're busy for lunch tomorrow?" Chief Gallant asked, following Helma behind Audrey's desk to the photocopy machine. Audrey was working at her computer and didn't look up. Long lists of numbers scrolled up her screen.

"Yes," Helma said, lowering the machine's lid on the first page of Stanley Plummer's notes. "Yes, I am."

Chief Gallant stood with legs wide. He put his hands in his pants pockets and Helma heard the jangle of coins and keys over the whir of the photocopier.

"With Aaron Hooke?" he finally asked. Jingle, jangle.

Helma copied another page. The machine's light blinked and flashed like lightning. "Is it of interest to the police?" she asked.

Wayne Gallant removed his hands from his pockets. "No, it isn't," he told her, sounding regretful.

Helma finished copying and gave Stanley Plummer's original notes to the chief. "I appreciate your letting me see these pages."

"Yeah. Sure," he said with unusual vagueness. "I'll see you again soon."

Helma stood by Audrey's desk and watched the chief of police leave the building. Holding his hat to his head, he unlocked and opened his car door with one hand. Once inside, his face was featureless behind the swishing windshield wipers.

At the same moment Chief Gallant turned on his headlights and backed out of the parking spot, Ruth and Tall Darkheart entered the front door, Ruth dashingly medieval in a green hooded cape that brushed her ankles. Tall Darkheart was coatless, his black braided hair dripping, his shirt damply clinging to his muscled chest. Ruth stamped her feet and shook her head so her hood fell back from her face while Tall Darkheart stood stoically beside her, impervious to his condition.

"I see you had a visit with the law," Ruth said to

Helma. "He looked a little low. Are you withholding information again?"

"Definitely not. What were you doing outside?"

Ruth pulled aside her cape. "Walking the dog. I didn't want her to get wet."

Tillie was nestled beneath Ruth's bosom, perfectly dry, her eyes blinking drowsily in the fluorescent light. She jumped from Ruth's arms and trotted to her chair beside Audrey.

Ruth fluttered her lashes at Tall Darkheart. A man taller than Ruth affected her to a giddy edge. "I've got my car," she told him. "Want to go . . ." With her right hand she pantomimed drinking from a beer stein.

Tall Darkheart inclined his noble head once, his dark eyes focused somewhere in the middle distance.

The two left and Helma allowed herself a small sigh of relief. It wasn't that she *didn't* want Ruth around, but Ruth had a way of disrupting the flow of order even when she was on her best behavior.

"Have you known Tall Darkheart long?" Helma asked Audrey.

"No," Audrey said.

"You don't like him," Helma said, not asking.

Audrey watched Ruth's Saab splash through a puddle in the driveway and turn onto the road. Ruth's original Saab had been destroyed but somewhere, somehow, she'd found another one, nearly as old, just as battered: "He's not what he seems," Audrey said, and before Helma could ask her what she meant, Audrey added, "but then none of us are."

In the Reading Room, Julianna sat in front of the typewriter, a *People* magazine balanced against the keyboard. She glanced up at Helma and turned the page to a black and white photo of a bare-chested man on a beach hoisting a bikini-clad woman over his head.

"I'm taking a break. It's the law. Fifteen minutes every four hours."

"I'm aware of that."

Helma stapled Stanley Plummer's notes together and set them on her desk. "What's the real reason you asked me to warn Ruth about Tall Darkheart?" she asked Julianna.

"Maybe I should warn *him*," Julianna said, licking her finger and flipping a page. "She's out for blood. You can almost see the dagger between her teeth. Ah, but Tall, he's playing the race card. Indian brave knocking white lady for a loop. There's a subtle hierarchy at work here. Maybe it's not visible to you or your friend Ruth but for some of us it's like wearing signs around our necks."

Helma sat down. "I don't understand. What kind of a hierarchy are you talking about?"

Julianna made a circle with her hands. "Just take our little cultural center here, for example. We're all outsiders except for Audrey and Tillie. Have you noticed there's a whole tribe of Indians just outside the city limits and the only member of the Nettles here is Audrey, and she's the center's receptionist? Not an adviser or a member of the board. Yet most of the exhibits in the Northwest wing have something to do with her people. Why would she be here except to keep an eye on what was going on?"

"Maybe she needed employment," Helma offered.

Julianna snorted.

"What about Raymond Corbin?" Helma asked, remembering the Indian who'd appeared in the Reading Room after the break-in.

"Ah. *There* is an important man. Low-key but very powerful in the Nettle tribe. Shelby keeps trying to woo him into the fold. If Raymond gave his nod to the center, it would be kosher."

"And your being part Indian doesn't count?" Helma asked.

"Might as well be a tourist," Julianna said, slapping closed her *People* magazine. "Members of the tribe welcome me—to a point. One class above white Cherokees."

"I'm not aware of that term," Helma said. "White Cherokee."

"Somebody who claims ties through a shaky Indian-in-the-woodpile connection, usually Cherokee. They're the coolest." And Julianna broke into a whining song that sounded distantly familiar, the last line of the chorus went, "So proud to diiiieee."

"It may be in my blood," Julianna went on, "but it's not in my background. If I *do* go for a degree in Native American studies I won't know much more than the kid sitting next to me. But then I knew a few Indians in New Mexico who'd never been near a pueblo and were learning to make pueblo pottery. Some people here do the same kind of thing."

"That's just learning your own culture," Helma said. "We all do that." She thought for a minute. "I'm Lithuanian," she told Julianna.

"That's still white, isn't it?"

"Of course. But before my grandparents left Lithuania the Russians outlawed the Lithuanian language and culture. Children went to Russian schools. People smuggled Lithuanian books. In a few years the culture my grandparents brought to America was more purely Lithuanian than the Lithuania they left behind.

"And after Lithuania became independent again, the people there turned to expatriate Lithuanians for their roots. My brother carves Lithuanian folk figures and once he shipped a batch to Lithuania itself."

"Weird, isn't it?" Julianna said. "Sort of like we

all have 'Man Made' stamped on the soles of our feet."

"And Young Frank?" Helma asked.

Julianna's mocking demeanor sobered. "He's caught in the middle. His carving might save him from tipping too far over the edge. His dad doesn't like him to come here but..." She stopped and looked outside. "Here comes the rain again."

Helma followed a city bus, its red and yellow taillights smeared through the rain. The bus windows were steamed and the figures inside appeared suspended in a greenish fog.

Bellehaven didn't really have a rush hour, more like twenty-five minutes of irritating slowdown. The bus pulled over and Helma passed it, glimpsing hooded, hunched figures hurrying from the bus stop into the darkness.

Downtown, she pulled into a parking space in front of the "Home Comfort" store and rushed inside, ten minutes before it closed.

She quickly chose two bright yellow dish towels, matching yellow oven mitts and a gaudy tablecloth covered with blotches of yellow sunshine faces. Near the counter where the clerk was already counting the change in her cash register, Helma passed the scented candle display. She stopped and added two yellow lemon-scented candles to her purchases.

Instead of saying thank you as she took Helma's check, the clerk said wearily, "I'm so sick of this weather."

"It *will* end," Helma told her.

"I hope I live that long."

In Helma's beige and wood-toned kitchen she hung the yellow towels in place of the neatly folded white kitchen towels. She replaced her tasteful blue pot holders with the bright yellow mitts. Beige natural-fiber placemats and a pottery vase of dried flowers sat on her oak table. Those she removed and covered the polished wood with the garish sunshine-happy tablecloth, smoothing it until it hung equally long on all four sides. The yellow clashed and over-powered her apartment. Very yellow, very bright.

While she prepared a dinner of broiled chicken breast, bright yellow corn and saffron rice, Helma played Vivaldi's "Summer" on Repeat on her stereo.

Finally, while the rain thudded monotonously on her roof and the damp air hovered beyond her walls and doors and windows, she lit her yellow lemon-scented candles on the table in front of her and sat down at her bright table to eat her dinner, humming to herself.

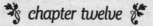

chapter twelve

FAITHFUL MEN

"The Moonbeam spilled the beans that she and Shelby Eaton worked out this exchange before Plummer bought the farm," George Melville told Helma. "I'll bet Plummer would have preferred a pink slip to a paper spindle." When he saw Helma's expression, he said, "Just kidding. Have you decided on a call number scheme for the collection?"

"I'm looking into an experimental system," Helma said, thinking of Plummer's notes. "If you wouldn't mind giving me your opinion, I'd appreciate it."

"I'd be honored to take part in the overthrow of standard cataloging practices." George took a step away and then turned back. "Oh. I saw your friend last night: all dressed up like Pocahantas. Feathers and beads and fringes. Clinging to some guy who looked like Sitting Bull so she wouldn't fall on her . . . the ground. Both of them pretty looped."

"Do you mean Ruth Winthrop?"

"The one and only. I'll bet she had a wingding headache this morning. At least the art world is safe for today."

* * *

In the staff lounge, Helma paused by the bulletin board to read the announcement of an upcoming tour of the Vancouver Public Library, then noticed the sinkful of dirty cups, the full trash basket, and the sugarless sugar bowl. Jack the janitor was home with the flu and everyone else had taken their cue from his absence.

Eve entered the lounge and removed a can of pop from the tiny counter-high refrigerator. "Hi," she said without enthusiasm.

"Hello, Eve," Helma said. "Is the weather finally having an effect on you after all?"

Eve shook her head. She poured her cola into a coffee mug and then tore open a bag of peanuts and shook those into the mug of cola. "Not me but the Moonbeam's on a tear. You're lucky you're out of this place."

Eve chewed a mouthful from her mug. "Until the sun comes out again she's going to be major cranky." Eve paused and said dreamily, "Maybe she'll go back to California and you could be director."

"Me?"

"Sure. Wouldn't it be fun? I know what I'd do . . ." Eve lapsed into a private fantasy, her eyes gone distant, chewing slowed. Helma left the lounge as silently as if the room held a sleeping librarian.

"Helma," Roberta called in a flurry, ushering a crying woman through the workroom toward the lounge. "Could you call a taxi and would you please take the reference desk for about fifteen minutes for me?"

"What happened?" Helma asked, pulling a tissue from her left pocket and giving it to the sobbing woman.

"Somebody cut in front of her in the checkout line and . . ."

"My husband's on a business trip in *Florida*," the

woman said, sniffing and wiping at her tears. "He's on the beach, and I'm *here*."

"Will you be all right?"

Roberta sang out over her shoulder, "Wait 'til the sun shines, Nellie."

After she phoned the cab company, Helma dialed Ginny's Tanning Salon and scheduled an emergency appointment for the patron. "Send the bill in care of the reference staff at the library," she told the receptionist.

After the cultural center, Helma found the reference desk to be a relief, as comfortable as a chat with an old friend.

"Telephone books are on the second low shelf to the right."

"There's a copy of the U.S. Constitution in this almanac. Page 456."

She looked up the formula for the volume of a pyramid, verified that this November was shaping up to be the second wettest November on record and helped a teenager find statistics on teenage versus forty-year-old drinking and driving arrests.

Fifteen minutes stretched to twenty-five.

"If I use these computers, will the government take a picture of me?" a tense man wearing a green garbage bag over his shoulders asked Helma.

"Which got here from Seattle first, the railroad or the highway?" another man asked.

Helma already knew it was the railroad but she never offered her own knowledge without written proof to back her up. In the local history titled *Beautiful Haven*, she found the answer and turned it toward the man. "The Forbes, Sands, and Moore railroad line arrived in 1888, the first paved highway in the 1920's."

The man shook his head. "I guess I just lost ten bucks."

"Helma!" Ms. Moon asked as Helma prepared to leave for the cultural center. "Have you had any moving experiences at the cultural center you'd like to share?"

Helma thought a moment. "I've eaten a frybread taco," she said.

"Oh," Ms. Moon replied.

Audrey gave Helma an inscrutable look when she entered the center and glanced down the wing toward the Reading Room.

Aaron Hooke sat in front of the locked door, rocking back in his chair, a wicker picnic basket at his feet. He waved to Helma, his teeth bright against his tanned face.

"You figured I wouldn't show, right?" he asked, rising and moving his chair as Helma approached.

"It crossed my mind," Helma said as she unlocked the door. In her bag she'd packed a banana and half a ham sandwich, just in case.

"Tch, tch," he said behind her. "Don't believe what you hear."

"About you?"

"About men. Some of us mean what we say and faithfully pay our child support on time."

"And do you pay your child support on time?"

"Exactly seven days in advance every month. Sometimes, when I'm in a good mood I add a little extra. Drives my ex-wife crazy."

"I'm sure it's a pleasant craziness."

Helma turned on the lights and made a quick survey of the Reading Room. Nothing had been disturbed during the night. Even yesterday's trash remained in the trash basket.

Aaron pulled a red and white checked tablecloth out of the wicker basket and spread it over the oak library table like a magician.

"For you I have a plain roast turkey breast on white bread, butter on the side. Plain potato chips, a Jonagold apple, and your choice of 7-Up: diet or non. Am I amazing or what?"

"That *is* surprising."

For himself, Aaron had packed a thick, pungent hoagie sandwich, spilling shredded lettuce and sliced olives.

"Forgot the candles," Aaron said, snapping his fingers. He moved the head of the flexible lamp on Helma's desk and shone it at the table. "There. Sunshine."

They sat opposite one another at Aaron's improvised picnic table, the basket open on the floor, the lamplight warm on Helma's back, while outside rain continued to fall and the sky hung barely above the rooftops.

"You seem to know several people in the Nettle tribe," Helma said as she reached for a pair of scissors from her desk and cut open her potato chip bag.

"A few. I go out to the casino sometimes. They're probably one of the most authentic tribes left in the country."

"Authentic in what way?"

"Think about it. The Nettles still live on their own lands—mostly. Our government couldn't have pushed them any farther west without drowning them in the ocean. They've kept their traditions— and they guard them with their lives."

"Are you privy to some of those traditions?" Helma asked.

"No way. Snooping is not appreciated." Aaron made a two-handed motion over his head, like a scalp being taken.

"Did your grandfather tell you the Raven tales when you were young?"

"Yeah, I don't remember them very well now. He used to tell me some great stories."

"What about Darren?"

"Oh, them," Aaron said, waving his hand in dismissal. "They never got along, even when we were little. Darren couldn't see that Mother and Gramps fought like crazy but they loved each other anyway, so he took Mother's side early on. Gramps called Mother a snob." Aaron grinned. "She is, too, but that's one of her charms. If you do it with complete self-assurance you might get away with it." He looked out at the mists and wet foliage. "This rain is snow up on Mount Baker, you know. I heard they might open the weekend before Thanksgiving this year. Do you ski?"

"Not anymore."

Helma had skied once, at age sixteen back in Michigan. Ruth had given her a day pass for her birthday and Helma didn't believe in wasting gifts. Michigan ski areas were gentle, "easy as pie," Ruth had claimed. Rope tows and snow machines. After her second triumphant run down the bunny hill, Helma was returning to the top when the rope tow gears slipped and, like a falling elevator, everyone landed in a huddle at the bottom of the suddenly very steep slope. She'd skied down the hill once more to prove she could and then retired from the sport.

Aaron smiled over Helma's shoulder and Helma turned to see Young Frank enter the Reading Room.

"I came to read," he said.

"Sure," Aaron told him. "Be our guest." He pulled out his wallet and set two twenties on the table. "I didn't pay you enough for that loon. Take this." He paused before removing his hand from the green bills. "Keep it to yourself, okay? It's *your* money."

Young Frank nodded and folded the twenties into tiny squares before he put them in his jeans. The shape of a jackknife was visible in his shirt pocket.

Helma watched Young Frank go straight to the shelf where the totem pole book was located, remove it, and settle on the floor with the book cradled on his lap.

"Now tell me why you're a librarian," Aaron said. He nodded toward Young Frank. "Don't worry. He's checked into another world. We're invisible to him."

Helma studied Aaron's face. He wasn't interested in why she became a librarian, not really, so she gave him *the* answer. True but incomplete. "Because I love books."

Aaron was satisfied, as she knew he would be. He popped the plastic lid on his chocolate cake and took two bites with a plastic fork, leaving a speck of chocolate on his chin.

"And you're not married because you haven't found the right man yet," he said.

"Or he hasn't found me," Helma told him.

"Whoever he is, he'd better hurry it up before somebody beats him to it," Aaron said.

Miriam Hooke stepped into the Reading Room, perfectly groomed, wearing a beige-pink suit and accompanied by musky perfume.

"The girl at the desk told me you were here, Aaron. I hope you're not interfering with Miss Zukas's work."

"It's lunch time, Mother. Even city employees get a lunch hour."

"Oh, I know, I know." She peered distractedly around the Reading Room, then at her gold watch. "Don't forget the two o'clock appointment with the lawyers to sign the scholarship fund papers. It'll only take . . ." Miriam spotted Young Frank huddled over his book. She raised her manicured hands to her cheeks. "Oh, isn't that *sweet*? Don't you wish you had a camera? They're such beautiful people."

A slight grin raised the corner of Aaron's mouth. He glanced at Helma, his expression unreadable.

Miriam clucked her tongue and said, "Just darling," before taking a tissue from her purse and dabbing at her lipstick. "I'll see you at Woodson and Gilbert at two, Aaron?"

"I'll be there."

"All right, dear. Good-bye, Helma."

When Miriam's voice faded into the distance, Aaron said, "Do you know when Mother divorced our father she cut her losses and changed all our names back to Hooke? She said it was a 'name with a better future.'"

"Or perhaps a better past?" Helma suggested.

Aaron laughed. "You said it. She's been working on a book about Gramps's family for as long as I can remember, her 'narrative.' Gramps called her Miriam Bronte."

"Can I take this home?" Young Frank interrupted. He held the totem pole book.

Helma hesitated. The book hadn't been cataloged yet. It wasn't that rare of a book but it was expensive. Either Colonel Hooke or Stanley Plummer had put a clear plastic cover over the colorful book jacket, which portrayed the closeup of a disintegrating totem pole. Round black eyes staring from split and mossy wood.

"What are you going to do with it?" Aaron asked. "Last I heard you were the school's worst reader."

"I'm going to carve some of these."

Aaron turned to Helma. "You don't want to be responsible for arresting artistic development, do you?"

"I think we could arrange an official borrowers' transaction."

Helma quickly typed up a facsimile check-out card with the author: Twitchell, John R., and the title: *Totem Poles*, and asked Young Frank to sign it, which he did in a laborious formal and fine hand: Franklin Bernard Portman.

"This is a special loan," Helma told him solemnly. "Is one week long enough for you?"

Young Frank nodded. "Can I stay here a while longer?"

"Certainly. I'll be here all afternoon."

Young Frank hugged the book to himself and returned to his seat by the window.

"Did you know Stanley Plummer was a collector?" Helma asked Aaron. "Rare books, spurs, trains . . ."

"And paper spindles, don't forget," Aaron said, grinning.

Helma rounded the corner near the restrooms and ran straight into Tall Darkheart.

"Excuse me," she said, taking a single step backward.

He nodded once and stopped where he was, waiting for Helma to go around him. Helma did likewise and they stood face to face, neither moving out of the other's way, neither looking the other in the eye.

"You're new to Bellehaven, I understand," Helma finally said. "Are you from the Northwest?"

Tall Darkheart turned his braided head, solemnly gazing eastward as if his home had once lain in that direction and was now forever gone. Still he didn't move.

"Are you doing research in the center?" she prompted. "I know you're not an employee."

"You're interested in my business," he said, looking down at her from the bottom of his eyes. "Why?"

"I have a natural curiosity about the people I meet," Helma told him.

"I'm here examining the pitiful remains of a culture," he said.

"Which one?" Helma asked.

Without another word or glance, he stepped around Helma and they both continued on their way.

As Helma pulled another book from the shelf, two stapled pages fell from between the volumes and fluttered to the floor. Helma retrieved the papers, reading the first page as she straightened.

What she held in her hands was an article from the *Journal of Native American Ethnology*: "The Finding of Two Hitherto Unreported Tales from the Nettle Indians," and the author was Stanley Carrol Plummer.

Published only a month earlier, one of the tales related to the creation of Mount Baker, the other told of two lovers who belonged to warring tribes.

Plummer had placed the article on the shelf—in order—as if he'd intended to include it in the Reading Room's collection. An author note at the bottom of the article read, "Stanley Plummer attended UCLA."

Now she knew the next career Stanley Plummer was preparing himself for at the cultural center: Native American folklorist.

While Helma impatiently waited for Audrey and Tillie to return to their posts in the reception area, she walked through the Plains Indians exhibits in the north wing, holding the folktale article and thinking of Frances Jay Plummer's little brother who "always cleaned up after himself."

She wiped a smear of fingerprints from a diorama and her attention was caught by the steam train emerging from fir trees along a trestled track against a mountain. She bent closer. No, that wasn't a lake beneath the train tracks but tidelands at low tide and the three Indians holding baskets and peering up at the passing train were gathering the tiniest white oysters. It wasn't a Plains Indian scene at all, but a

Northwest location. The diorama was in the wrong wing of the center.

"Coming into Home, the Forbes, Sands, and Moore Railroad, 1886," the narrow brass plaque read. The scene was so realistic, Helma made out the shadowed outline of heads inside the train, one woman pressed close to a window holding up her baby to see the Indians gathering oysters.

The trains versus highways reference question was still fresh in Helma's mind. Colonel Hooke had supplied the incorrect date. The Forbes, Sands, and Moore line began in 1888, not 1886. She was surprised the colonel had made such an error. She noticed the year he'd built the diorama and made a quick calculation. He'd been ninety-seven years old. She supposed a lapse was understandable when you were nearly a hundred years old. Still . . . She'd inform Shelby Eaton of the discrepancy.

A single bark came from the reception area and Helma returned to find Audrey seated at her desk and Tillie trotting down the hall to meet Young Frank.

"Do you know anything about this?" Helma asked, showing Audrey Stanley Plummer's folktale article.

Audrey glanced through the pages, exhibiting no surprise but her face darkening, and Helma was sure this wasn't the first time Audrey had seen the article. She handed it back to Helma. "I know who you can talk to. I'll call him."

In the Reading Room, Helma's eye was caught by a golden shadow on the floor where Young Frank had been sitting: a scattering of wood chips. In their center sat a small figure carved from the wedge that used to block open the Reading Room door. It was rough and unfinished but it was unmistakably a bust of Miriam Hooke, her hair a smooth cap, her face a suggestion of cheekbones, lips pursed as if she were about to kiss the air. It wasn't a rude carving but neither was it flattering—or particularly kind. Helma slipped the little figure into her desk drawer and cleaned up the wood chips as best she could without a vacuum.

Audrey entered the Reading Room and placed a map on Helma's desk. "Raymond Corbin's waiting for you at his house," she said. "And can you take Young Frank home on your way?"

"Mr. Corbin lives on the reservation?" Helma asked, studying Audrey's neatly drawn directions.

"A mile from my family's house," Audrey offered.

"Then you grew up in your tribe's traditions," Helma said. "That must have shaped your life."

Audrey shrugged. "I grew up on the reservation but who shaped my life the most was my grandmother. She worked in the fields, following crops around the state. My grandmother taught me to be a person. The traditions are secondary." She gave Helma a long look. "I'm a person first."

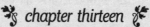

chapter thirteen

RESCUES

Young Frank sat with the totem pole book held on his lap, occasionally stroking the plastic-protected cover as if he were petting a sleek-skinned animal.

They followed a pickup with a blue tarp flapping over a load of furniture. Between each sweep of the windshield wipers, the tarp blurred, fluttering like the wing of a giant bluebird. Helma flashed her lights twice, alerting the driver to the mattresses being rained on but the pickup lumbered onward, ten miles below the speed limit.

"The other guy wouldn't let me read the books," Young Frank said.

"Did you have to wait until Mr. Plummer was gone?" Helma asked.

Young Frank nodded. "But I never took a book out of the room."

"Where would you like me to take you today?" Helma asked him.

"To my grandfather's, the same place you dropped me off last time."

"Isn't your grandfather dead?"

Young Frank nodded. "But it *was* his. Can't it still *be* his?"

"I suppose." Helma knew the answer to her next question but she asked it anyway, giving Young Frank the opportunity to respond in his own way. "Did your grandfather carve too?"

Young Frank gazed down at the totem pole book. "Better than these. He showed me how."

"My brother carves," Helma told him. "He believes that when he carves an especially beautiful figure, it's a gift from the wood."

Young Frank nodded eagerly. "The wood shows you what it wants to be. You have to be still so you can see and hear. Wood has its own story, too."

"What do you like to carve best?"

He looked out his window at a cat stalking through the weeds in the rain, then back to Helma. "It changes. Someday totem poles," and he thumped the totem pole book.

"You're very talented," Helma said. "You . . ."

Young Frank turned his head away, gazing out the window again and Helma realized she was making an error of some kind so she quit speaking. The pickup truck carrying the furniture turned onto a gravel road and Helma sped up.

"How fast does this car go?" Young Frank asked.

"The speed limit," Helma told him.

"My cousin put twin pipes on his car like this."

Helma didn't know what twin pipes were but she gathered from Young Frank's grin that they either made a car go faster or sound louder, neither one a goal of hers.

"Do you know Raymond Corbin?" Helma asked.

"Grandfather said that long ago Raymond would have been a holy man."

"A shaman?" Helma asked.

"Grandfather carved spirit figures sometimes, for medicine bundles, to help cure people," he said, ignoring Helma's question.

"Does Raymond cure people?" Helma asked.

Young Frank snorted as if Helma were being ridiculous. "Want me to tell you a shortcut to his house?"

"No thank you. Shortcuts are only short to people who already know their way."

Young Frank thought about that, then nodded gravely. "You have to go the long way first," he said, "to compare."

"It's all relative," Helma agreed.

This time Helma recognized the faint trail through the blackberry bushes and evergreens and pulled off the road beside it. "I have something in the trunk for that book," she said. "Wait here."

As she unlocked her trunk in the dank and cold air that carried a faint odor like burning trash, Helma saw through the wet rear window the shape of Young Frank slip from the passenger seat to the driver's side. She paused, watching. The emergency brake was set and she held her keys so there was nothing mischievous he could do. His outline swayed back and forth as if he were turning the steering wheel of a car racing along a winding road.

In Helma's trunk, next to her bright yellow plastic highway emergency kit, she kept a cardboard box of useful items: paper towels, plastic bags, rope, bottled water, a first-aid kit, a Swiss army knife, and a tire iron that didn't fit her wheel lugs but felt just right in her hand.

She removed a large plastic bag and closed the trunk in time to see Young Frank jump back to his side of the seat. She gave him a few seconds to situate himself before she opened the driver's door, shook out her umbrella, and got inside.

"Here," she said, handing Young Frank the plastic bag. "Put your book in here. Keep it wrapped tightly so it won't warp."

"Got it," he said. He slid the book inside the bag,

folded over the end, and then zipped it inside his jacket. "Thanks," he mumbled at her as he slammed the door.

Helma waited to start her car until Young Frank disappeared into the gloomy trees, a figure in a bright blue jacket suddenly swallowed by winter green dissolving to black.

Over the river and onto the reservation, Helma followed Audrey's directions. Past the wood frame church and beyond the mobile home with the collapsed barn and a pile of eerily translucent green fish netting in the yard. At the next corner, where an unpainted picnic table sat tipsily beside the road, she turned left.

"One mile," Audrey's note directed. "Cedar house on left." Trees grew close to the road, hanging over deep narrow ditches on either side. There was no shoulder, no place to pull off the road if she was forced to.

At 1.1 miles from the corner, the trees opened to a clearing holding a tall cedar house with a slanted roof and a narrow porch. A fishing boat on a trailer was parked beside it, a towering stack of crab pots leaned against a shed. Another building stood closer to the road, smoke wafting from a metal chimney. From its door emerged a man in a brown jacket who Helma recognized as Raymond Corbin.

She parked her car by the shed and got out, greeted by a husky black dog that rounded the front of her car, its head low and hackles raised.

"Stop," Helma ordered the dog and the black dog immediately sat on its haunches, tipping its head quizzically at her.

"Good dog," Helma said and walked past it, allowing it plenty of room. Helma never touched unfamiliar animals.

Raymond Corbin was younger than she'd first thought, the wrinkles around his eyes and mouth

more from weather than age. A scar bisected his left
cheek, deepening when he smiled, which he did as
he shook her hand.

"You're good with animals," he said, nodding at
the dog who still sat by the front tire of her Buick,
rain beading on his glossy fur.

"I don't confuse the species," Helma told him.

"Come on inside," he invited, leading her into the
building from which he'd just emerged.

It was a studio, its interior fragrant cedar, the
floors wooden planks. A fire hissed and crackled in
a woodstove, and rain trip-tripped on recessed sky-
lights above their heads.

And all around the room, hung on the walls in
plain metal frames, others mounted and some
merely tacked to the walls, were black and white
photographs. Of the land, the Nettle people. Long
canoes, dances, teenage boys playing basketball,
girls in heavy makeup, babies nestled against mothers in native costume, a decrepit mobile home with
a soaring totem pole in the front yard, two elderly
women holding hands and seated in webbed lawn
chairs, clam digging, a fishing boat emptying its
hold, a blurry-eyed man panhandling in downtown
Bellehaven, the gates of the Nettle cemetery.

Each photograph stood starkly on its own, causing
the viewer to pause and wonder: why? or who? or
what will happen next? The contrast between light
and dark was sharply defined, powerful. Helma
moved from one photo to the next, smiling at three
little girls giggling into the camera, uncomfortable at
the slitted staring eyes of a young tattooed Indian in
a ponytail. She stopped before a young boy deep in
concentration as he used an adze on the rough blank
of a mask, his tongue between his teeth, totally
oblivious to the camera; it was Young Frank.

"These are . . ." Helma said, waving toward the
rows of photographs.

"Thank you," Raymond told her. "Would you like a cup of tea?"

"What kind do you have?" she asked, turning regretfully from the photos to the subject at hand.

"Green," he said. "Did you expect cedar bark?"

Actually, Helma had. "Green is fine," she said. "My Aunt Em always drinks green tea."

He took two thick mugs down from a shelf and poured steaming water from a kettle that sat on the woodstove. "Supposedly, the polyphenols in green tea inhibit cancer growth," he said. "It's not fermented like black teas."

Helma sat on a caned straight back chair beside a small wooden table and Raymond pulled up a stool opposite her.

"Audrey tells me you found Plummer's article," he said as he squeezed honey from a plastic bear into his cup.

"I found it in the Reading Room," Helma told him. "You've read it then?"

"The *Journal of Native American Ethnology* has used my photographs off and on for years. One of the editors sent me a preprint of the article—too late to stop its publication," he added wryly.

"Did a member of the Nettle tribe tell Plummer the tales?" Helma asked.

"I confronted him." Raymond blew lightly across the surface of his tea. "Plummer didn't deny a thing. The stories were in a hand-written manuscript in Colonel Hooke's collection, transcribed by a nun in one of the Indian schools."

Raymond offered Helma the honey, which she politely refused. "Bee spit," her cousin Ricky had called honey.

"A couple of generations ago," Raymond said, "the schools were little boot camps: take away all you've got and give you a new foundation. Most of the people here over the age of sixty spent time in an Indian school, away from their family, forbidden to speak their own language. Who knows why the nun committed these tales to paper? Her church would have considered them blasphemous."

"Perhaps she just thought they were beautiful," Helma suggested. "Not every nun had a limited view of culture."

"Whatever her reason, it's lost now. There aren't any copyright laws for a tribe's oral tradition and we hold our stories and traditions very close. This," and here Raymond disdainfully waved a hand toward the Plummer article, "is theft, plain and simple. The tales were taken in the first place without anyone's knowledge and then reshaped and published without any input from anyone in the tribe. No effort to discover if they're true or simply fabricated. Just stolen."

Raymond Corbin's voice hadn't risen nor had the rhythm of his speech changed but the anger was evident in his tightly held mouth, the grip on his mug.

"Did Stanley Plummer understand how grievous an act this was?" Helma asked.

The black dog climbed in through a swinging dog door cut into the human door and settled with a grunt on the floor beside the stove.

"All that mattered to him was that he got the stories into print first. His attitude reminded me of the academic shenanigans I saw in graduate school."

"Where was that?" Helma asked.

"University of Washington. I didn't finish."

"And you came back home?"

"I never intended to leave permanently. I figured an education would help me help the tribe. But in a way, it separated me. Even though I came back, some see me in a different light now. Can you understand that?"

Helma did. "You returned a different person than the man they knew."

"But only in their eyes, not here," and he pressed a fist against his heart.

"Do other people on the reservation know about Stanley Plummer's article?"

"Most do," Raymond said.

"And were they upset about it?"

Raymond stopped himself in the midst of a nod. "Are you taking this conversation to a specific conclusion?" he asked.

"I was curious whether anyone was upset enough with Stanley Plummer to murder him."

Raymond Corbin turned his mug in his hands, double frown lines appearing between his brows. After a few long moments he said, "Maybe. But I doubt it. Plummer's crime isn't exactly shocking, is it?"

"But his death is," Helma reminded Raymond.

"Death is serious business," Raymond agreed.

"He wrote me a letter before he was killed," Helma said. "I think he was trying to tell me about something that's hidden in the Reading Room."

"Have you searched for it?"

Helma nodded. "But I haven't found it. I'm going through the books now. He told me to uncover the Raven; does that mean anything to you?"

Raymond opened a tin of fig bars and offered it to her. Helma disliked all those little black seeds but she politely took one.

"No," Raymond said, biting into a fig bar. "It's too general; the Raven can turn himself into any being. He's a trickster. You might say that's his stock-in-trade."

"Did you know Colonel Hooke very well?"

"He bought a few of my photographs. Two of them are on display in the cultural center."

"But did you *know* him?" Helma persisted.

"He was already an old man when I met him." Again Raymond Corbin thought, the frown reappearing. "He wanted to do something good, I think."

"His grandson said it was to make amends for buying up reservation land between the world wars."

"Maybe. But it's impossible to know another man's motivations."

"I don't agree. Some actions have very obvious motivations. Do you support the cultural center?"

Raymond smiled. "Support it? How do you define 'support'? Financially, no. The concept, yes. Exposing people to another culture is always good, unifying. But it depends on who's interpreting the culture, doesn't it?"

"Then perhaps you should interpret your own culture and create your own center."

"What makes you think we haven't?"

Helma was confused. "I haven't heard of it," she said.

Raymond said nothing, the words resonant between them, reminding Helma the reservation was a foreign country to her. Homes, a school, fish cultivation, a casino, chronic land and water rights battles with the surrounding communities. News through the local paper as sparse as from across the ocean.

He laughed. "But even here, we can't agree on what's most important or who's the most reliable interpreter of the past."

"That's a conundrum everywhere," Helma said. "I brought Young Frank home."

"To the trailer?" Raymond asked, suddenly alert.

"To his grandfather's," Helma said, watching Raymond's expression. It didn't change, yet he seemed to relax.

"Thanks," he told her.

Raymond walked Helma to the car. The rain had subsided and in the surrounding trees, water gently dripped, mists rose from the ground into the branches like lazy steam.

Helma slowed her Buick when she came to the spot where she'd dropped off Young Frank. The afternoon light, although directionless, had dimmed and she could only see a few feet into the brambles before it turned dark and fathomless.

Every Tuesday evening after dinner, Helma changed all the trash bags in her apartment, putting a new paper sack in each plastic container, squaring the paper top, and folding over the opening to stiffen the bag.

As she worked, she imagined Stanley Plummer, not as a dead man but as a living man. On one side: dishonest, vindictive, arrogant, an intense loner. On the other: intelligent, meticulous, a man who taught himself one complex area of knowledge after another, obsessively committed to each undertaking, ethical or not.

Helma had no doubt that given the opportunity, with or without a library degree, Plummer would have completed cataloging Colonel Hooke's library and done a credible job of it. He would have been bitterly disappointed to discover he was about to be fired.

She turned over the edge of the bag in her bathroom trash basket and had another thought. If Stanley Plummer was murdered for something he *knew*, perhaps something in the Reading Room, would the murderer now suspect that Helma had discovered this secret, that she knew the same thing?

Her phone rang at ten-thirty, just as she was turning off her lights. She hesitated and then picked it up on the third ring.

"Helma, this is Wayne Gallant."

Chief Gallant at ten-thirty at night. Dark thoughts raced through Helma's mind. Her mother, an accident, danger. "What's wrong?" she asked.

"It's not an emergency," he hastily assured her. "It's your friend, Ruth Winthrop. She's here at the station."

"Why?"

"Detective Houston brought her in. He found her walking down the middle of Third Street. She's inebriated."

"Carter Houston arrested her?" The detective had suspected Ruth of violent activity the previous spring. Ruth had called him a "relentless little bulldog" and there weren't many warm feelings between the two.

"Actually," Wayne Gallant said, "he didn't arrest her at all. He brought her to the station to sample our late-night coffee. Then he called me."

"May I come get her?" Helma asked.

"That's why I phoned."

Helma hastily combed her hair and pulled on her rain jacket. She left her umbrella behind and hurried down the steps, her feet clattering and the shades of 2C parting as she passed.

Chief Gallant met her in the lobby of the police station. "She's lying down," he said, "but I don't think she's reached the sleeping-it-off stage yet."

"Can you tell me again *how* Carter Houston picked her up?"

"He was off-duty, coming home from a movie and saw Ruth dodging cars in the middle of Third Street. She told him she was on her way to Wisconsin or Minnesota to kill somebody."

"Oh," Helma said.

Chief Gallant looked at Helma quizzically. "You know about the situation?"

"She's mentioned it."

Ruth lay stretched on a too-small couch in a waiting area next to the chief's office, her legs hanging over the arm, humming "On Top of Old Smoky" and waving her arms out of rhythm. She wore the clothing George Melville had described: beads and feathers and fringes.

Ruth struggled to sit up when Helma and Wayne Gallant entered her field of vision, then surrendered and collapsed back on the couch.

"Oh, Helma," Ruth greeted her in a loud voice. "Haven't we met in these hallowed walls before?"

"Halls," Helma corrected. "It's 'hallowed halls.' "

"All I see are walls." Ruth giggled. "No halls. Did you bring bail money?"

"You're not under arrest, Ruth," Helma said. "I've come to take you home."

"I won't go," Ruth said and set her lips.

Wayne Gallant pulled Helma aside. "I tried to take her home before I phoned you," he said quietly. "She refused."

"Stop talking about me," Ruth called from the couch. "I'm not dead."

Helma was tired. She had a long day tomorrow. "Ruth," she said firmly. "Which do you prefer: to go home or go to jail?"

"What's the difference?"

"Ruth."

"I'm *not* going home. The walls are crushing the life out of me. I can't paint; the phone doesn't ring. I don't get any letters. Jail, hah! You might as well seal me in a pine box and bury it."

"I'd call this severe self-pity," Helma said without sympathy. "If you won't go to your home, will you come to mine?"

"Oh cute. A sleepover. Can I bring my bunny jammies? Will you pop popcorn and make grape Kool-aid?"

But Helma could tell Ruth was weakening. "Whatever you want," she told Ruth. She turned to the chief. "Can you help her to my car?"

"Sure."

With one of Ruth's arms over his shoulder and his arm gripping her waist, Wayne Gallant maneuvered Ruth out of the station to Helma's Buick.

"I suppose this is as close as you and I'll ever get," Ruth said as the chief buckled her in.

"Good night, Ruth," he said. "Pleasant dreams." And closed her door. Over the roof of the car he said to Helma, "Can I call you tomorrow?"

"About the cultural center?" Helma asked.

"Partially."

"I'll be home by five-thirty," she told him.

"I'll talk to you then," he said and slapped her car's roof with the palm of his hand, police short-hand for "go," Helma suspected.

On the boulevard, Helma swerved through a long puddle to avoid a garbage can lid that had blown into the street. Water sprayed up against the bottom of her car like a timpani drum.

"You know what the detecto-bot did?" Ruth asked. "I oughta have him arrested."

"If you're talking about Detective Houston, he probably saved your life."

"Oh yeah? What he *really* did was point his gun at me and tell me if I didn't get out of the street and into his car, he was going to shoot me."

"What did you do?"

"Whaddaya think, Sherlock? I obeyed, all meek and mild."

Helma doubted *that*. "Were you with Tall Dark-heart?" Helma asked.

"At some point. Lost him somewhere before I started heading east."

"On your way to kill Paul or the woman he was with?"

"Take your pick."

"If you . . ." Helma began.

"I don't want to talk about it, okay? I'm drunk

and that makes me unreasonable and irresponsible."

Helma definitely agreed with that assessment and they drove in silence until Helma turned into the parking lot of the Bayside Arms. "What about my toothbrush?" Ruth asked.

"I keep extra toothbrushes," Helma told her.

"And guest soaps, too?" Ruth asked. "Maybe a supply of nice new combs and personal-sized deodorants?"

"Of course."

Helma opened the door to her back bedroom for Ruth. Ruth looked inside and backed out. "Do you mind if I sleep on the couch?" she asked. "If I'm going to be sick I'd like to look at the sea and pretend I'm seasick."

Helma gave Ruth blankets and a pillow and then, while Ruth was in the bathroom, discreetly placed a dishpan beside the couch.

Once, when Helma got up in the night to use the bathroom she saw Ruth in the dark living room sitting cross-legged on the floor in front of the sliding glass doors. Ruth's head was bowed and Helma heard her friend quietly sobbing.

❧ chapter fourteen ❧

VISITORS

Helma found herself wide awake at five in the morning, staring at the slowly changing digital numbers on her clock radio, thinking she may as well get up. It was Wednesday, and on Wednesday mornings, Audrey arrived at the center at seven o'clock and left early in the afternoon. Helma could make uninterrupted progress on the book collection before the rest of the staff arrived.

Ruth was asleep on Helma's couch, her mouth open, the blankets pulled to her chin, but not high enough to hide Boy Cat Zukas. He lay in the crook of Ruth's arm, eyes closed, the top of his head touching Ruth's cheek. When Helma opened her drapes, Boy Cat Zukas opened his eyes, yawned, and drew back beneath the covers until he was invisible. Ruth didn't stir.

There was no sign of a let-up in the weather. Helma twisted her hands together, then made fists and jammed them in the pockets of her robe. It wasn't daylight yet but looking out at the few lights was like peering through gauze. Mists and rain, congealed air. Water, water everywhere.

She left a note on her table explaining where the

juice and cereal were kept and ending with a reminder for Ruth to "please lock the door and put out the cat" when she left.

Walter David had left his Christmas lights on all night and they randomly blinked on and off in his window with a gaiety out of place so early in the morning.

Audrey's white Toyota was the only car in front of the center and Helma parked beside it and climbed out, glancing inside at Tillie's basket and squeeze toys on the front seat.

A light drizzle fell and Helma ignored it. What was the point? No matter what she did, her hair was frizzed within two minutes from the moist air anyway.

She was nearly to the door when she was stopped by the odd light coming from inside the center: flickering orange. She frowned, puzzled, attempting to recall an orange light fixture in the reception area.

And then she noticed the gray, misty air through the glass doors. No. It wasn't mist; it was smoke and the orange flickering light was a fire.

Audrey and Tillie. Helma reached for the door handle, then turned and ran back to her car. She threw open the driver's door and felt beneath the car seat for her fire extinguisher.

Like a soldier advancing toward the enemy, swinging her weapon forward, pulling the pin and pointing the nozzle, Helma jerked open the front door and ran toward the flames. The orange flared upward, fed by the air she'd let inside.

"Audrey?" she cried before she pulled her coat over her mouth and squeezed the lever of the fire extinguisher, sweeping the red canister from side to side as she aimed at the base of the fire.

Helma's aim had always been accurate. Fire retardant foam frothed and bloomed and before her the orange flames dampened and sputtered and melted.

Her eyes burned; she could barely see in the billowing smoke. "Audrey?" she cried again, and then, "Tillie?" and began to helplessly cough, her throat seared, bending low and searching vainly for the fresh air the fire monitors had always promised hovered at floor level.

Suddenly a hand grabbed her arm and jerked her backward. Helma had no idea which way she was being dragged and she struck out desperately, fearing she was being pulled farther into the building. Somewhere an alarm began to desperately jangle. She couldn't stop coughing, couldn't get enough air.

There was a bump and Helma tumbled helplessly backward, hearing a yelp beneath her. She reached out and grabbed a handful of fur.

"Breathe," a voice commanded.

Helma did and sucked in the sweet morning air, gratefully gasping the moisture. When she was able to open her eyes, she found herself looking into Audrey's face, with Tillie at her elbow.

"I thought you were inside," Helma said.

Audrey shook her head. "I went over to Kelly's to get a cup of coffee."

"The fire," Helma told her, coughing again. "I think it was on your desk."

Audrey frowned. "All I had . . ." She raised her head, listening to the screams of the approaching sirens.

Someone had brought folding chairs for Helma and Audrey and they sat on the lawn in front of the center, wrapped in blankets and sipping coffee as the sky lightened and passing traffic slowed down for a good look.

The center's doors stood open and the smoke had dissipated although a smell like burned chemicals remained. Firemen in yellow slickers stood in a bright clump while a flat white hose lay unfurled—

and unused—across the lawn. Radios crackled over the scene.

"Thanks for pulling me out of the building," Helma told Audrey.

"You were trying to save Tillie and me," Audrey replied, her face solemn and thoughtful. "And you didn't even know whether we were inside."

"I didn't expect you to be anywhere else," Helma told her.

Chief Gallant, in a yellow slicker, emerged from the building and joined Helma and Audrey, with Shelby Eaton at his heels.

"Congratulations, Helma," Wayne Gallant said. "You definitely saved the day. There's some ash throughout the building and it's going to smell for a few days but there's no serious damage." He nodded apologetically to Audrey. "Except to your desk."

"What about the Reading Room?" Helma asked.

"Some ash. We're lucky—in this instance—that the sprinkler system malfunctioned. The door was open."

"Open?" Helma repeated. "I locked it last night. The door was open, you're positive?"

"Yes."

"How did the fire start?"

"On Audrey's desk, like you thought. Newspapers and wood chips were ignited."

"I wasn't gone more than ten minutes," Audrey told the chief. "I just ran over to Kelly's for a coffee-to-go."

Wayne Gallant glanced across the road at Kelly's flickering neon sign. "You left the door unlocked?" he asked.

Audrey bowed her head. "Yes, I did."

"May I go inside?" Helma asked. "I need to inspect the Reading Room." The Reading Room door had been open. Helma *knew* she'd locked it the night before.

Chief Gallant glanced inside the building where two firemen and official-appearing men stood in the reception area. "Not yet," he told Helma, "but you'll be one of the first allowed inside." He turned to the uniformed policeman beside him. "Don't permit anyone to enter the library area before Helm . . . Miss Zukas. She's the person best able to tell us what's been disturbed."

"I appreciate it," Helma told him.

"It won't be long."

Tillie sniffed the air and whined, struggling to get down from Audrey's arms. "She doesn't like the smell," Audrey said.

"Neither do I," Helma agreed. "Maybe your ex-husband would take her."

"Today's *my* day to have her," Audrey said, holding Tillie tighter.

Finally, Chief Gallant ushered Helma and Audrey—minus Tillie—inside. The air was acrid. The surface of Audrey's desk was a heap of unrecognizable contours and blackened lumps. Her computer screen sagged like a cartoon shape, partially melted. The desk was the only area actually burned but soot darkened the walls and filled the air with a gritty gray cast. Color had been leached away, inside and out, as if the weather had finally conquered the world.

Audrey held her nose and the fireman behind her said, "Try this," offering her a white paper mask on a rubber band.

Helma took one, too. Relief wasn't total but it helped. She studied the ravaged desk, then the floor where a few shreds of burnt newspaper lay sodden among scattered wood chips.

She pointed to the smoke detector above the desk.

"Whoever started the fire *wanted* to set off the alarm."

"And the sprinklers," the chief added. "Don't touch anything, please."

Helma cautiously made her way toward the Reading Room. As Chief Gallant had said, the door stood open. The doorjamb was intact, the door itself unscratched. There was no sign of forced entry.

"Someone had a key for this door," Helma said.

Chief Gallant nodded and jotted that fact in his notebook.

Inside the Reading Room, only the odor and a thin dusting of ash were apparent. Helma stood by the door and scanned her desk, the shelves, her stacks of pamphlets and notes.

"What do you see?" Chief Gallant asked from behind her. He wasn't wearing a mask and Helma removed hers, breathing shallowly.

"Nothing appears disturbed. But the door *was* open. That's irregular," she mused. Then Helma felt the moist stirrings of air at her ankles and traced the sluggish breeze to an open window in the lower portion of the floor-to-ceiling windows. She walked over and reached out to pull it closed.

"Don't," Chief Gallant warned.

She dropped her hand. "I *know* this wasn't open when I left last night. And the screen's intact so no one used it for entrance or egress."

The chief looked over his shoulder toward the reception area. "If a fire began out there and a window was open in here . . ."

"In combination with the hallway, it would act like a chimney, pulling the fire straight through the wing," Helma finished.

"That's right," he agreed, excitement raising his voice. "That's why the Reading Room door was open: to encourage the fire."

"And if the fire didn't reach the Reading Room,

the sprinklers would have done serious damage to the materials," Helma suggested. "Stanley Plummer was murdered because of something he knew, something in this room. The fire is one step beyond the earlier vandalism. Whoever did this is growing desperate."

"Then why not set the fire in here?" he asked. "Be *sure* you've destroyed the room?"

"No, that would be too deliberate. The arsonist hoped to deflect your attention *away* from the Reading Room, toward a fire flagrantly set on Audrey's desk."

Wayne Gallant held his pencil to his notebook. Helma could tell from its movement that he wasn't notating her observations, only drawing circles.

"You don't think Plummer was murdered because of his past shady dealings?" he asked.

Helma shook her head. "He was too meticulous of a person to leave loose ends that would get him killed. Except if he were forced to leave loose ends through his own death," she amended.

"You sound like you knew the man."

"I'm beginning to," Helma said.

Wayne Gallant closed his notebook. "You may as well take the day off," he told her. "We'll need to spend time in here going over this development."

"May I take this stack of papers?" Helma asked him, pointing to her notes on enhancing the classification system Stanley Plummer had outlined.

"Go ahead."

Helma gingerly picked up the papers, blowing off the fine gray dust that speckled the top white sheet. "You'll be sure the door is locked when you're finished?"

He nodded and suddenly asked, "Would you like to go to dinner with me tomorrow night?"

She looked at him in surprise. "To discuss my theories of Plummer's death?"

"I thought we could just enjoy an evening together."

"I'd be happy to," Helma told him.

Helma had already turned the nose of her Buick into the parking lot of the Bellehaven Public Library when she decided she could work on the classification scheme just as well at home, perhaps even better than in the cramped library workroom with all its interruptions. She glanced at her watch. It was ten-thirty. She hoped Ruth had remembered to let out Boy Cat Zukas. In fact, it was prudent to return to her apartment and check.

She backed out and drove through town, stopping at swaying traffic lights, passing a man standing on the corner by the post office. He held a placard, the writing protected by plastic. "Repent!" his sign read, "or the sun will never shine."

In the empty bay whitecaps flipped up one after the other, driven to shore by the relentless winds. Turnouts scooped along the boulevard, where sunset watchers gathered during the warmer months. Cars sat facing the water, occupants of the steamy vehicles now viewing the rough water.

Plump Mrs. Whitney sat in her overstuffed chair with a red and gold granny afghan across her lap. Her feet rested on a doily-covered footstool.

"Welcome home," Helma told her.

"Thank you, dear. It's good to be here." She leaned forward and whispered with a hand to the side of her mouth. "And not down *there*. It was a narrow escape."

The apartment smelled of cinnamon and baking. "You're not up to baking already, are you?" Helma asked.

"That's me," Cassandra told her, laughing. "I inherited the tendency."

"Did Meg leave?"

"This morning. I'm staying until Thanksgiving. Brad's taking the kids to his parents for the holiday; we all could use the break. If you don't already have plans, will you join us for Thanksgiving dinner?"

"My mother . . ." Helma began.

"Invite her, too. And if you have friends at loose ends, them, too."

"How's your work at the cultural center?" Mrs. Whitney asked. "Do you have the day off?"

"There was a . . . heat problem this morning," Helma told her. "I'm doing work at home today."

"Mom took me with her to visit Colonel Hooke a few times when I was a girl," Cassandra told Helma. "The colonel's son and Mom were once lovebirds, you know. He told me I would have made a fine granddaughter."

"Oh, that poor man," Mrs. Whitney said, her eyes tearing up.

"I loved those little scenes he made." Cassandra looked dreamily past Helma. "All those tiny people and their houses, like if you could just make yourself small enough you could step right in beside them. The colonel told me if I looked very carefully, I'd discover a secret story."

"And did you?" Helma asked.

"No, but those miniature lives were mysterious enough to me."

Suddenly a deep rhythmic booming reverberated from the walls and floors, like the beat from the cars of teenage boys. Helma had never heard it so close before.

"What's that sound?" she asked.

Cassandra bit her lip. "Well, actually, we've been hearing it for the last hour. I think it's coming from your apartment. Do you have company?"

Helma picked up her bag and stood. "It appears

so. I'll go see what it is. I'm sorry if its bothered you, Mrs. Whitney."

"Nonsense. It reminds me of when Meg and Cassandra were young. The house used to shake with that rock and roll music."

Ruth stood at the stove in Helma's kitchen, her body bobbing to the music's beat. The blankets on Helma's sofa were draped onto the floor, with Boy Cat Zukas curled in their midst. Helma's radio was tuned to a station *she'd* never tuned to before; it was loud, deafening. So loud, Ruth didn't hear Helma enter the apartment.

Ruth screeched and spun around when Helma switched off the radio. Boy Cat Zukas scrambled out of the blankets and ran to the sliding glass door, his scraggly tail as fluffed as a bottle brush.

"You scared the hell out of me," Ruth accused Helma, holding a frying pan and spatula. "You could have rung the doorbell instead of sneaking up on us like that. Look at your poor cat."

Boy Cat Zukas hunched beside the door, staring at Helma with cold gold eyes.

"He looks normal to me," Helma said. She crossed her living room and unlatched the door. As soon as the gap was wide enough Boy Cat Zukas slipped through.

Helma sniffed the half familiar cooking odor. "What are you frying?" she asked, spotting the open bottle of olive oil on the counter.

"Hot dogs," Ruth said, tipping the frying pan so Helma could see the three blistered frankfurters rolling on the bottom of the pan.

"I didn't have any hot dogs," Helma said.

"I know that. I called Tommy, the bagger at the Green Apple and he ran them over to me. Sweet, huh?"

"I thought you'd have gone home by now,"

Helma said as she hung her coat in her closet.

"Can't," Ruth told her. "What am I supposed to do when I get there: shuffle blank canvases? Stepping inside my house is like a knife in the belly, or maybe a paper spindle to the chest. That's what a broken heart does for you. Turns you ineffectual, robs you of your artistic skills."

"You could feed your cat," Helma suggested.

"I leave the food bag out for Max, he knows what to do. What are you doing home in the middle of the work day?"

"There was a fire at the cultural center."

Ruth switched off the burner and gave Helma her full attention. "No lie? Did it burn down?"

"No. Only the reception area was involved. Someone set a fire on top of Audrey's desk while she left to get a cup of coffee."

"An inside job," Ruth said with certainty.

"Do you have reason to believe that, Ruth?" Helma asked. "I notice you're friends with Julianna and Tall Darkheart. Have they mentioned anything about dissatisfaction at the center?"

Ruth shook her head. "They're outsiders, really. Tall wouldn't dirty himself setting a fire. What about the kid? Everybody says he's a firebug."

"Young Frank?"

"The one and only."

"But he's a gifted carver."

Ruth snorted. "What's that got to do with it? Wasn't Hitler a credible artist? Wasn't Hannibal Lechter a good cook?"

"Hannibal Lechter is a fictional character. From what I understand, Young Frank's fires were set when he was bored, wherever he happened to be. He didn't go out of his way to commit arson. His fires didn't get out of hand."

"Yeah, like he'd tell you if they had. You like this kid?"

Helma thought for a moment. She didn't have any reason to like or dislike Young Frank. She hardly knew him. "Yes," she admitted. "I do like him."

"That's nice. But your liking someone hasn't stopped him or her from turning out to be a criminal in the past, has it?" Ruth reminded her smugly.

"Young Frank is a child."

"Criminal children are common these days, even hip."

"This fire had some curious elements," Helma told Ruth, explaining about the open window and door of the Reading Room, and the way the air would have drawn the fire through the wing like a chimney.

"Or like in a tunnel." Ruth shivered. "Do you ever think about that when you're driving through a tunnel? One wrong move, one little explosion and everybody in there is caught in a chimney fire. Poof. Toast."

"Some of life's possibilities are so remote we're better off not even considering them," Helma told her.

"The remote possibilities are what make life interesting," Ruth retorted. "Do you think this was what Plummer was talking about in his letter? Maybe he knew who wanted to destroy the center and now he expects you to 'un-cover' who it was. Woooo, the Raven did it."

"If that's what he wanted," Helma said, "he should have left clearer information. I *do* think the fire is connected to Plummer's death, though. Stanley was killed for something he knew and now his murderer wants to make sure I don't learn the same thing."

"Stanley?" Ruth squawked, waving the spatula. "You called him 'Stanley.' He was a creep, Helma. You make him sound like your *friend*."

"I'm attempting to comprehend him as a person

so I can understand why he was murdered."

"Yuck."

"The key to whatever he knew is in the Reading Room. That's why it's been disturbed since Plummer's death."

"And naturally you've looked high and low for it," Ruth said.

Helma nodded. "I've been through most of the books. I've checked desk drawers and cabinets, under shelves. But I haven't found anything except the folktale article which he made no effort to conceal."

"So his ending up dead doesn't have much to do with his letter to you?"

"If Plummer knew he was being fired and I was replacing him, he meant for me to uncover facts *after* he was gone, and 'gone' to him didn't mean dead."

"He could still be talking about his big system for all the books," Ruth offered. "Classifying or numbering or whatever you call it."

"Maybe, but . . ."

"I mean, this system was his little creation, right? His baby. Did he have the kind of ego to play the primal mother guarding her young?"

"I believe he did," Helma admitted.

"Mmm." Ruth forked a frankfurter and bit into it with relish. "Rumor is that Aaron Hooke's been hanging around the Reading Room making eyes at the librarian."

"He's visited the Reading Room a few times," Helma acknowledged.

Ruth swallowed her mouthful of hot dog. "He's got three ex-wives, Helma, and a reputation."

"There's no danger, Ruth. I assure you."

"Guys are funny about nuns and librarians. Maybe under all that he sees a sex goddess."

"Under all what?" Helma asked.

Ruth shrugged, biting the last of her hot dog off the fork and Helma changed the subject. "If you're not going home, what do you intend to do?"

"Honest, I don't plan to move in with you. But," Ruth looked out at the gray sky, "I feel a need to be part of the flock of humanity. So when the cultural center's visitable again, you may see me out there."

"Are you still seeing Tall Darkheart?" Helma asked.

Ruth bridled a little. "So what if I am? What have you got against the man, anyway?"

"I don't trust him."

"*Trust* him? You don't even *talk* to him. If you stay out of my love life, I'll stay out of yours, okay?"

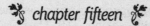

DINNER TALK

"**L**ast night's rag called your fire 'probable arson,'" George Melville said on Thursday morning. "Bet it was an inside job."

"Why do you say that?" Helma asked. That was exactly what Ruth had called it: an inside job.

"It makes sense. If I were the police, I'd check the insurance policies. See who wins big if the place is destroyed. Are you going out there today?"

"Yes. It was scheduled to reopen this morning."

Roberta walked by, her head high. George didn't turn but he watched Roberta from the corners of his eyes. "Then life goes on as smoothly as ever," he said in a voice too loud to be just for Helma's benefit and which she didn't feel it necessary to answer.

"Our circulation statistics are going through the roof this month," George continued in a normal voice. He glanced out at the dripping lawn. "Bellehavenites are reading their little hearts out. Every book we own about the deserts, the jungles, and the southern, sunnier climes is checked out."

Ms. Moon wandered from the staff lounge carrying in one hand a cup with a teabag string hanging from it and in the other a large brownie on a paper napkin. She stopped in the center of the workroom, a bewildered expression on her face.

"Is something wrong?" Helma asked her.

Ms. Moon's eyes widened. "Yes," she said and like a sleepwalker, continued into her office.

Helma set aside the list of associations she was compiling—she'd reached the L's—and followed Ms. Moon into her office in time to see Ms. Moon set down her tea and drop her untouched brownie in the trash basket—a compelling indication of her troubled mind. A tear slid down her cheek.

"Is there anything I can do?" Helma asked, pulling the director's door closed.

Ms. Moon slumped in her chair. "It's Pat," she said, her voice low and choked.

Pat, who Ms. Moon called her "life partner," had accompanied Ms. Moon from San Diego two years earlier and worked in the budget office for the Bay Hospital.

"Pat's seeing another woman," Helma guessed.

Ms. Moon nodded. Tears sparkled along the rims of Ms. Moon's blue eyes. "I worked late one night and stopped by Saul's for a cup of coffee and they were there, together."

"Perhaps it was coincidental," Helma suggested.

"They were sharing a piece of pie—with one fork."

"Oh," Helma said. "A single fork between two people does indicate a certain intimacy."

"I know," Ms. Moon agreed, her head bowing.

"Have you confronted Pat?"

"I'm afraid to. What if . . ."

"Knowing the worst news is better than tearing yourself apart with worry," Helma said reasonably. "You could get on with your life, move forward." She inwardly flinched but said anyway, "Regain your holistic balance in the universe."

"I suppose," Ms. Moon said. "I just hoped it would solve itself."

"Life rarely does solve itself, at least not if you intend to maintain your self-respect and a healthy state of mind."

"I'll think about it." Ms. Moon wiped her eyes on her voluminous sleeve. "Thank you, Helma."

"You're welcome."

Audrey sat at her new desk, which had been pushed forward into the reception area, while behind her three overalled painters had draped spattered drop cloths over the stripped floor and were repainting the walls and ceiling. The odor of burnt materials still hung in the air, only now it was overpowered by the paint fumes, definitely a preferable condition.

"I can't get a new computer until next week," Audrey said, pointing toward the beige IBM Selectric beside her desk.

Helma glanced down each wing. The portrait of Colonel Hooke had disappeared and in its place remained a rectangle of lighter paint. Signs had been removed from the walls. Other men and women in coveralls scrubbed and dusted, most of them wearing white dust masks.

Shelby Eaton came out of his office, casually dressed, a smudge of dust on the sleeve of his shirt, a dust mask on his forehead, and headed toward the south wing, his face preoccupied.

"The police questioned Young Frank," Audrey said as casually as if she were commenting on the weather.

"And what did Young Frank tell them?" Helma asked.

"The truth."

"Which is?"

"That he was at his grandfather's, busy at carving, but . . ."

"But he can't prove it because his grandfather's dead and no one saw him," Helma finished.

Audrey nodded. "Miriam Hooke is coming in to talk to Shelby about Young Frank."

"The police will sort it out," Helma assured her.

Audrey glanced at Helma without expression, then returned her attention to the open folder on her desk.

Helma surveyed the cleanup process, walking through the Plains exhibits in the north wing and stopping beside a red-haired woman cleaning the glass that protected Colonel Hooke's incorrect steam train diorama.

"These are the cutest things," the woman said. "Like dollhouse people I had when I was a little girl."

"They *are* fascinating," Helma agreed, thinking of how Colonel Hooke had told Cassandra—who'd been like a granddaughter to him—that the dioramas depicted secret stories. What had he meant? The tellers of the stories were gone; who had the right to say which stories were true and which weren't? "But this diorama is in the wrong wing," Helma said. "It should be in the south wing with the other Northwest exhibits."

"Well, *I'm* not going to move it," the woman told her. "I could lose my job for pulling a stunt like that."

Miriam Hooke entered the exhibit area, wearing a pale blue painter's smock over her clothing. "Why do you think it should be in the south wing?"

"This diorama's a scene from the Northwest, not the Plains," Helma explained. "The Indians are gathering oysters and see the Madrona trees among the firs?"

Miriam leaned over and peered into the diorama,

then rose and smiled at Helma. "You're right. I'll ask Shelby to relocate it as soon as the cleaning's finished."

"One other thing," Helma said, pointing to the diorama's bronze plaque. "The date's also incorrect. Perhaps someone else besides your father was responsible, but the Forbes, Sands, and Moore railway line entered Bellehaven from the south in 1888, not 1886. I recently answered that question at the library."

Again Miriam bent low, studying the plaque, then the name of the line on the smoking locomotive. "That's correct," she murmured.

"Were you looking for me?" Helma asked her.

"No. I was surveying the damage." Miriam rose. "All the work that's gone into this center, and yet ever since its inception, it's been plagued by problems." She shook her head. "I should be grateful it wasn't worse, I suppose."

"We were fortunate," Helma agreed.

"This episode didn't interfere with your work, I hope."

"The project is progressing well," Helma told her. "Stanley Plummer was very organized."

Miriam didn't conceal her distaste for the subject of Stanley Plummer. "He misrepresented himself," she said tersely.

"As a librarian or a distant relative?"

Miriam looked only momentarily surprised. "Both. If you'll excuse me, please, I'd like to continue my survey."

Helma left the exhibit room, leaving Miriam among her father's dioramas.

The smell in the Reading Room wasn't masked by paint or cleaning compounds and Helma reopened the windows she had so carefully closed the morning before. The damp air crept inside and Helma turned up the room's heat.

She donned a smock and cotton gloves to protect herself, even an old sun hat that had gone floppy, and began cleaning the room without further delay.

"The brothers Hooke approach," a voice called out, and Helma looked up as Aaron and Darren entered the Reading Room, both wearing light gray coveralls over their clothing. Aaron's eyes sparkled; Darren looked like he'd rather be anywhere but in the cultural center.

"Cute outfit," Aaron said. "We're doing a detailed damage inspection for a report to Mother." He raised a clipboard with a calculator attached to the side.

"She was here a while ago," Helma said.

"Mother doesn't poke and pry around in rubble. The bottom line here is money. Do you have any damage that's going to cost the board more than a dollar ninety-eight to repair?"

"This is serious, Aaron," Darren told his brother.

"Don't I know it," Aaron said, waving his clipboard.

Helma shook her head. "Only the odor which will disappear in a few days."

"The door was open, the police said?" Darren asked, swinging the door back and forth on its hinges.

"That's right. And a window."

Darren nodded and walked up and down the aisle, running his hand in that curious way people had, along the spines of the shelved books.

"Are you familiar with these books?" Helma asked him.

"No. I didn't share my grandfather's interests," Darren said.

"Just Gramps's love of money," Aaron added, smiling mischievously at Darren.

Darren opened his mouth and then closed it and Helma detected a lifelong torment between the two brothers, with the more dour, less charming Darren the frequent loser.

The brothers gave the Reading Room a cursory inspection, Aaron stopping and making a few marks on his clipboard while Darren stepped ahead of him out the Reading Room door. Aaron glanced once down the hall after Darren and then turned back to Helma.

"How about dinner tonight, Helma?" he asked.

"I'm sorry but I already have an engagement," she told him.

Aaron stuck out his lower lip. "Damn," he said. "I was counting on you to get me out of an evening with Mother and the evil twin."

"I'm afraid you'll have to find some other excuse."

Aaron hung his head in exaggerated humility. "I deserved that. Break your 'engagement' and I'll make it up to you."

Helma laughed. It was impossible not to. "Another time, Aaron."

He shrugged. "Okay. I'll call you. So long."

"How does seafood sound tonight?" Chief Gallant asked as they pulled away from the Bayside Arms.

"Delicious," Helma said. And it did. There was an element to seafood that reminded her of sunshine and cloudless skies, the clean uncomplicated succulence of the pale tender meat.

They drove to a restaurant at the tip of a long spit popular with kite flyers and also where the Snow to Surf carnival was raised in a wild tumble of neon every Memorial Day holiday. She blushed and glanced away from the now bare and sandy carnival site, remembering the Tilt-a-Whirl ride she'd shared last Snow to Surf with . . .

"When's the last time you saw a sunset?" Wayne Gallant asked.

Helma laughed. "My head says it was only a

month ago but my heart thinks it's been years."

The restaurant was circular, with tall windows that on fair days overlooked the marina with a long view of the bay and the islands beyond.

But now it was dark outside and in the window beside their table, all that could be seen were their own smoky images reflected back to them by candlelight.

"Let's get our business out of the way first," Chief Gallant said after they ordered, him choosing crab-stuffed prawns and Helma choosing broiled salmon.

"Do you mean the business of murder, arson, breaking and entering, and letters from the dead?" she asked.

Wayne Gallant poured white wine into her glass from the carafe on their table. "The very same. How well do you know Young Frank Portman?"

"If you suspect him of the arson, I don't agree. From what I hear, he doesn't fit the profile that well. He doesn't go out of his way to set fires. He doesn't get involved in fights and he's not prone to temper tantrums or revenge. He's not really disruptive at school, more independent. His behavior is very even. He has one major passion: carving, and to have an absorbing interest like that is totally outside the profile."

Wayne Gallant listened, nodding. "Have you recently read information on arsonists' profiles?"

"Yes," she admitted. "Specifically for children nine to twelve."

"Those profiles aren't ironclad."

"I'm aware of that," Helma said. "But I'd expect him to fall more in line with them than he does, wouldn't you?"

"We know that whoever did it had a key to the Reading Room, but from what we've learned, there was little control over the keys. Very easy to come by."

"I still believe the arson was connected to Stanley Plummer's murder," Helma said.

"Possibly. We're not ruling out anything at this point."

"Or anyone?"

"Or anyone," he agreed. He grinned and raised his glass toward Helma. "But I *do* exclude you."

"Thank you. I did discover Stanley Plummer's newest avocation," Helma said and told him about the stolen Nettle folktales.

"Ah, those are the kinds of crimes that are rarely prosecuted," he said. "Academic horseplay. Major crime in a very small world."

"And my letter from Stanley Plummer?" she asked.

"Now *there* was someone who fit the profile of a loner. Maybe he saw you, felt romantic, and wanted to let you know."

"So much so that he slipped an unaddressed letter into the mailbox on the way to his death?"

"Is that so unbelievable?" he asked.

"Yes."

Chief Gallant smiled and Helma unaccountably and clumsily brushed her napkin from her lap. Wayne Gallant motioned to the waiter, who retrieved Helma's napkin and brought her another.

"Stanley Plummer's last act was to ask a favor from me," she said. "He felt time was essential."

"We're not bound by requests from the dead."

"I'd still like to discover what he meant," Helma told him.

"If you think this is leading you beyond library matters, Helma, don't do it on your own."

"I'll request help the instant I need it," she assured him.

Helma's broiled salmon was perfect: moist, the pink flesh firm and too delicately flavored to dash with lemon. She savored each perfect mouthful before swallowing. Wayne Gallant's prawns were stuffed with a crab filling, then wrapped in bacon and broiled. Too many contrasting flavors for Helma's tastes. She preferred to indulge one flavor at a time.

Helma grew more relaxed as the meal progressed but she was surprised that Wayne Gallant seemed to grow *less* relaxed. He bumped his wine glass against his plate, smeared butter on his hand, and shifted uncomfortably in his chair. Helma subtly glanced at her watch—it was still early evening— certainly he didn't have another appointment? She ate her meal quietly, setting her fork down between each bite, a habit she'd acquired after reading the tip in an article about indigestion and weight gain.

The chief cleared his throat. "Helma," he said.

"Yes?" she replied.

"I noticed you were having lunch with Aaron Hooke. Are you . . . Did . . . well, are you seeing him socially?"

The thought hadn't crossed Helma's mind prior to that moment. Seeing Aaron Hooke socially? Of course she wasn't so she was stunned to hear herself say, "It wasn't a business lunch."

"I see," he said. "Then you two . . ."

"We're just friends," she said, grimacing a little at the triteness of the phrase.

"You and I have known each other a long time," he said.

"Two years and seven months," Helma said.

"Right. Almost three years."

"But it does seem like a long time," she hastily added. "We've shared some interesting experiences. And when people share experiences, the effect is to become closer, better acquainted. Time is intensified," she ended lamely.

He nodded. "I admire you," he said.

"It's mutual," she told him, glancing once into his eyes and away.

They paused while a waiter stopped at their table and poured more lemon-tinged water into their goblets.

The chief wiped at the sweat on his water goblet with his thumb and distractedly turned the glass. "My divorce was final seven months ago," he said.

Ruth had called Wayne Gallant's divorce "long and brutal." Helma said nothing, waiting. She could feel her heart beating.

"It's been rough sometimes," he said in a voice lower in timbre and authority than usual. Helma glanced at his downcast eyes in surprise, searching vainly for the professional policeman.

"Good friends are invaluable in situations like this," he continued.

"Good friends are always invaluable," Helma replied.

"It's just that certain situations remind you of that fact," he said.

Helma wasn't sure where the conversation was heading so she cut her red potatoes into smaller pieces while she waited for him to continue his thought.

"There are times when you wish some people could be more than friends," he said, his voice cracking a little.

Helma's knife sliced through her potato and snicked against the plate. She froze, holding it there.

"But then you realize you've got a long way to go before you think about anything more than friendship, that you might even be keeping another person from going forward with her own life. And that's not fair."

Helma left her red potatoes untouched and tidily laid her fork and knife at the edges of her plate, careful not to get any food on the handles. She was finished.

She folded her hands in her lap. "When you say 'you,' you mean yourself, not the general indefinite form of the pronoun 'you,' am I correct?" Helma asked.

"Yes," he said.

"I see."

"I value your friendship more than I can tell you, Helma," he said, leaning toward her across the table, his eyes now intent on her face.

She unclasped her hands; the bite of her nails into her palm was growing painful. "And you'd like us to remain friends," she said, "with no mistake about our friendship developing any further."

He pulled back, visibly uncomfortable again. "That's not what I mean at all. It's just too soon. My life . . ."

"I know exactly what you mean," Helma said, feeling the slow, somber beat of her heart. "I understand completely." A gust of wind dashed rain against the window and the water ran down the glass like tears.

Wayne Gallant actually looked relieved. He smiled warmly and thrust his right hand across the table. "Then we're friends?" he asked.

Helma took his hand and shook it. "Yes," she said, amazed at the words issuing so calmly from her mouth. "We're friends." She pulled back her hand and glanced at her watch, her vision too misty to read the numbers. "Look what time it is already," she said. "I hope you don't mind if this evening ends early. The next few days are going to be very difficult for me."

Wayne Gallant returned Helma to her apartment, hugging her briefly at her door. Instead of going to bed, she retrieved the red chevron afghan Aunt Em had knit for her from her back bedroom and wrapped it around herself. It fell from her shoulders to her ankles.

She opened her curtains so she was only separated from the wind and rain of the night sky by the thin glass of her window and stood for a long time in her dark living room watching the lights along Washington Bay blink off one by one.

❧ chapter sixteen ❧

THE WEATHER CONSIDERED

Helma woke up with a headache at 6 a.m. to an instrumental version of "O Come All Ye Faithful" on her clock radio. She ran a washcloth under cold water, wrung it out, and carried it to her dark living room. There, she sat in her rocking chair, still in her night clothes and pressed the washcloth to her forehead.

It would be dark for another hour. She'd neglected to close her drapes the night before and now she sat facing the black morning, oblivious to the cool room, her bare feet, and the washcloth slowly rising to skin temperature.

She gazed at nothing, vaguely aware of the bump and growl of the unsteady winds that rattled loose items and met immovable objects. Her balcony door shuddered in its tracks, the glass shivering.

Helma removed the washcloth from her forehead, her attention caught by Boy Cat Zukas meowing at her balcony door.

Without thinking, she rose and let him in. He entered, then sensed her distraction. Instead of climbing into his cube he sat beside the door while she resettled in her rocking chair. When she said nothing he slunk toward her, staying low to the floor, approaching from an angle. Still not impeded, he slipped beneath her chair and curled there, one paw outstretched and touching Helma's bare heel so lightly she didn't feel it.

Helma thought of other storms she'd known, of blizzards that shrieked off Lake Michigan and drifted roads closed for days, of thunder so loud it pounded against her heart, of hail and warm rain and hoar frost and ice storms that weighted the electric lines until they snapped, of sticky sultry days when her shirt stuck to varnished chairs and her clothes stiffened with salt.

Then she pondered falling library budgets, the weakening dollar, clearcutting, carpal tunnel syndrome, and the odd mole on her knee. Everything but Chief of Police Wayne Gallant who wanted to be friends.

When she truly took note outside her window it was to see a stocky black and white tugboat bucking and plunging through the waves toward the mouth of the bay and to realize suddenly it was light and if she didn't hurry she was going to begin this Friday by being late for work at the cultural center.

Helma tackled the shelves of material with what some might call a vengeance. Stanley Plummer receded to the realm of Dead and Gone, with Wayne Gallant momentarily at his elbow.

Even though she wasn't hungry—in fact the thought of food made her a little queasy—she stopped precisely at noon and laid out her sandwich, chips, and apple.

Laughter and loud voices interrupted her as she peeled her Macintosh apple, the rest of her lunch untouched. Helma recognized Ruth's and Julianna's voices and in a moment they appeared bodily in the Reading Room, Ruth leading the way. Each of them was brilliant in her own fashion: Ruth in plaids and stripes, her dark hair in a high knot; Julianna in a flowing pumpkin-colored tunic over black stirrup pants. Both of them in makeup suited to the theater.

"Well, it smells better in here," Ruth said, taking exaggerated breaths. "Take a break and go out to lunch with us."

Helma held up her nearly peeled apple, the red skin a single curved strand. "I have my lunch here, thank you."

"She eats while she toils," Ruth said in a conspiratorial voice to Julianna.

"I'm impressed."

"I intend to finish this project before Christmas," Helma told Ruth.

"So you can start the new year without loose ends?" Ruth asked.

"And so I can enjoy the holidays."

"That's right. You're going back to your Aunt Em's. Back to the bosom of our old hometown. I'll bet your Aunt Em is already baking those potato thingees."

"*Kugelis,*" Helma said.

"Right. Bring some back, okay?"

"What are you doing for Christmas?" Helma asked Ruth.

"Sulking, probably. Having a blue Christmas, a silent night, no joy in the world, stuck in O little town of Bellehaven."

"Stop!" Julianna cried. "You're breaking my heart. If I wasn't going to Albuquerque, you could spend it with me."

"Thanks but it wouldn't have the same dramatic appeal."

Julianna and Ruth together made Helma physically tired. She suppressed a yawn and finished peeling her apple, dropping the peel into the waste-basket where it curled itself among the scrap paper like a loose, gutted fruit.

"Are we boring you?" Ruth asked.

"No. Well, yes, a little."

"Tsk, tsk." Ruth turned to Julianna. "Have you ever shown Helma 'the room'?" she asked.

Julianna shook her head, a warning look on her face which Ruth plainly intended to ignore. Ruth's eyes sparkled. "Do you know there's a sub-museum here, Helma?"

"If there is, it's probably not your place to show me."

"What? Isn't this a public institution? Come on."

Julianna shrugged. "You might as well see it," she told Helma. "It's no big deal."

Helma's apple would be brown by the time she returned, but Ruth was already out the door. In res-ignation, Helma wrapped the apple in a piece of plastic from a stack of catalog cards and wiped her hands.

"You might not like this," Julianna said as she walked with Helma down the hall toward the recep-tion area.

"Does it matter?"

"No," Julianna said, grinning.

Ruth stood in the short corridor of offices directly behind the reception area. She held open the door of the third office back, behind and across from Shelby Eaton's.

"Welcome to the Colonel Hooke Submuseum of Native American History," Julianna said, bowing Helma inside.

Helma stood in the doorway of a small window-less room, barely big enough to hold a desk. Two walls were lined floor to ceiling with attachable shelves.

Helma stared. First, she noted a three-foot-high to-tem pole on the floor, the figures all brightly painted overendowed women. Leaning against it was a plas-tic bow and arrow set. On the shelves stood plastic figures of cleavage-exposing native women, a trick bank that scalped an Indian when a coin was in-serted, a ceramic teepee with a bare bottom sticking out the door flap, a weather rock, plastic Indians with Chinese features. The walls were hung with big-eyed Indian children, wooden bar signs with risque Indian jokes, crude cocktail napkins and post-cards. Indians of impossible cheekbones and solem-nity whose untangled raven hair dissolved into eagle feathers and rainbows or were accompanied by surreal wolves and white buffaloes. Indian maid-ens of uncommon beauty wearing buckskin with im-practical fringes.

It was dizzying. "Who put this collection to-gether?" Helma asked.

Julianna touched a finger to a plastic blue-eyed brave with a rippling GI Joe chest. "Everybody. It grew unintentionally. Somebody sent that war bon-net nightlight as a donation and it expanded from there."

"But this has less to do with Native American cul-ture than the exhibits in the center."

"Do you think so?" Julianna asked.

"It's not . . . actual," Helma explained. "Not *from* Native Americans, only somebody else's jaundiced view. It's insulting."

"You're right!" Julianna said, smiling as if Helma had said something very clever.

"Did Stanley Plummer know about this?" Helma asked.

"Mm hmm. He donated the big-busted Pocahon-tas doll up there."

"This collection's not historically accurate."

"It depends on how you look at it," Julianna

agreed, seriously peering around the room. "These little artifacts definitely exist in *somebody's* perception of history."

All those grinning foolish faces, the crude jokes and rude toys and over-romanticized pictures. A mishmash of foolishness.

"I'm offended by this," Helma said.

Julianna pushed the feather on the head of a wooden carving. The figure's loincloth dropped. Too casually, she knocked over the carving, leaving it toppled on the shelf, and said, "I'm hungry, Ruth. Let's get something to eat."

Ruth was examining a teepee barometer. When barometric pressure was high, a dainty squaw emerged. When it was low, out popped a loin-clothed brave wielding a tomahawk. "Tall's supposed to meet us here," she said, poking the brave, who swung into the teepee and right back out again.

This was the room where the fire should have started, Helma thought as she followed Ruth to the reception area.

Tall Darkheart stood solemnly beside Audrey's desk, his gleaming black hair braided, turquoise rings glowing on his fingers. He nodded to the three women, not a muscle moving in his dark face. Ruth turned back to Helma and winked, fluttering her hand over her heart.

Again, Helma was struck by the certainty that something about Tall Darkheart wasn't quite right. Unbidden, the words "mirage" and "chimera" came to mind.

Tall Darkheart turned his proud head to the left, slipping into profile.

And Helma saw it, the uncanny resemblance to that movie star. She bit her lip, trying to remember. It started with a C. No, a P. As was her habit, she constructed names in alphabetical order and luckily, it was situated near the beginning of the alphabet of

P's: Pacino. Al Pacino, star of *Scent of a Woman* and *The Godfather*. The nose, the chin, the lips. Uncanny. Al Pacino: he was Italian, wasn't he?

"Bye," Julianna said to Helma.

"See ya," Ruth called over her shoulder.

Tall Darkheart was last. Before he could say goodbye, Helma said, "*Ciao.*"

"*Ciao,*" he returned. Just that one word but said with such natural assurance, such subtlety of accent, that there was no doubt Tall Darkheart had grown up, at least for a time, among native Italian speakers.

Silence descended the hall. Audrey busily moved papers from one side of her new desk to the other. Helma turned and walked down the south wing toward the Reading Room. She had a great deal of work to which she must attend.

Ruth returned at four-thirty. She dropped into the oak swivel chair near Helma's desk, turned it back and forth, and said, "Aren't you the clever one?"

"I don't know what you're talking about," Helma said.

"*Ciao,*" Ruth spat out. "*Ciao.*"

"And?"

Ruth threw her hands in the air. "Don't be coy. You unmasked Tall Darkheart with one brutal thrust to his language center. He wilted like the Wicked Witch of the East."

"West," Helma corrected.

"Whatever. All I had to do next was ask him if he preferred lasagna to spaghetti and he confessed. He had me fooled. Pretty tall for an Italian though, don't you think?"

"Where is he?" Helma asked.

Ruth shrugged and swung the chair from side to side. It creaked. "Packing for Sedona, Arizona, to commune with the spiritual center of the universe or draw prayer wheels in the dirt or pick up rich women, who knows. He's been planning this little trip for a while, it seems, but you turned it into sooner rather than later. Don't expect any fond farewells from him. He doesn't look kindly on your knack for public humiliation."

"I refuse to take responsibility for Tall Darkheart's actions or deceptions."

"Bravo. Well said." Ruth stared out at the nearly dark afternoon. "I didn't eat lunch after all. Wanta walk over to Kelly's with me and have an early dinner?"

"I still have work to do."

"C'mon Helm, be a friend." Ruth's eyes were dark and sorrowful, not manic but quietly sad. Helma looked away, guessing that her own eyes reflected Ruth's.

"All right," she said. "I didn't eat lunch either. As long as we're back here by five-thirty."

"No problem."

When Helma told Audrey she was taking a break, Audrey pulled a key off her metal key ring and said, "Take this. I have to leave early tonight, so if I'm gone, can you be sure all the lights are turned off?"

"Certainly. Did Mr. Eaton leave?"

"He never stays all day on Fridays."

Kelly's was less than a block from the center, but walking on the shoulder of the road in the wind and darkness, with her coat pulled tight and one hand holding her knit hat to her head, Helma felt like it was a good half-mile distant.

Gravel and humps of wet grass and oncoming headlights made walking clumsy and perilous. Traffic had picked up as five o'clock approached and the cars drove too close to the shoulder. Giant shiny wet shadows with blinding headlights.

Ruth rarely wore anything as conventional as a button-up coat and her green hooded cape billowed with each passing car. Drivers honked: quick-spirited toots that Helma doubted were aimed at her smaller, neater figure.

Kelly's was a combination bar/restaurant/deli. Far enough on the edge of town, it tried to be all things to all potential customers, from farmers to reservation Indians to those approaching hip.

It was warm inside, a fetid warm, musky with the odor of beer, hot grease, and wet clothing.

"Ruth!" a man's voice called. "I'll buy you a drink."

"Not tonight," Ruth called back. "I have to comfort a friend."

"What does that mean?" Helma asked as she removed her coat and folded it over an empty chair at a table farthest from the bar. "Who do you have to comfort?"

Ruth sat down and threw off her cape, letting it fall over the back of her chair and ripple into folds on the black tile floor.

"You. Who else? What happened?"

"What makes you think anything happened?"

"Suit yourself. Let's order."

All Helma'd had to eat all day was a dry piece of white toast and two bites of a slightly brown Macintosh apple. The thought of salad gave her a stomachache. Definitely nothing fried. Finally she settled on a bowl of chicken vegetable soup while Ruth mumbled, "What in hell does free-range veal mean: the little calves frolicked in the buttercups before they whacked them?" and ordered a double cheeseburger with bacon, and onion rings. "And bring us a carafe of red wine, two glasses," Ruth finished.

"I don't want . . ." Helma began.

"Then don't drink any," Ruth snapped. "Do you think I'm going to force you?"

Their table sat by a window, and on the wet road outside, the traffic steadily increased, a long line of lights fleeing town while music, sounding like a mix of country western and Irish folk, played in the bar area.

Ruth drummed her burgundy fingernails on the table. "So now *my* heart is broken once again," she said, looking accusingly at Helma.

"I doubt that," Helma told her.

The waitress brought wine glasses and filled them with deep red liquid before she left the carafe in the center of the table.

"Cheers," Ruth said, raising her glass to Helma.

"Cheers," Helma replied, taking a single sip of the soft liquid.

"It's okay, though," Ruth continued after swallowing a third of her glass. "He was just a diversion while the real object blithely continues on his merry way through the frozen north, snipping my heart to shreds. Death by long distance."

"He probably feels you broke his heart," Helma said.

"How could he possibly?"

Helma took another sip of wine, a deeper one this time. "He asked. You said no. What do you expect him to think?"

"If he'd *really* wanted me to live with him, he wouldn't have given up so easily. Or *he* would have moved out here. No, he shrugged it off too easily; he *wanted* me to say no."

"That's convenient logic," Helma said.

"Convenience is the only way to logicize."

"Logicize isn't a legitimate word."

"Legitimate, logical. La la la."

"One too many la's," Helma said.

"What?"

"You had two alliterative adjectives and three la's. I was only equalizing them."

Ruth poured more wine into both their glasses. How had Helma's glass emptied so quickly?

"Matching sets," Ruth commented. "Like we used

to do on those intelligence tests when we were kids." She licked a drop from the rim of the carafe. "So tell me. What did the white-knight–chief-of-police-in-shining-armor say to you to make you look like somebody's lost dog?"

"Nothing. Well, nothing *that* terrible."

Ruth screwed her mouth to one side, tapped her cheek, and said, "The two worse things a man can tell a woman are 'There's no reason to be jealous; she's only a friend,' or 'I think we should just be friends.' Which one was it?"

"The latter."

"No lie? The jerk. What was his excuse?"

Helma set down her half empty wine glass. What was taking their food so long? "He's not over his divorce yet."

"Oh. It might be legitimate."

"And logical?" Helma asked.

"La, la."

The waitress delivered their food, plates balanced up her arms. A slick of shiny grease floated on the surface of Helma's soup. She pushed away the bowl, unwrapped a saltine cracker, and nibbled off all four corners.

Ruth bit into her hamburger. A lettuce leaf slid out the other side and dropped onto her plate. Still chewing, she said, "If a wife dies, a man just replaces her, but if she divorces him, he takes it personal and is wounded for life. You might have to give our valiant chief a little time."

"It's been almost three years since they separated and seven months since their divorce was final," Helma said, adding a little more wine to her glass.

"Try seven *years*."

"No thank you. I'm not *that* interested."

"You've waited thirty-nine already. What's a few more? Sorry, bad joke."

"Yes, it was," Helma agreed.

"I hear gossip, well actually, I seek it out, and I haven't heard that Wayne Gallant is seeing anyone." Ruth shrugged. "He might be worth waiting for. Some guys are."

"But what exactly would I be waiting for?"

"Good question. Sort of like investing in the stock market." Ruth rearranged her onion rings, piling them in a tower on her plate. "An Italian Indian," she said. "Tall Darkheart's *Italian*."

"What's his real name?" Helma asked.

"Paul Stromboli or Pepperoni or something like that. He wasn't very clear on the details. I did get it out of him that he came out here on the train. All the way from the East Coast by himself, isn't that cute. Seeing America. Choo choo."

They must have turned up the heat in Kelly's; Helma was growing uncomfortably warm. She unbuttoned the top buttons of her blouse. "Colonel Hooke came to Washington state on the train," she told Ruth. "He was born on the trip out, in the 1880's."

"On Amtrak?" Ruth asked.

"That was over a hundred years ago, Ruth," Helma carefully explained. "There was no Amtrak then."

"I bet there was; they just called it something different. They're always changing the names of things. You just get used to it being one thing, and wham, it changes. What's the point?"

"There were a lot of little lines," Helma went on. "Railroading was big business in the 1800's but most of the lines didn't last."

"Like computer stores?" Ruth asked.

"Exactly. Everyone wanted in on the ground floor." She thought a moment. "Or on the fast track."

Ruth groaned.

"That's what a lot of the trails around Bellehaven

are," Helma explained. "Old railroad beds."

"Yeah, yeah," Ruth said. "Save it for the library."

But Helma's mind had meandered off on its own siding, to Colonel Hooke's incorrect train diorama with the Indians gathering oysters. The railroad line's name had been on the engine. But there'd also been writing on the tender. Another name. Helma's mind fuzzily and vainly struggled to make connections. Her normally sharp recall failed her. She simply couldn't remember. But suddenly she felt a deep compulsion to *know*.

Stanley Plummer had trusted her train of thought. Trains, engines, tenders, and cabooses.

"We have to return to the center," she told Ruth. "Right now."

"I'm not finished," Ruth said, holding up her half-eaten hamburger, "although we did go through that wine damn fast."

"Bring your sandwich," Helma said. "Let's go." She stood and nearly tipped over her chair. She grasped the table edge and gingerly sat down again. "I drank too much wine," she said.

"Drank it?" Ruth snorted. "You *guzzled* it. Deadly on an empty stomach."

"That's immaterial. We must get back to the center."

"Can't you just give me a teensy clue why?"

"I have to check a name in one of the colonel's dioramas."

Ruth resignedly wrapped her hamburger in a napkin. "I'd say go yourself but you'd probably end up on your face in the street. Can't have that on my conscience."

"Wait. We have to pay for this," Helma said, reaching for the tab.

"I left my wallet at home," Ruth said. "Sorry."

Helma opened her own wallet and removed a plastic card.

"That's not a credit card for pete's sake, is it?" Ruth asked. "*You're* paying with plastic?"

"Of course not. It's a gratuity chart, to calculate tips. Beulah at the hospital library put it in my Christmas card last year." Helma ran her finger down the amounts on the left side of the card, squinting over the numbers but unable to read them, which was absurd; she didn't even wear glasses.

"Don't be so cold-blooded," Ruth said. "I've got it." She took two crumpled dollar bills from her pocket and dropped them on the table.

"I thought you forgot your wallet."

"I did. This is my emergency fund."

Helma left the correct amount of cash to cover the tab and pulled on her coat. Ruth, totally engulfed by her cape, snickered.

"What's wrong?" Helma asked her.

"You've buttoned your coat wrong."

Helma looked down. Her coat hung askew, off by one button, but too complicated to fix. "Let's go," she said.

"Geesh."

They hurried through the darkness toward the center, cars whizzing past, throwing up water, wind blowing, beams of light flashing and blinding. Helma stumbled and Ruth grabbed her arm, shouting words Helma couldn't make out. The surrounding earth was unnaturally tipped, off-cant and oversized.

In front of the center, Helma leaned against the totem pole and suspiciously regarded the building. It was dark, totally dark, not even lit by the usual night lights. The only car in the parking lot was her own and that she'd left at the north end of the lot, beneath the last light post.

"Is that building dark?" she asked Ruth, not trusting her own alcohol-tinged perceptions.

At their backs a truck rumbled past and Ruth waited until it was gone before she answered.

"Definitely," Ruth said. "Definitely dark."

❧ chapter seventeen ❧

AFTER HOURS

"**L**et's hop in your little old car and go home," Ruth suggested.

"I promised Audrey I'd check to see if the lights were off."

"Well, just look, would ya? It's darker than a boot in there. The lights *are* off. Trust me."

"They shouldn't *all* be off," Helma said.

"Make up your mind, please. Off or on?" Ruth stumbled and veered into the gloom toward Helma's Buick. "Forget it. Let's go home."

"I can't drive in this condition," Helma said. "And neither can you," she added while Ruth's mouth was still open but before words had issued forth. "Besides, I have to check something, I told you that."

A gust of wind winged Ruth's cape outward as if she were about to take flight. "Do it tomorrow."

"Tomorrow's Saturday. You can wait out here for me if you want. I'll unlock my car."

"I don't think I'd like waiting out here any more than going in there." Ruth stalked toward the dark center. The totem pole leered with passing car lights, strobing in and out of the night. "At least it'll be dry in there," Ruth said over her shoulder.

Even the light under the portico was off. Helma carried a small flashlight attached to her key chain and it only took her a few seconds to insert Audrey's key in the lock and open the door. It swung forward into the darkness soundlessly, well oiled. The air inside was less acrid, smelling more of ammonia and paint, a clean odor Helma sniffed with pleasure.

"Where are the light switches?" Ruth whispered.

Helma shone her light along the walls until the beam found a single switch plate and she turned the toggle upward. The outside portico light came on, casting shimmering light through the glass doors and into the hallway, illuminating their figures without color.

"One down," Ruth said aloud.

There was a crash somewhere in the building. One quick sound of two hard objects meeting.

Ruth gasped. "Oh lordy. What's that?" she cried, grabbing Helma's arm.

"It came from the south wing," Helma told her. "We'd better investigate. Ruth, you're hurting my arm."

Ruth released her. "It's dark down there. Maybe the exhibits came to life. You know the guy with the tomahawk? Or all those weird little figures in the colonel's diabolicals?"

"Dioramas," Helma said.

"Yeah, like in that story where the little warrior statue slashes the woman's ankles right through her stockings with his itty-bitty knife? Wait a minute. Where are you going?"

"I told you. To see what the noise was."

"What if it's your buddy Stanley come back to haunt you?"

"Don't be silly."

"Okay," Ruth said, "but you go first."

Helma moved in shortened steps toward the reception area where she recalled the panel of light

switches. Her flashlight projected a yellow pinprick
of light four feet in front of them before it was lost
in darkness.

Ruth loomed behind Helma, her presence marked
by heavy breathing. "I hate it when you do this kind
of stuff," she said. "Did you ever sneak inside a
school after everybody'd gone home?"

"Of course not." Helma remembered the night
she'd reenacted Stanley Plummer's death and shivered. "Did you?"

"I might have."

The flashlight beam crossed a shiny object and
Helma stopped, slowly moving the light over the
shapes until she could identify them.

"Ladder and bucket," she warned Ruth. "The
crash was just the wind through the building when
we opened the door. Something loose fell over."

"Slow down," Ruth said. "This is bottled courage,
Helma. You may not know the signs but I do. Remind me never to let you drink again."

"This has nothing to do with drinking or any type
of courage," Helma told her. "It's simply common
sense to investigate unknown noises."

"Not in my book."

In the miniature light beam, Audrey's desk was
indecipherable angles and shadows. Helma flashed
her light along the walls. Around them, the center
was silent, deserted. There it was: a panel of four
switches, and, with her palm flattened, Helma
flipped them all at once.

The center burst into normalcy and both Helma
and Ruth released held breaths. A can of pop sat on
Audrey's new desk; her chair was slid in, a new
chair sat beside her desk for Tillie.

"See. Everything's okay," Ruth said. "Now let's
go home."

"You're being impatient, Ruth," Helma said. "I
told you I have items I need to check."

"I know: names. Well, do it then."

"I'll check the south wing first."

"I'll cover you from back here," Ruth said and sat on a rung of the aluminum ladder left by the cleaners.

Helma quickly passed through the Northwest exhibits in the south wing, from where she speculated the crash had come. The masked figures stood at fixed attention, the dioramas were all in place. At the end of the hall, the door to the Reading Room stood properly closed. While she couldn't spot the source of the sound, Helma saw nothing unusual in the south wing, nothing suspicious.

It was the north wing Helma was most interested in at the moment and she turned and headed in that direction.

"Now what?" Ruth asked from the ladder.

"The name in the diorama. Colonel Hooke left it behind for someone to find."

"Left what name behind for who?"

"I suspect for one of his grandsons if they'd been interested."

"So why are you?"

"I'm not sure yet."

"Okay, lead on," Ruth said and rose clumsily from her perch. The aluminum ladder rocked and chimed against the metal bucket beside it.

The Plains exhibit, too, appeared in perfect order, untouched. The painted buffalo robe and beaded moccasins, the leather-clothed figures and dioramas in a straight line.

Helma moved directly to the train diorama with the young woman holding the baby to the window as the train passed above the three Indians gathering oysters.

Steadying herself against the base of the diorama, she crouched down, peering in at the miniature scene.

The cliffs were soft and fanciful, formed of real sandstone. And the baskets of the Indians along the tidelands bulged with white oyster shells so proportionately tiny that Helma thought the colonel had portrayed wild Olympia oysters, before they were fished out.

But it was the name Helma was most interested in, the name and the initials on the gleaming tender car.

"So what's so intriguing?" Ruth asked from behind her.

"Read the name on the tender for me, will you?" Helma asked her. "Just to confirm what I'm seeing."

"What's a tender?"

"The car behind the engine."

"John R. Twitchell and T. Poles, Cert," Ruth read aloud. "So what's significant about that?"

"Along with the fact that Colonel Hooke purposely misdated the inauguration of the Forbes, Sands, and Moore train line into Bellehaven; it's very significant. The line entered Bellehaven in 1888 not 1886."

"So Colonel Hooke wasn't infallible. Big deal."

"No. He wouldn't have made that gross of an error. Colonel Hooke left a message. He said as much to Mrs. Whitney's daughter: a 'secret story,' he said."

Ruth rolled her eyes. "People say that to kids all the time. Trying to keep their interest."

"But Cassandra wasn't any 'kid,' she was the daughter of the woman the colonel's son hoped to marry. He considered her to be almost a granddaughter. Plummer knew," Helma went on. "Remember his letter?"

"Not really."

Helma had memorized it. " 'I've seen you at work and I trust your train of thought. Time is essential. Un-cover the Raven.' He was talking about trains and time."

"I don't get it," Ruth said.

But Helma was following her own train of thought. *Time is essential,* Stanley Plummer had written. Could he have been referring to *dates,* not the *passage* of time? 1888, not 1886?

"See this name on the tender car? I . . ." Helma jerked upright, alert. Ruth turned toward the entrance to the exhibit room. "Shh," Helma warned.

"I heard it."

"It was a door opening. Someone's in the building."

"I told you that," Ruth said. " 'It's the wind,' you said."

Helma raised her finger to her lips but it was unnecessary. The silence was again broken, this time more violently and the crashing was identifiable: the aluminum ladder against the bucket. Whoever was in the building was hurriedly departing.

Helma turned too quickly and lost her balance, her equilibrium undone by alcohol. She caught herself against the train diorama, dangerously rocking it.

"Watch out!" Ruth cried, leaping forward and steadying the glass case with both hands.

Together they ran from the north wing past the aluminum ladder lying beside the metal pail. The doors at the front entrance were closed, the portico light turned off. Helma flicked it on again and wrenched open the doors.

A moist, cold wind blew against her. She closed her eyes, then opened them again, trying to clear her vision, to keep the headlights of the passing cars from creating trails that glistened like oil on water.

"He's gone," Ruth said behind her. "Vanished."

"He can't be far," Helma told her. "It's only been a few seconds."

"So take your matchstick flashlight and go searching through the bushes." Ruth pointed back inside

the center. "Come back inside so you can see what
I see—or saw."

"What was it?"

"Come in and I'll show you."

Helma glanced vainly around the center's dark
grounds again. Shrubbery rustled and moved. Whoever had been inside was gone, or else hidden well
enough Helma wouldn't find him, not with what
Ruth called her "matchstick flashlight." She reluctantly turned and followed Ruth back into the center.

Ruth raised her arm and pointed down the south
wing. "There," she said.

The door of the Reading Room stood open.

"But it was closed when we . . ." Helma began.

"That's right," Ruth said with unnecessary smug-
ness.

Helma warily approached the Reading Room. She
stepped through the dark doorway and reached for
the light switch, bracing herself. All her work, her
plans, the shelves of rare materials.

The lights showed nothing unusual. Helma didn't
trust the illusion of serenity; she stepped toward her
desk, eyes alert.

"This little library seems to be of interest to somebody. What do you keep in here anyway?"

"Only books, that *I* know of, but I've felt for some
time that Plummer was killed because of something
here," Helma told her, her attention on her desk.
Nothing was out of order, yet . . .

She walked around the desk, shaking her head a
little, struggling to clear the muzzy edges. Her blotter was straight, sharpened pencils stood properly in
the snakeskin pencil holder; her notes and notebook
were as neatly stacked as before she and Ruth departed for Kelly's.

Finally, she sat down at her desk to view the room
from her usual angle. Ruth shrugged out of her

green cape, dropped it on the floor, then slid down to sit on it, her back against the wall.

"You're better than a bloodhound," Ruth said.

"Not unless I find whatever our guest was looking for."

"Maybe he wasn't looking for anything. He just slipped in here to avoid us."

"The door was locked."

She opened her desk drawer and looked inside. Paperclips, ink cartridges, notepaper. Still . . .

"The names on the tender car?" Helma said to Ruth as she continued to search her desk. "John R. Twitchell and T. Poles? That's the author and title of a book I checked out to Young Frank. *Totem Poles* by John R. Twitchell. Plummer found it, too. That's what he meant by 'train of thought,' and the word 'time' signified dates: 1888, not 1886." Helma reached for Young Frank's checkout card in the file on her desk.

"Why'd he make it so tough?"

The checkout card was gone. Helma flipped through her cataloging notes, the excess three-by-five cards, her forms. The card wasn't anywhere on her desktop, nor the floor nor trash basket.

"What's wrong?" Ruth asked.

"I allowed Young Frank to check out the totem pole book. I typed the author and title on a card and he signed it. And now the card's gone."

"So whoever was in the building took the card and knows Young Frank has the book?"

"That's right."

"But you saw the book. What was it? Was it rare? Valuable?"

Helma shook her head. "It was about twenty years old. Beautiful color photographs of totem poles. Not scholarly, more of a coffee table book."

"I don't get it. Why did the colonel put the names on the train. What's in . . ."

"Hello!" a man's voice called. "Anybody here? Helma?"

Helma didn't shout inside buildings, but Ruth did.

"We're back here in the Reading Room," she called with substantial volume. "Is that you, Aaron?"

"Yeah."

While they waited for Aaron, Helma realized what was different about the contents of her desk drawer: the wooden caricature that Young Frank had carved of Miriam was missing, too.

Aaron entered the Reading Room, fashionably dressed in slacks and leather jacket, his hair blown across his forehead.

"Funny time for you to turn up," Ruth said.

"I was driving by and saw all the lights. What's going on?"

"Not much," Ruth told him. "We surprised an intruder in the building and then Helma found a cryptic message from your dead grandfather that nicely goes along with her love letter from the dead Mr. Plummer."

"Messages from Gramps?" Aaron asked. "What's this all about?"

"Beats me. You tell him, Helma."

But Helma's thoughts were elsewhere. "Ruth and I have both imbibed alcohol," she told Aaron, ignoring the way Ruth mouthed the word "imbibed." "Neither of us can drive. Would you drive us—or at least me—to Young Frank's?"

"Sure. Is he expecting you?"

"No, but it's very important."

"She's searching down an improperly checked out library book," Ruth told Aaron.

"My car's out front," Aaron said. He paused. "It's the Porsche. The back seat's a little tight."

"I'm long but bendable," Ruth told him. "I'll volunteer."

Helma paused long enough to turn off all the lights except the usual night lights, then slipped Audrey's key onto her own key ring for safe keeping.

Aaron opened his car door for her, and in the car lights, Helma saw the small smile on his lips, the eager gleam in his eyes.

🌿 chapter eighteen 🌿

FAST CARS

"**A**re we going to Young Frank's trailer or his grandfather's house?" Aaron asked as he turned the ignition key and the Porsche came to life with a powerful growl that involuntarily brought Helma's hand to the dashboard.

"His grandfather's," Helma told him. "Have you been there?"

"Not really. I dropped him off once but I didn't make the trek through the bushes, how about you?"

"No, I only dropped him off there, too."

"How sweet," Ruth muttered from the back seat. "You have something in common. Can we go now?"

The little car leapt forward into the night. Helma had the sensation that instead of giving the car gas, Aaron was holding it back, keeping it from racing away on its own. She felt low to the ground, swift and dangerous. Surely they were traveling far beyond the speed limit.

"Can't you go any faster?" Ruth asked over Aaron's shoulder. "There's some urgency to the situation, right, Helma?"

"Ruth's right; this may be an emergency. The sooner we're there, the better."

"Gotcha," Aaron said and Helma gasped as the Porsche effortlessly shot forward, pressing her into the passenger seat. She clasped her hands tightly in her lap and concentrated on the projection of the headlights, not on the speed of the passing scenery.

"Are either of you going to tell me what this is about?" Aaron asked as he casually accelerated around a slower car, pulling back into the right lane moments before oncoming headlights.

"Ask Helma," Ruth said. "Something about your grandfather writing on trains, and Young Frank and library books and Stanley Plummer, the murdered librarian."

"He wasn't a professional librarian," Helma reminded her. "It's important we talk to Young Frank as soon as possible."

"He's not in trouble again, is he?"

"Not in trouble, but he may be in danger."

The Porsche turned the corner toward the reservation, shimmying, the tires squealing. Water arced up behind them. Helma swallowed and asked, "Did your grandfather ever tell you the story of his birth?"

Aaron laughed. "On the trip out from Boston? It's gospel. His father died of food poisoning along the way—bad chicken, the story goes. His mother got off the train in Nebraska somewhere with the body, went into early labor, gave birth to Gramps and named him Soldier in gratitude to an unknown soldier who helped her and then disappeared."

"Like Clint Eastwood," Ruth added.

"But was it your grandfather who told you the story, or your mother?"

"Mostly Mother, I guess. She loves the tragedy of it. 'One died and one was born,' she says, like it was the second coming. I think Gramps was amused by the tale. His mother was a stubborn old terror, I gathered from him, a real hard-liner, despite Mother's rhapsodizing about the beautiful, glorious, and legendary pioneer. It's all in Mother's book, her 'Hooke Narrative,' if she ever finishes it."

They were far enough from town that the darkness on either side of the headlights was only broken now and then by yard lights. It wasn't raining but mists clung to the trees in front of them like hanging smoke.

"Not too far ahead," Helma said. "I gather Young Frank doesn't spend much time at home."

Aaron nodded. "Depends. His mother lives in town, his father out here. Everyone's close-mouthed about it but I think he gets leaned on at home. Out of sight, out of mind."

"Why doesn't he just live with his grandfather?" Ruth asked.

"His grandfather's dead," Aaron explained. "He left his place in trust for Young Frank. The land's off the reservation. A boy caught between two worlds."

"There," Helma said, spotting the subtle parting in the bushes, recognizing the looming fir tree by the road. "You just passed it."

Aaron braked the Porsche and backed up. Farther ahead Helma caught the glint of the auto beams reflecting from a metallic surface.

"There's a flashlight under your seat, Helma," Aaron said.

Helma reached beneath her seat and pulled out a long black metal flashlight.

"A man who's prepared," Ruth said. "I'm impressed."

"If you tell me what I'm supposed to be doing," Aaron said, "I'll go ahead in and you two can wait here and stay dry."

"Okay," Ruth said.

"We'll come with you," Helma told Aaron. "I'm not certain myself what we're looking for—or what we'll find."

Helma wore ankle-high boots but by the time she'd walked ten feet along the slick and narrow path through the bushes with their dead-leaved fingers and the tall pulpy grasses, her legs were wet, the hem of her wool coat was weighted with moisture, and a fine mist dampened her face.

It had been dark for almost two hours and it was only six o'clock. The forest around them dripped, dark and ancient, trees towering above them so dense and thick they blocked the sky.

Aaron led the way, holding the beam low, then Helma, and finally Ruth, who muttered fierce expletives every few steps. After weeks without sun, with continuous rain and wind and muddy gray skies, most anyone else wouldn't have left her house in open-toed shoes.

"Where *is* this place?" Ruth demanded.

"It can't be far," Helma told her.

"Why in hell can't it be?" There was a slap of bushes behind Helma. "Ouch!" Ruth cried out.

"Put your hand on my shoulder if you can't see," Helma said.

"I can see fine; I just need to be two feet shorter. This trail, if that's what you call it, might not even lead to Young Frank's house."

"I saw Young Frank use it," Helma said. "I dropped him off here."

"So you said." Ruth raised her voice. "Hey, Aaron, would you lead us astray? You're not the enemy, are you?"

"Why would..." Aaron began. Suddenly the flashlight dropped from his hands and Aaron tumbled to the ground.

Ahead of them, a bell began clanging. Ruth screeched and Helma, without thinking, crouched in the wet bushes.

"Duck!" Ruth cried, still standing. "It's a booby trap!"

As the clanging subsided and the forest returned to silence, Helma rose and helped Aaron to his feet. The flashlight lay in the dripping grasses, its beam flickering on shiny tree trunks.

"Thanks," Aaron said. "It was a trip wire. I hope the kid didn't land mine the place."

A rectangle of light appeared fifty feet in front of them. A doorway.

Aaron brushed at himself and called, "Young Frank, are you there? It's Aaron Hooke and a couple of friends. Can we approach?" he asked, sounding like he would next offer up a secret password.

A back-lit figure stepped into the doorway of light, beckoning them forward.

"Are you sure that's the kid himself?" Ruth asked.

"Young Frank?" Aaron called.

"Yeah," the figure answered.

Aaron turned off the flashlight and they gratefully walked forward and entered Young Frank's home.

It was a one-room building, half old man's retreat, half young boy's clubhouse. Wood plank walls, old kerosene lamps on the table and windowsill, a battered woodstove with its door open, a fire crackling inside, filling the room with a dense piny smell. A narrow bed stood against one wall, a metal table and two chairs with torn plastic seats against the other. Rough shelves were filled with carvings: loons, chickadees and eagles, foxes and coyotes and bears, masks and miniature totem poles, fanciful creatures, too. Two-headed beings, creatures Helma recognized from mythology: the Mintaur, Medusa. "Star Trek," Aaron said, lightly touching a squat figure with a ridged and distorted face.

Young Frank stood watching them without comment.

"You're damn talented for such a surly kid," Ruth told him.

"Has anyone been here to ask about the totem pole book?" Helma asked him.

He shook his head and glanced at the table where the totem pole book lay open. In front of the book, with shavings all around, sat the rough beginnings of a frog figure.

"May I look at it?" Helma asked.

He stared into his fire for a few moments and Helma hastily said, "It's not overdue, I just need to check something."

Young Frank marked his place with a wood shaving and gave the book to Helma.

Helma skimmed the pages for handwriting or inserts, discovering neither. "Did you find anything in the book?" she asked Young Frank. "A piece of paper, perhaps?"

"No," Young Frank told her.

She closed the book, discouraged, idly gazing at the disintegrating closeup of the totem pole on the cover. "What's this figure?" she asked Young Frank, touching the blank-eyed, beaked depiction.

"The Raven," Young Frank said.

"I thought the Raven's beak pointed upward," Helma said.

"Sometimes."

Un-*cover the Raven*, Stanley Plummer had written. Un-cover. Stanley Plummer had not only invoked the Raven as a trickster but as a literal figure.

Helma sat at Young Frank's table and gingerly ripped off the tape that held the plastic cover to the book jacket.

"Un-cover," she said aloud. "It's *under* the *cover*."

"What is?" Ruth asked. She and Aaron and Young Frank crowded around Helma in the warm room.

Helma laid the book jacket flat on the table and pulled up the tape of the lower inner fold.

"Ta da!" Ruth said.

Beneath the crease lay two folded sheets of paper.

One yellow, brittle along its edges and corners, the other white, newer. Helma extracted both and set them side by side on the table.

"Can't you do this any faster?" Ruth asked.

"Savor the moment," Aaron told her. "I think we're onto something big."

Helma unfolded the older sheet of paper first.

"Birth Certificate," it read at the top of the page, the handwriting thin and slanted with precise loops and whorls, the ink gone brown.

Helma took a breath and read aloud: " 'Born on September 6, 1888 in North Platte, Nebraska to Rosemary O'Riley Hooke, a son, Soldier Patrick Hooke. Father unnamed.' The brief document was signed by 'Elizabeth Peterson, Midwife.' "

"Father unnamed?" Ruth asked.

"1888?" Aaron repeated. "Gramps was born in 1886. He died just after his 101st birthday in 1987, the same year my son was born. Does this mean he had a younger brother? Born on Gramps's birthday? I don't get it."

"This may explain it," Helma said and unfolded the other sheet of paper. " 'Now I write the truth,' " the first line read.

"Uh oh," Ruth said, leaning against the wall. "The truth. That's synonymous with trouble."

"Go ahead," Aaron urged Helma. Read the rest."

" 'Who will find this?' " Helma read. " 'It should be Aaron but if it's Miriam, these facts will never see the light of day. Only Aaron, although not the brightest of young men, would see the humor and irony in this story.' "

Here, Aaron grunted and said, "Pure Gramps. Pat you on the head with one hand and poke his fingers in your eyes at the same time."

" 'My mother,' " the letter went on, " 'a young Irish immigrant the Hookes wouldn't accept, *did* get off the train in North Platte, Nebraska, and oversee the return of her young husband's body to Boston, and she *was* broken-hearted. But she wasn't pregnant, nor did she continue west—at that time. She had no money. Despite her frantic entreaties, the Hooke family refused to help her, leaving her stranded without funds in Nebraska, hoping she'd fade away forever into the Wild West.

" 'A few months later, my mother took up with a young Sioux half-breed named Soldier Half Man, whose father had been a soldier at Fort Kearny. She became pregnant. She was mum about what became of my real father but after my birth, she continued her trek west, two years late.

" 'She kept me at home during those first few years, telling folks I was sickly, small for my age. A new birth certificate was made. Years later, the Hookes pleaded for contact, "for the sake of the grandson," but she refused to forgive them. When she finally told me the whole story before she died she thought it was a hilarious trick on the Hookes. You might say she died laughing.' "

"Wow," Aaron said. "Oh wow. Can you believe it?"

"He *did* leave you clues," Helma told Aaron. "The train diorama. He portrayed a Forbes, Sands, and Moore train traveling into Bellehaven in the year 1886, also the supposed year of his birth, but the train line wasn't inaugurated until 1888, the actual year of his birth."

Aaron shook his head. "I blew that one. Gramps left me a diorama and a few books and I donated them to the center. I never *really* looked at that diorama and I'll bet the totem pole book was one originally left to me."

"The author's name and the title of this book was printed on the tender behind the engine," Helma said. " 'John R. Twitchell and T. Poles,' it said."

"Hide in plain sight," Ruth commented.

Aaron's eyes sparkled; his smile widened. "That old coot kept a secret like that all those years. What a riot."

"And it's going to stay secret."

Aaron's twin brother, Darren, stood in the doorway of Young Frank's shack. Behind him, Helma made out the pale, hatted figure of Miriam Hooke. Ruth and Helma exchanged startled looks while Aaron greeted Darren's stony gaze as casually as if their meeting had been planned.

"Hey, Darren," Aaron said, pointing to the letter Helma still held. "Isn't this a kick? We're not Boston Hookes; we're shanty Irish and Sioux and a few other genes which Mother probably stomped into oblivion." He saluted the shadowy figure of his mother. "Sorry, Mother dear," he said.

Miriam stepped forward, her manicured hand outstretched.

"Give those letters to me," she said.

"I don't think so," Helma told her, refolding the letters and holding them close to her body. "They're evidence."

"Evidence of what?" Aaron asked.

"Ask your mother."

"Evidence of what?" Aaron asked his mother. "That you've been living a lie all these years? How long have you known about our great-grandmother's little deception?"

"Since shortly before your grandfather died," Miriam said in a pleasant social voice. "Now, Aaron, please take the letters from Miss Zukas and give them to me."

"Come on, Mother. This is no big deal. It's very 'in' to have Indian blood. Let's see. Gramps was a quarter so you're an eighth and Darren and I are only a sixteenth. Just enough to brag about."

"You'll do nothing of the sort. This little tale ends here and now and it will never be mentioned again."

"But what if it *is* mentioned?" Ruth asked. "I could tell lots of people."

"No one will believe it once those papers are destroyed. It would be a silly rumor. There's no other copy of the birth certificate. And I have proof of our Hooke background: ancestry charts, census records. Even local histories in the library."

"Psst," Ruth hissed at Helma. "Even the library's in on it."

"Give the letters to Mother, Aaron," Darren urged his twin. "What difference does it make now, after all these years? Let's let the past lie."

"You're forgetting that *I* don't intend to give the letters to Aaron," Helma reminded them. "The police may be interested in them."

"The police?" Aaron asked. "Why should the police care about nineteenth-century hanky panky?"

"Oh," Ruth suddenly said, snapping her fingers. "Stanley Plummer."

"You can't prove anything," Darren said.

"Darren," Miriam said sharply. "Be quiet."

"Stanley Plummer figured it out," Helma said. "He wrote a letter to me, and unwittingly ended up asking for help in solving his own murder."

"That's impossible," Miriam said with authority. "What letter? Where is it?"

"I gave the original to the police," Helma told her.

Miriam's confident face faltered. She stared hard at Helma who gazed back at her in total self-assurance.

"Plummer worked out your father's puzzle and found the birth certificate hidden in the totem pole book, didn't he?" Helma asked.

"This is absolutely ridiculous," Miriam said. Her eyes lowered. She fidgeted with the collar of her coat.

"You knew the birth certificate was somewhere in the Reading Room. Did Stanley Plummer threaten you with it? You were responsible for the break-ins and the fire, trying to destroy Plummer's proof when you couldn't find it yourself."

"I've spent my whole life as a Hooke," Miriam said, actually stamping one black-booted foot, her voice rising. "I wrote their history, spent years researching all the branches. And all I . . ."

"Just because one old lady wanted to get even with a cruel family," Helma said.

"Rosemary Hooke was the only one who knew the truth until she told her son," Ruth said. "You have to admire her for that. Secret revenge is the sweetest."

"She *should* have kept it to herself," Miriam said angrily. "She didn't have to tell Daddy; he didn't have to tell me. Her revenge ended up being on her own family."

"You're forgetting the person who was hurt most," Helma reminded her. "Stanley Plummer."

Miriam waved her hand in dismissal. "He was a petty criminal."

Aaron's mouth dropped open. "*You* really were involved in his death, Mother?"

"She had nothing to do with it," Darren interjected. "I went to talk to him after he found the birth certificate. His death was an accident."

"You accidentally chased him into the handicapped stall in the women's restroom and shoved a paper spindle into his heart?" Helma asked. "And then threw a Barbie doll beside his body to assist the police in discovering Plummer's past?"

"He was blackmailing Mother," Darren said.

"I don't believe that," Helma told him. "Stanley Plummer wasn't a blackmailer. He worked alone and didn't leave untidy ends. Blackmail would have been too entangling for him. No, it wasn't blackmail."

"It was," Darren insisted. "You never met Plummer."

"But I knew him," Helma said. She turned to Miriam. "He discovered your plan to fire him. In revenge, he passed his clues to the birth certificate to me, trusting my curiosity. Instead, his note became a clue to the identity of his killer."

"That's very fanciful reasoning, Miss Zukas," Miriam said, her voice warming up to charming. "But surely you can see the Hooke family history is unimportant in Stanley Plummer's death. He wasn't trying to blackmail me at all." She laughed prettily. "Heavens no. Darren discovered Stanley Plummer was selling rare books from the colonel's private collection. There was a fight. Darren was trying to protect the colonel's collection. It was all just a silly accident, a little misunderstanding."

Darren and Aaron stared at their mother as if she were a stranger.

"Plummer wasn't interested in selling books," Helma said, "only in cataloging them. If his death *had* been an accident, you would have gone to the police, not pretended to be ignorant."

"Our family has so little experience with the police we just didn't know what to do. Now, of course, I realize I should have. And we will, too. Right away. Tonight we'll explain everything to your chief of police as soon as we leave here."

"He's not 'my' chief of police," Helma said.

"He says he's her 'friend,'" Ruth added.

"How nice. Now will you please give me the documents?" Miriam asked Helma.

"No," Helma told her.

From someone else, she might have suspected it, but not from Miriam Hooke. Helma was totally unprepared when Miriam casually unsnapped the gold clasp on her black leather handbag, reached in one manicured hand, and pulled out a small stylish pistol.

"Mummy!" Darren cried out.

"Is that real?" Aaron asked.

"I'm a *Hooke*!" Miriam wailed. The gun wavered between Helma and Ruth. "I won't let you take that away from me just because of some silly piece of paper."

"Mother, this is crazy," Aaron told her. "Give me the gun and let's go home."

"You be quiet, Aaron," she said, actually pointing the pistol at her son. "You think life is so humorous. You wouldn't lift a finger to save your name."

Unnoticed by everyone in the crowded shack except Helma, Young Frank had sidled around behind Darren and Miriam. He stood close to the open door of the woodstove, one hand in his pocket.

"It's still our name, Mother," Aaron reasoned. "We just got rid of a load of relatives, that's all."

"You'll never understand," Miriam said scornfully. "You're just like your father." She turned the gun toward Helma again. "Now, Miss Zukas, give me those papers immediately."

At that moment, Young Frank's hand shot out toward the fire. Three sharp explosions resounded in the shack. Billowing, eye-burning smoke poured from the woodstove. Helma had suspected something of the sort and had marked a mental path to the door.

With one hand she grabbed for Ruth but Ruth was no longer beside her. A grunt sounded and Helma reached toward the sound, gripping a handful of fabric.

"Follow me," she ordered.

She closed her eyes, held her breath and pulled whoever's clothing she held directly to the door and outside into the damp night. Young Frank was already outside, standing beneath a tree a few yards from the building, illuminated by the smoky light.

It *was* Ruth's arm Helma had grabbed but Ruth wasn't alone. She in turn held tightly to the gun-wielding arm of Miriam Hooke who was undaintily hacking and coughing.

Darren emerged next, with Aaron right behind him, one hand on his twin brother's shoulder.

"Took a minute to find the door," Aaron said between coughing. "Are you okay?" he asked his mother.

Miriam's coughing turned to sobs and she released her hold on the gun. It fell to the ground, glinting.

Ruth dropped Miriam's arm and bent over, scooping up the gun.

"Your fingerprints, Ruth," Helma warned.

"Oh," Ruth said, juggling the gun from palm to palm.

"Please point it in another direction."

"Sorry," Ruth said, finally making a pouch in the front of her cape and enclosing the pistol inside the fabric.

Aaron turned to Young Frank. "Smartass kid," he said and shook Young Frank's hand. "Thanks."

"Is this going to hurt your building?" Helma asked Young Frank. "Or your carvings?"

"No," he told her. "I do it all the time."

"I've never seen fireworks like that," Ruth said.

Young Frank puffed a little. "I make them myself," he told her.

"What will I do?" Miriam wailed, asking no one.

Helma handed Darren a tissue from her left coat pocket.

"Here, Mother," Darren said as he took the tissue, his voice gravelly from coughing. A gold watch flashed on his wrist.

"That was you at the library the night before I began working at the center, wasn't it?" Helma asked. "Standing in the dark on the loading dock? Were you planning for me to have an accident?"

"I only wanted to warn you to stay away from the center," Darren said indignantly.

"But in the center's parking lot. My battery. That was you, too."

He busily wiped at Miriam's tears, turning his back to Helma. Miriam jerked the tissue from his hand and dabbed at her own face.

"Well, bro," Aaron told Darren. "Don't try anything stupid."

"Yeah," Ruth said. "I've got the gun right here . . . somewhere."

"I'll call the cops on my car phone," Aaron told them.

"I wish you wouldn't do that," Darren said to his brother.

"I wish you hadn't made this mess. Geez. You *killed* Plummer, didn't you? What were you thinking? Paper spindles and Barbie dolls?"

"Mother was broken-hearted," Darren said. "I did it for her." He kicked at the thick layer of needles and rotting leaves. "That Hooke business getting out scared her to death." Darren shrugged. "Plummer really was a weasel."

"Lousy excuse. Poor Gramps, though. He never really did get to make it to a hundred years old like he dreamed, did he?"

It was late and Helma's wine-induced muzzy-headedness had metamorphosed into a throbbing headache. She sat in the front seat of Aaron's Porsche with the motor running and the heat on, the interior lit by dash light. Lining the road were three police cars and an ambulance. She didn't know who had thought of the ambulance, only that it was unnecessary.

Darren and Miriam each sat in the back seat of a

different police car. Young Frank, Aaron, and Ruth were back at Young Frank's cabin, airing it out, she supposed, perhaps celebrating their close call under the vigilant eyes of the police.

Aaron hadn't appeared unduly shocked by the crimes of his brother and mother and had trouble keeping the twinkle from his eye as the events unfolded. On his fourth "Oh, wow!" Helma had excused herself and retreated from Young Frank's cabin to wait in the Porsche. Aaron hadn't even removed his keys from the expensive vehicle.

A tap sounded on the Porsche's window. Helma turned the window crank. It was Chief Gallant.

"Mind if I talk to you for a few minutes?" he asked.

"No," she told him.

He was bigger than Aaron and couldn't close the driver's door until he moved the seat farther back and his legs fit beneath the steering wheel. By that time, the warmth had escaped and he turned up the heater.

"You should have called the police before you came out here," he said.

"But I didn't," Helma said wearily.

Wayne Gallant rubbed his hands around the steering wheel. "I always wanted a car like this," he said.

"But not anymore?" Helma asked.

"I don't think about it as often now," he said. He dropped his hands into his lap. "This is going to shake up Bellehaven society."

"Maybe even cause a ripple in Boston, too," Helma said. "I don't suppose Miriam will donate her Hooke historical research to the East Coast branch of the family."

"Probably not."

"A hundred years ago, deception was a lot easier to practice," Helma said. "A plot like Rosemary O'Riley Hooke's could hardly succeed now, not with computers and so much documentation."

"Don't underestimate the deviousness of humanity," Wayne Gallant told her. "Where there's a will . . ."

"Maybe."

A sudden flurry of raindrops blew from the trees onto the roof of the Porsche in a pounding wave. Helma glanced up at the upholstered ceiling.

"You probably saved Young Frank's life," Wayne Gallant told her.

"I can't believe Miriam or Darren would have harmed him."

"Maybe not physically but they were campaigning pretty strenuously for his being responsible for the fire at the center. Trying to deflect any blame from themselves."

"It was actually Darren, wasn't it? Miriam was willing to destroy the center in order to hide proof of her father's parentage."

"Miriam didn't know the birth certificate existed until Stanley Plummer found it. She thought the secret died with her father."

"Was I wrong?" Helma asked. "*Did* Plummer try to blackmail Miriam?"

"Not according to Darren. Plummer didn't tell Miriam about the birth certificate until he discovered he was being fired. And then it wasn't to use it as leverage but to let her know it existed, liable to be accidentally stumbled on by anyone. He was trying to scare her, to get even."

"So she'd always be in fear it might turn up?"

"Right," the chief said.

"That's a severe revenge. So originally, he wrote me the note when he learned about the negotiations between the library and the center. He was deliberately vague to pique my curiosity and continue Miriam's torture, knowing I'd keep looking until I eventually found the birth certificate."

"Long after he'd moved onto another scheme. It obviously didn't take Plummer long to develop a high regard for your curiosity and tenacity."

Helma smiled.

"What are you thinking?" Wayne Gallant asked.

"That Stanley Carrol Plummer and Rosemary O'Riley Hooke could have been partners; they both relished long-term revenge."

The chief turned down the heater. "Can I take you home?"

Helma looked through the windshield at the police car in front of the Porsche. "No thank you," she said.

Wayne Gallant sat very still. "Helma . . ." he began and then asked softly, "Are you sure?"

"Positive," Helma told him.

"Helma, did you hear what happened to George and Roberta?" Eve asked.

Helma glanced from George Melville's empty desk to Roberta's vacant cubicle. Both chairs were pushed in and their desk lamps were turned off.

"Are they all right?" Helma asked, alarmed.

Eve leaned closer. "They didn't come back from the library tour in Vancouver!" Her voice squeaked with excitement.

"They're still in Canada?"

"It was so exciting. You know those little walkways between sections of the floors in the library where you can look all the way down to the ground floor?"

Helma did. Walkways like gangplanks on all six floors. Waist-high railings. Not for the vertigo-prone.

"On the sixth floor," Eve went on, "Roberta started across the walkway and *fainted*. George swept her into his arms like a knight—or maybe a cowboy. The last time I saw them they were in a corner, all snuggly."

"And Ms. Moon left without them?"

"She was madder than heck but when we tried to find them, they were *gone*. Isn't that romantic?"

"I hope so," Helma said.

Eve glanced at the labels Helma was sorting on her desk and read aloud, ⬧ 'Raven, carved by Young Frank Portman.' Are those for the new exhibit?"

Helma nodded. "His carvings will be displayed in the cases in the front lobby. You can meet the carver at the reception Thursday night."

"Cool."

Ms. Moon joined them, holding Helma's description of the call numbering scheme she was using at the cultural center. "I've never heard of the Carrol Classification system, Helma."

"It's fairly new," Helma told her. "It was developed for collections concentrating on a single topic." When Ms. Moon still looked doubtful, Helma said, "I believe by someone who was employed at UCLA."

"Oh," Ms. Moon who was from San Diego, said in satisfaction. "I hope it doesn't take long for life to stabilize again at the center. Such shocking news. Miriam Hooke and her sons." She looked at Helma, waiting.

"Only one of her sons," Helma corrected. "I believe Aaron may develop more of an interest in the center. In the meantime, the board of directors is perfectly capable of keeping the center going."

"And I heard they're happy to finally have the opportunity," Ms. Moon said naughtily.

"We don't usually pick up animals," the receptionist at the Meow Medic said into the phone.

"I'll pay extra," Helma told her. "He needs a complete physical, inoculations, and whatever preventative medicine is available. Plus a bath and grooming and please eradicate any fleas or parasites.

Trim his toenails, and he has a profusion of hair in his ears—one ear is torn so be careful. Oh, and do you carry labels to hang around his neck?"

"Is this your first cat, Miss Zukas?" the receptionist asked.

"He's not . . . well, yes, I suppose it is."

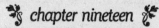

TURKEY

"**H**appy Turkey!" Ruth said when Helma answered Mrs. Whitney's door. "Am I late?"

"You're exactly on time," Helma told her as she held the door open.

From beneath her green cape, Ruth pulled a bottle of red wine and an apple pie. "I baked this myself," she said, handing the warm pie to Helma, "so treat it like the rare and precious thing it is."

Beneath Ruth's cape she wore a calf-length print purple dress. It took Helma a minute to realize the print was a multitude of weavy, wispy jellyfish swimming upward toward Ruth's neck.

"Ah, Ruth," Mrs. Whitney said from her recliner chair in the living room. "Just a glimpse of you cheers me up."

Ruth bent down and hugged Mrs. Whitney. "Seeing *you* looking so good definitely cheers *me* up," Ruth told her.

Helma's mother and Cassandra were huddled over the open oven, poking at the browned turkey. "I think it's done," Lillian was saying.

"It feels like spring in here," Ruth said, gazing around Mrs. Whitney's bright apartment.

"Don't we wish," Cassandra said.

"The weather's supposed to change this weekend," Mrs. Whitney told them. "A forty percent chance of sunshine. That weather girl on channel five said so. She's almost always right."

"Just as I leave," Cassandra grumbled. "I haven't seen sunshine here in years."

"Visit more often and you will," Ruth told her.

Ruth helped Helma set the table. "Guess who called me this morning?" she whispered as she laid out seven sets of silverware.

"Guess who sent me a bouquet of flowers this morning?" Helma whispered in reply as she followed behind Ruth, moving the forks from the right to the left side of the plates.

"See, they can't get us out of their minds."

"It might be the season," Helma suggested. "Holidays make people nostalgic."

"Not this time. Trust me."

"Tomorrow's the big Christmas shopping kick-off," Helma's mother said as she cleared a place in the center of the table to set the turkey. "I have my shopping list ready."

Cassandra groaned. "I haven't even *thought* about Christmas shopping yet. I always swear I won't get caught up in the commercialism, but every year, with three kids . . ."

"I'm nearly finished making my gifts," Mrs. Whitney said.

Ruth was looking at Helma, one corner of her mouth raised. "Go ahead, Helma. Tell them."

"Tell them what?"

"When you finished your Christmas shopping."

"I still have a few last-minute items to purchase," Helma said.

"She finished in *August*," Ruth said gleefully.

"You're exaggerating. It wasn't until mid-September."

Mrs. Whitney's doorbell jangled the same way Helma's did when Ruth rang it.

It was Julianna. "Now that I'm here, this Thanksgiving can be deemed traditional," she said. "I brought corn. Is that fitting or what?"

A few minutes later, the doorbell rang again. "All present and accounted for," Ruth said.

Ms. Moon was the last to arrive. Pat, her "life partner," had flown to a family Thanksgiving in Colorado. "It'll do us good to be apart for a few days," Ms. Moon had said.

Ruth had called the Thanksgiving dinner "the feast for lost souls."

"Hello, Ms. Moon," Helma said, accepting a hot casserole dish wrapped in a towel.

"Please," Ms. Moon said, hands struggling with her coat buttons. "Today call me May or May Apple, not Ms. Moon." She paused. "And not 'Moonbeam' either, please," she said, grinning at Helma's surprised face.

They sat at Mrs. Whitney's round table, their chairs squeezed together, elbows occasionally bumping, the turkey fragrant and brown before them. Helma sat across from her mother, facing the bay. The sky was gray, the islands mere suggestions. Somewhere behind all that, the sun was about to set. She *might* be seeing a lightening of the sky, the slightest shift from pewter to silver.

"A toast," Lillian said, lifting her wine glass. "To good health and good friends."

"And the good men who aren't present," Ruth added.

"Not this time, anyway," Cassandra contributed.

They raised their wine to one another, glasses chiming together like music.